A
MURDER
IS
FOREVER

A
MURDER
IS
FOREVER

THE DIAMOND DISTRICT MYSTERY SERIES

ROB BATES

Kenmore, WA

CAMEL PRESS

A Camel Press book published by Epicenter Press

Epicenter Press
6524 NE 181st St.
Suite 2
Kenmore, WA 98028

For more information go to:
www.Camelpress.com
www.Coffeetownpress.com
www. Epicenterpress.com
www.robbatesauthor.com

All rights reserved. No part of this book may be reproduced or transmitted in any form or by any means, electronic or mechanical, including photocopying, recording, or any information storage and retrieval system, without permission in writing from the publisher.

This is a work of fiction. Names, characters, places, brands, media, and incidents are the product of the author's imagination or are used fictitiously.

Cover and interior design by Scott Book and Melissa Vail Coffman

A Murder is Forever
Copyright © 2020 by Rob Bates

ISBN: 978-1-60381-221-4 (Trade Paper)
ISBN: 978-1-60381-222-1 (eBook)

Printed in the United States of America

*To Susan, Mikey, and the rest of my family,
including the real Max and Mimi.*

ACKNOWLEDGMENTS

THANK YOU TO MY PARENTS for always supporting me in what I wanted to do, even if that was an impractical thing like writing a book.

Thank you to my super-cool agent Dawn Dowdle and Camel Press for taking a chance on a first-time author.

Thank you to all my writing group companions for your support and encouragement, and having the patience to critique three (!) drafts of this book.

Thank you to all my coworkers at the various jewelry publications I've worked at over of the years, for being such great editors, mentors, and companions, and for putting up with me talking loudly on the phone.

Thank you to all those in the diamond and jewelry industry who have dealt with my annoying questions over the years and answered them with good humor and patience (mostly). And a special shout-out to all the good, honest, and ethical people earning a living in an industry where that can be hard to do.

Finally, all my love and gratitude to my incredible wife, Susan, and my beautiful son, Michael, for letting me spend way too much time at my computer to write this, and for all your support, encouragement, and love along the way.

This book has taken a long time to come together. It means a lot to me to see it published. I hope you enjoy it. I got a lot out of writing it.

CHAPTER ONE

As Mimi Rosen exited the subway and looked out on the Diamond District, she remembered the words of her therapist: "This won't last forever."

She sure hoped so. She had been working on Forty-Seventh Street for two months and was already pretty tired of it.

To outsiders, "The Diamond District" sounded glamorous, like a street awash in glitter. To Mimi, who had spent her life around New York, Forty-Seventh Street between Fifth and Sixth Avenues was a crowded, dirty eyesore of a block. The sidewalk was covered not with glitz, but with newspaper boxes, cigarettes, stacks of garbage bags, and, of course, lots of people.

Dozens of jewelry stores lined the street, all vying for attention, with red neon signs proclaiming "we buy gold" or "50 percent off." Their windows boasted the requisite rows of glittery rings, and Mimi would sometimes see tourists ogling them, their eyes wide. She hated how the stores crammed so many gems in each display, until they all ran together like a mess of kids' toys. For all its feints toward elegance, Forty-Seventh Street came off as the world's sparkliest flea market.

Mimi knew the real action in the Diamond District was hidden from pedestrians, because it took place upstairs. There, in the nondescript grey and brown buildings that stood over the stores, billions in gems were bought, sold, traded, stored, cut, appraised, lost, found, and argued over. The upstairs wholesalers comprised the heart of the U.S. gem business; if someone bought a diamond anywhere in America, it had likely passed through Forty-Seventh Street.

Mimi's father Max had spent his entire life as part of the small tight-knit diamond dealer community. It was a business based on who you knew—and even more, who you trusted. "This business isn't about sorting the diamonds," Max always said. "It's about sorting the people." Mimi would marvel how traders would seal million-dollar deals on handshakes, without a contract or lawyer in sight.

It helped that Forty-Seventh Street was comprised mostly of family businesses, owned by people from a narrow range of ethnic groups. Most—like Mimi's father—were Orthodox, or religious, Jews. ("We're the only people crazy enough to be in this industry," as Max put it.) The Street was also home to a considerable contingent of Hasidic Jews, who were even more religious and identifiable by their black top hats and long flowing overcoats. Mimi once joked that Forty-Seventh Street was so diverse, it ran the gamut from Orthodox to ultra-Orthodox.

Now Mimi, while decidedly secular, was part of it all. Working for her father's diamond company was not something she wanted to do, not something she ever dreamed she would do. Yet, here she was.

SHE HAD LITTLE CHOICE. SHE HAD not worked full-time since being laid off from her editing job a year ago. She was already in debt from her divorce, which had cost more than her wedding, and netted little alimony. "That's what happens when you divorce a lawyer," said her shrink.

Six months after she lost her job, Mimi first asked her father for money. He happily leant it to her, though he added he wasn't exactly Rockefeller. It was after her third request—accompanied, like the others, by heartfelt vows to pay him back—that he asked her to be the bookkeeper at his company. "I know you hate borrowing from me," he told her. "This way, it isn't charity. Besides, it'll be nice having you around."

Mimi protested she could barely keep track of her own finances. Her father reminded her that she got an A in accounting in high school. Which apparently qualified her to do the books at Max Rosen Diamond Company.

"We have new software, it makes it easy," Max said. "Your mother, may she rest in peace, did it for years."

Mimi put him off. She had a profession, and it wasn't her mother's.

Mimi was a journalist. She had worked at a newspaper for nine years, and a website for five. She was addicted to the thrill of the chase, the pump of adrenaline when she uncovered a hot story or piece of previously hidden info. There is no better sound to a reporter's ears than someone sputtering, "How did you find that out?"

"It's the perfect job for you," her father once said. "You're a professional nosy person."

She loved journalism for a deeper reason, which she rarely admitted to her cynical reporter friends: She wanted to make a difference. As a girl, she was haunted by the stories they told in religious school, how Jews were killed in concentration camps while the world turned its head. Growing up, she devoured *All the President's Men* and idolized pioneering female muckrakers like Nellie Bly.

Being a journalist was the only thing Mimi ever wanted to do, the only thing she knew how to do. She longed to do it again.

Which is why, she told her therapist, she would tell her father no.

Dr. Asner said she understood, in that soft melancholy coo common to all therapists. Then she crept forward on her chair.

"Maybe you should take your father up on this. He's really throwing you a lifeline. You keep telling me how bad the editorial job market is." She squinted and her glasses inched up her nose. "Sometimes people adjust their dreams. Put them on hold."

Mimi felt the blood drain from her face. In her darker moments—and she had quite a few after her layoff—she had considered leaving journalism and doing something else, though she had no idea what that would be. Mimi always believed that giving up her lifelong passion would be tantamount to surrender.

Dr. Asner must have sensed her reaction, because she quickly backtracked.

"You can continue to look for a journalism job," she said. "Who knows? Maybe working in the Diamond District will give you something to write about. Besides,"— here, her voice gained an edge—"you need the money." That was driven home at the end of the forty-five minutes, when Dr. Asner announced that she couldn't see Mimi for any more sessions, since Mimi hadn't paid her for the last three.

By that point, Mimi didn't know whether to argue, burst into tears, or wave a white flag and admit the world had won.

IT WAS A COLD FEBRUARY MORNING as Mimi walked down Forty-Seventh Street to her father's office, following an hour-plus commute from New Jersey that included a car, a bus, and a subway. With her piercing hazel eyes, glossy brown hair, and closely set features, Mimi was frequently told she was pretty, though she never quite believed it. She had just gotten her hair cut short to commemorate her thirty-eighth birthday, hoping for a more "mature" look. She had always been self-conscious about her height; she was five foot four and tried to walk taller. She was wearing a navy dress that she'd snagged for a good price on eBay; it was professional enough to please her father, who wanted everyone to look nice in the office, without being so nice that she was wasting one of her few good outfits. She was bundled up with multiple layers and a heavy coat—to protect against the winter chill, as well as the madness around her.

Even though it was before 9 AM, Forty-Seventh Street was, as usual, packed, and Mimi gritted her teeth as she bobbed and weaved through the endless crowd. She sidestepped the store workers grabbing a smoke, covering her mouth so she wouldn't get cancer. She swerved around the stern-looking guard unloading the armored car, with the gun conspicuously dangling from his belt. And she dodged the "hawker" trying to lure her into a jewelry store, who every day asked if she had gold to sell, even though every day she told him no.

Finally, Mimi reached her father's building, 460 Fifth, the most popular address on "The Street." After a few minutes standing and tapping her foot on the security line, she handed her driver's license to the security guard and called out, "Rosen Diamonds."

"Miss," growled the guard with the oversized forehead who'd seen her three days a week for the past two months, "you should get a building ID. It'll save you time in the morning."

"It's okay. I won't be working here for long," she chirped, though she wasn't quite sure of that.

Next stop, the elevator bank. Mimi had an irrational fear of elevators; she was always worried she would die in one. She particularly hated these elevators, which were extremely narrow and perpetually packed. She envied those for whom a subway was their sole exposure to a cramped unpleasant space.

As the car rose, one occupant asked a Hasidic dealer how he was finding things.

"All you can do is put on your shoes. The rest is up to the man upstairs."

Only in the diamond business. Mimi's last job was thirty blocks away, yet in a different universe.

At each floor, dealers pushed and rushed like they were escaping a fire. When the elevator reached her floor, Mimi too elbowed her way to freedom.

As she walked to her father's office, she marveled how the building, so fancy and impressive when she was a kid, had sunk into disrepair. The carpets were frayed, the paint was peeling, and the bathroom rarely contained more than one functioning toilet. If management properly maintained the building, they'd charge Midtown Manhattan rents, which small dealers like her father couldn't afford. The neglect suited everyone.

She spied a new handwritten sign, "No large *minyans*, by order of the fire department." Mimi produced a deep sigh. She had long ago left her religious background behind. Somehow, she was now working in a building where they warn against praying in the halls. She was going backward.

Perhaps the dealer in the elevator was right. You could only put on your shoes and do your best. She grabbed her pocketbook strap, threw her head back, and was just about at her father's office when she heard the yelling.

"I'm so tired of waiting, Yosef! It's not fair!"

Max's receptionist, Channah, was arguing with her boyfriend, Yosef, a small-time, perpetually unsuccessfully diamond dealer. Making it more awkward: Yosef was Mimi's cousin.

Channah and Yosef had dated for nearly eighteen months without getting married—an eternity in Channah's community. Still, whenever Channah complained, Mimi remembered how her ex-husband only popped the question after three years and two ultimatums.

"Give me more time," Yosef stuttered, as he tended to do when nervous. "I want to be successful in the business."

"When's that going to happen? The year three thousand?"

The argument shifted to Yiddish, which Mimi didn't understand, though they were yelling so fiercely she didn't need to. Finally, tall, skinny Yosef stormed out of the office, his black hat and suit set off by his red face. He was walking so fast he didn't notice his cousin Mimi standing against the wall. Given the circumstances, she didn't stop him to say hello. She watched his back grow smaller as he stomped and grunted down the hall.

Mimi gave Channah time to cool down. After a minute checking her phone in vain for responses to her latest freelance pitch—editors weren't even bothering to reject her anymore—she rang the doorbell. She flashed a half-smile at the security camera stationed over the door, and Channah buzzed her in. Mimi hopped into the "man trap," the small square space between security doors that was a standard feature of diamond offices. She let the first door slam behind her, heard the second buzz, pulled the metal handle on the inner door, and said hello to Channah, perched at her standard spot at the reception desk.

Channah had long dark curly hair, which she constantly twirled; a round, expressive face, dotted with black freckles; and a voluptuous figure that even her modest religious clothing couldn't hide.

"Did you hear us argue?" she asked Mimi.

"No," she sputtered. "I mean—"

Channah smiled and pointed to the video monitor on her desk. "I could see you on the camera." Her shoulders slouched. "It was the same stupid argument we always have. Even I'm bored by it."

"Hang in there. We'll talk at lunch." Mimi and Channah shared a quick hug, and Mimi walked back to the office.

She was greeted by her father's smile and a peck on the cheek. If anything made this job worthwhile, it was that grin. Plus the money.

"How are things this morning?"

"*Baruch Hashem*," Max replied. Max said "thank God" all the time, even during his wife's sickness, when he really didn't seem all that thankful.

Sure enough, he added, "We're having a crisis."

Mimi almost rolled her eyes. It was always a crisis in the office. When Mimi was young, the family joke was that business was either "terrible" or "worse than terrible."

Lately, her dad seemed more agitated than normal. As he spoke, he puttered in a circle and his hands clutched a pack of Tums. That usually didn't come out until noon.

"I can't find the two-carat pear shape." He threw his arms up and his forehead exploded into a sea of worry lines. "It's not here, it's not there. It's nowhere."

Max Rosen was dressed, as usual, in a white button-down shirt and brown wool slacks, with a jeweler's loupe dangling on a rope from his neck. His glasses sat off-kilter on his nose, and two shocks of white hair jutted from his skull like wings. When he was excited about something, like this missing diamond, the veins in his neck popped and the bobby-pinned yarmulke seemed to flap on his head.

Mimi stifled a laugh. That was the crisis? Diamonds always got lost in the office. As kids, Mimi and her two sisters used to come in on weekends and be paid one dollar for every stone they found on the floor. "They travel," Max would say.

It was no surprise that things went missing in that vortex of an office. Every desk was submerged under a huge stack of books, magazines, and papers. The most pressing were placed on the seat near her father's desk, what he called his "in-chair."

When Mimi's mother worked there, she kept a lid on the chaos. After her death, Max hired a few bookkeepers, none of whom lasted; two years later, the job had somehow fallen to Mimi.

Eventually, Channah found the two-carat pear shape, snug in its parcel papers, right next to the bathroom keys. The only logical explanation was that Max was examining it while on the toilet.

Max sheepishly returned to his desk. Mimi loved watching her father at work. She was fascinated by how he joked with friends, took grief from clients, and kept track of five things at once. It felt exotic and forbidden, like observing an animal in its natural habitat.

For the most part, they got along, which was no small thing. Over the years, there had been tense moments as he struggled to accept that she was no longer religious. Lately, he rarely brought the topic up, and she didn't want him to. Her split from her non-Jewish ex probably helped.

On occasion, the old strains resurfaced, in subtle ways. Max's desk was covered with photos—mostly of Mimi's mom and her religious sisters and their religious broods. One time when Max was at lunch, Mimi tiptoed over to glance at them, and—not incidentally—check how many were of her. It made her feel silly, yet she couldn't help herself. She was a professional nosy person.

She got her answer: out of about twenty photos, Mimi was in three, an old family photo and two pics from her sisters' weddings. That was less than expected. She tried not to take it personally. She had no kids and her marriage was a bust. What was there to show off?

Mimi spent most of the morning deciphering her father's books—a task made more difficult by his aging computer system, which regularly stalled and crashed. Her father's "new" software was actually fifteen years old.

Sometimes she wished he gave her more substantial tasks to do. While her father would never say it, he didn't consider the diamond

industry a place for women, as it had always been male-dominated—
even though, ironically, it catered mostly to females. That was fine with
Mimi. She didn't want to devote her life to a rock.

AT 1 PM, CHANNAH AND MIMI headed for Kosher Gourmet, their usual
lunch spot. Mimi always joked, "I don't know if it's kosher, but it's not
gourmet."

In the two months Mimi had worked for her father, she and Channah
had become fast friends, bonding over their shared love of mystery
novels, crossword puzzles, and sarcastic senses of humor.

Channah was not Mimi's typical friend. She was twenty-three and her
parents were strictly religious, even more than Mimi's. She commuted to
Forty-Seventh Street every day on a charter bus from Borough Park, a
frum enclave in Brooklyn. The Diamond District was her main exposure
to the wider world. She reminded Mimi of her younger, more religious
self, under her parents' thrall yet curious what else was out there.

Mimi was not Channah's typical friend either. During their lunches,
Channah quizzed her on the taste of non-Kosher food (it didn't taste any
different, Mimi told her); sex ("When the time comes," Mimi said, "you'll
figure it out"); and popular culture ("Can you explain," Channah once
asked, "why Kim Kardashian is famous?" Mimi just said no.) Today, as
usual, they talked about Yosef.

"I don't get it." Channah wrapped sesame noodles around her white
plastic fork. "I love him. He loves me. Why not get married?"

Mimi took a sip from her Styrofoam cup filled with warm tap water.
She preferred bottled water but couldn't afford it. "Have you thought of
giving Yosef an ultimatum? Tell him if he doesn't marry you by a certain
date, that's it."

"Yosef wouldn't take that seriously." Channah turned her eyes to her tray.

"Why not?"

"Cause I've done that already. Three times! I backed down every
time." Her fork toyed with her food. "I believe it is *beshert* that Yosef and
I will end up together. I've thought so since I first met him at your father's
office, and he smiled at me. What choice do I have?" Her elbow nudged
her tray across the table. "I understand why he's waiting. He wants to be
a steady provider. That's a good thing, right?"

Actually, Mimi found it sexist. She didn't say that, because she found
many things in Channah's world sexist.

"He just needs to sell that pink," Channah said, spearing a dark brown cube of chicken.

Mimi took a quick sip of water. "That pink" was an awkward subject.

One month ago, Yosef had bought a three-point-two carat pink diamond. It was the biggest purchase of his career, the kind of high-risk move that could make or break his business. Max was overjoyed. "Do you know how rare pink diamonds are?" he exclaimed. "And it's a three-carater! Sounds like a great buy!"

That was, until Yosef proudly presented it to his uncle Max, who inspected it under his favorite lamp, muttered "very nice," and quickly handed it back.

It was only after Yosef left that Max dismissed his nephew's score as a *strop*, a dog of a diamond, the kind of unsellable item that gathered dust in a safe.

"It has so many pepper spots," Max lamented. "The color's not strong at all. No one will buy that thing."

"Maybe he got it for a good price," Mimi said.

"I'm sure whoever sold it to him said it was the bargain of the century. Anytime someone offers me a *metziah,* that's a sign they can't sell the stone. There's a saying, 'your *metziah* is my *strop.*'" His face sagged. "I wish he talked to me first. That stone is worthless. I don't have the heart to tell him."

When Channah brought up the big pink at lunch, Mimi didn't want to dwell on the subject. "What's happening with that?" she asked, as casually as possible.

"Didn't you hear?" Channah jerked forward. "It got the highest grade possible on its USGR cert."

"You'll have to translate." Mimi tuned out most diamond talk.

"Cert is short for certificate, meaning grading report. The USGR is the U.S. Academy for Gemological Research, the best lab in the industry."

Mimi just stared.

"That stone's worth four million dollars."

That Mimi understood. "Wow." A lot of money for a dog of a diamond.

"Four point one million, to be exact." Channah laughed. "Don't want to leave that point one out!"

"I thought that stone was—"

"Ugly?" Channah chuckled. "Me too! I don't understand how it got that grade. I guess it doesn't matter. As your father says, 'today the paper is worth more than the diamond."' She slurped some diet soda.

"Is Yosef going to get four million dollars?"

"Who knows? He isn't exactly an expert in selling such a stone. Your father convinced him to post it on one of the online trading networks. Someone called him about it yesterday."

"That's great!"

"Hopefully. If anyone could screw this up, Yosef could." Channah's mouth curled downward. "I keep checking my phone to see if there's any news." She flipped over her iPhone, saw nothing, and flipped it back. "The way I figure, if he sells that stone, he'll have to marry me. Unless he comes up with some new excuse. He wouldn't do that, right? Not after all this time. Would he?"

Mimi struggled to keep herself in check. She was dying to shake Channah and scream that if Yosef wasn't giving her what she wanted, it was time to move on. She didn't. Yosef was her cousin. Mimi was in no position to critique someone else's love life. She always told people hers was "on hold." It was basically non-existent.

Plus, she remembered how, weeks before her wedding, her friends warned her that her fiancé had a wandering eye. That just strengthened her resolve to marry him, even though in retrospect, they were right. "With situations like that," her therapist said later, "I always recommend not to say anything. Just be a supportive friend."

Mimi waited until Channah stopped speaking. She touched her hand. "I'm sure it will work out," she said.

CHAPTER TWO

AROUND 11 AM, ONE OF MAX'S OLDEST DEALER FRIENDS, Sol, stopped by the office. Sol was tall, tan, lean, wrinkled, and, like Mimi's dad, in his 70s—though, unlike him, he spoke in a distinct Israeli accent and dyed his hair shoe-polish brown.

Sol parked himself in a chair across from Max's desk, crossed his legs, and, after he and Max asked about each others' families, opined on world events, and complained how cold it was, they started talking business.

"How are things?" Max asked.

"I'm *schlepping* along, like everyone."

"The entire industry is going down the tubes."

Mimi laughed to herself. Her father had been saying that for thirty years.

"I heard some awful news yesterday," Sol said. "Chaim from the eleventh floor was riding home when he realized he was being followed by one of the South American gangs. They banged his rear bumper until he swerved off the road. They ran up to his car, jammed a metal bar through his window, stuck a pistol against his head, and made him hand over all his merchandise."

The "South American gangs" was the non-P.C. way the industry referred to the theft crews that preyed on diamond dealers. They regularly robbed them at appointments, when they stopped to get a bite to eat, even at their homes.

"I must have told you the story of my robbery," Sol said, before launching into it regardless. "I was calling on this jeweler in Dallas. I had knowing how much Channah was hoping for a sale.

"Didn't someone contact you about it yesterday?" Mimi called from her desk.

Max and Yosef's heads both snapped toward Mimi, who tensed up at the sudden attention.

"They didn't want to buy it." The contours of Yosef's face hardened. "They knew the truth."

Mimi was mulling this over when Max broke in. "You gotta move that stone. Did I ever tell you the story about Yeheskel?"

He didn't wait for an answer. "Yeheskel was a young man entering the diamond trade. His father told him, 'here's your first lesson. Take off your pants.' Yeheskel was a little surprised but did it. The father commanded, 'now, take off your underwear.' Yeheskel did that too. The father pointed to a pile of diamonds and told him to sit on it. Yeheskel sat perched on the pile of pointy rocks for five minutes. It really started to hurt. Finally, his father said, 'get up.'

"He put his arm around his son's shoulders and said, 'I've taught you an important lesson. Don't sit on your goods!'"

Yosef laughed, even though he'd no doubt heard that joke several times before. Mimi had. Afterward she thought: *Yosef, if you know what's good for you, you won't sit on your girlfriend either.*

"Anyway," Yosef declared, "we have news to share." He called to Channah in the reception area.

She sprinted back to the office. "I was talking with my family." She stood next to Yosef in a direct horizontal line. Her smile stretched out to her ears. Something was up.

"I'm happy to announce," Yosef declared, "Channah and I are getting married."

Mimi sat shocked. The news seemed pretty sudden, given Channah's complaints at lunch, and the argument this morning. Regardless, she and her father uttered enthusiastic "*Mazal Tovs.*" Max gave Yosef's hand a hearty shake, and Mimi hugged Channah. She wanted to embrace Yosef, too, though Yosef would never touch a woman who wasn't his wife. Cousins included.

After both Mimi and her dad sat down, Yosef declared, "I always believed, good things come to those who wait. Channah has waited a long time for me."

Channah burst in, "That's for sure."

Everyone laughed.

"I can be slow." He shrugged. "I hope I'm worth every second that you've waited. I know you will be for me." He turned toward Channah and his grin grew wide and his face seemed to melt, and Mimi felt ashamed she ever doubted him.

At this point, a secular couple might engage in a showy public smooch. Yosef and Channah had never kissed, never held hands, and, needless to say, never had sex. Watching them banter, they appeared as comfortable as any couple who'd done those things. As they circled each other's space, it seemed like they very much wanted to.

"Let's see the diamond," Max said.

"Haven't gotten one yet," Yosef said.

"Right." Channah theatrically groaned. "It's not like you work in the diamond business or anything."

"I've had it with diamonds," Yosef said. "I only want to do business with people I trust, like my uncle Max."

"Sorry. All out of diamonds today." Max smiled. "Let's have a toast to celebrate. There's a bottle of Schnapps stored in the closet for just such an occasion."

"Sorry, I have an appointment to get to," Yosef said. "Thank you for everything." He waved good-bye with a big smile, the congratulations pouring down around him like confetti.

Post-announcement, Mimi felt melancholy. She was happy for her friend, yet knew things would be different from now on. After Channah got married, she would cover her hair with a *sheitel*, a wig to preserve her modesty. Mimi would miss her wild beautiful locks.

Channah would likely soon have children, because that was what religious women did. She would probably work following the first and stop after the second and third. Channah and Mimi had only known each other for two months, and they were that very specific kind of acquaintance, the work friend. This would spell the slow death of their friendship. They might see each other at family functions or keep in touch through intermittent emails or phone calls or, more likely, through Facebook. Work friends tended to drift apart after they stopped working together, particularly if marriage and kids were involved. It was a shame; Mimi enjoyed talking with Channah. It had been a while since she had a friendly confidant, who wasn't a doctor she paid for the privilege.

Before she left for the night, Mimi gave Channah one more congratulatory hug.

"Thank you for being such a wonderful friend," Channah said. "I couldn't have survived this waiting period without you."

Mimi swallowed nervously and wet her lips. "This might seem like a weird thing to say." She exhaled. "I hope we stay friends after you get married."

"Of course we will, Mimi." Channah tilted her head and emitted a forced laugh. "Why wouldn't we?"

"Sometimes when people get married, they drift away from other people in their life. I've seen it happen with my friends. When I got married, I did it to my friends."

"Come on, Mimi." Channah took her hand. "We'll always be close."

Mimi smiled. "I'm really happy that things worked out. I guess Yosef didn't have to sell that pink."

"Strange, huh?" Channah threw up her hands. "*Hashem* works in mysterious ways." She giggled. "So does Yosef."

THE NEXT MORNING, CHANNAH WALKED BACK TO THE OFFICE, wringing her hands. "I don't get it. Last night, Yosef and I were supposed to have a celebratory dinner at our favorite restaurant. He never called, even after I left a million messages.

"Yosef wouldn't back out, would he? After all this time, he wouldn't change his mind? Right?"

"Of course not." Mimi tried to sound reassuring. Inside she winced. Yosef was sometimes flaky, but this was a bit much, even for him.

Channah wrapped her fist around a strand of curls. "We just got engaged. Why is he avoiding me?"

Mimi had reached her limit. She had to say something. The last two days were like a roller-coaster for her, she could imagine how they felt for Channah.

She pulled Channah aside. Her friend seemed to know what was coming. She turned her face away.

"This isn't easy for me to say." Mimi spoke softly so her father wouldn't hear. "I went through a lot of bad stuff with my ex-husband. I kept thinking things would get better. They never did. At some point, you have to stand up for yourself." Her voice grew lower. "I care about Yosef. And I care about you. He's strung you along for some time. You don't deserve that."

Channah didn't look up.

"The other day, you asked me, 'what choice do I have?' You always have a choice. You can always choose to do right by yourself. If Yosef keeps acting this way"—Mimi took a deep breath—"find someone else."

At this, Channah lifted her head. "I understand what you're saying." She slipped her hand out of Mimi's. "It's not like that. It'll be fine. He won't back out. I'm just a worrier."

There was no point saying more. It might sink in later. Mimi gave Channah a hug, and Channah returned to reception.

An hour later, Channah walked to the back office. "It's Yosef. He—"

"Oh God, Channah." Mimi put her hand to her mouth. "Don't tell me he backed out."

"No, he . . ." She stood frozen and pale. "Died."

Then she fainted.

CHAPTER THREE

Less than twenty-four hours after Channah collapsed on the floor of Max Rosen's office, Mimi and her father attended Yosef's funeral. When she was younger, Mimi asked her father why Jews buried their dead so quick. "So you face it," he replied.

The service was held in a weathered wooden box of a synagogue, with a simple color scheme: brown. Its décor was stubbornly free of flourishes, apart from a few washed-out stained-glass windows and the ceiling, which formed a triangle pointed at the heavens. This was a no-nonsense place of worship. Today, it was a place of grief, as an entire community tried to absorb the news that a young man had been killed in a robbery.

Men and women sat in separate sections, on hard wooden benches not meant for comfort. The sanctuary usually sat about one hundred. This afternoon, it drew far more, and a few dozen people stood in the aisles and against the back wall. Despite the overflow crowd, it was eerily quiet, except for the constant creaking of old wood. It was like everyone had been stunned into silence.

The rabbi, an overweight man with dark eyes, wild untrimmed eyebrows, and a white beard that stretched halfway down his stomach, lumbered to the podium. He was dressed in the standard black hat and black suit, with a white shirt that refused to stay tucked in. His fingers curled around the lectern and his beard brushed the podium, as if he were wiping it off. Even on this cold day, his forehead was dotted with sweat, and his words, and delivery, were raw. He was more than a clergyman. He was a mourner.

"Two days ago, I spoke with Yosef." He tilted his head skyward, like he was asking God for help. "We had a long talk, just as I'm talking to you now. And now this!"

A stark wail rang out from a corner of the synagogue, followed by another —the sobs spread in a chain reaction, like yawns.

"Yosef in the Torah was known for his visions," the rabbi said. "He had the ability to see things others could not. Our Yosef was like that too. While others chased after material things, Yosef knew what was most important in life—being the best person you can, caring about others, and living in accordance with the laws of *Hashem*.

"The name *Yosef* is derived from the Hebrew word 'to add.' Yosef added something to the lives of everyone he came into contact with. That is why it's so painful that he has been taken from us." He delivered the last part in a voice soaked with sobs.

My God, Mimi thought, *even the rabbi can't hold it together.* The tears flowed.

The worst came last. Everyone left the *shul* for the cemetery, where they stood in the cold and recited the *Kaddish* as the unadorned brown pine box that contained Yosef was lowered into the ground. As is tradition, Yosef's brother Bernard lifted a shovel, scooped a pile of dirt, and poured it in the grave. Max joined him, filling the hole with such grunting exertion Mimi was worried he'd hurt himself. Mimi was not a praying woman, but she begged God to blot out what she was seeing, to make it all a dream.

AFTERWARD, EVERYONE HEADED TO THE *SHIVA*, held in the Riverdale section of the Bronx, at the home of Yosef's only sibling, Bernard. Like Yosef, Bernard was a diamond dealer. Unlike his brother, he was successful at it. Visiting his house underscored just how successful. Instead of the standard modest religious home, Bernard's place was upscale and well-decorated, highlighted by clear tables, glass bookshelves packed with Judaic ornaments, and freshly vacuumed white rugs.

Following custom, Mimi and her father had picked up food for the mourners—a plate of bagels and egg salad. Mimi was so beside herself that she nibbled on a bagel when her car stopped at a traffic light. Her father shot her a dirty look.

A candle stood on a table in the center of the living room, a symbol of Yosef's short life. It was meant to burn for the entire seven-day length of the *shiva*. All the mirrors were covered, to prevent mourners from getting distracted by vanity. The bereaved sat on low stools, which brought them close to the ground to show the depth of their sorrow. It all gave Mimi flashbacks to sitting *shiva* for her mom two years ago. While Mimi tried to respect the religious traditions, those stools were butt-numbing and uncomfortable. She used every excuse not to sit on them.

Mourners are not supposed to change their clothes for a week or even wash. On the third day of her mom's *shiva*, Mimi took a shower and changed her shirt. It was her favorite part of the whole miserable week.

The sexes were divided into different rooms, with the men stationed in the living room, and the women, as usual, relegated to a smaller spot, the den. When Mimi entered, the ladies' room was packed. Most of the women were muted and somber, although a few laughed and gossiped like it was a cocktail party. Peering through the crowd, Mimi spied Channah, stuck in a kind of *shiva* limbo. As Yosef's fiancée, and only a fiancée for half a day, she wasn't considered an "official" mourner, which meant she sat on a regular chair, with her hand on her chin. She'd been as devastated by this as anyone. Mimi wondered how long it would take her to get over this. Probably her whole life.

Mimi pushed through the throng to greet her friend—two months in the Diamond District had improved her ability to shove—and the two shared a warm, tearful, tight hug.

"How are you?" Mimi sat on a metal folding chair and put her hand on Channah's knee.

"I feel numb." Channah had a quarter-sized bruise on her head from when she'd fainted. "I'm surviving, I guess."

"I'm so sorry about this. I'm in shock."

"My parents gave me a couple of Xanax so I could make it through everything. I may have to take some the whole week. You might think I'm a bad person,"—which for her meant bad Jew—"I didn't attend the funeral. I was walking over and realized I would have to see Yosef's coffin. I couldn't handle that."

Mimi didn't know a sensitive way to ask the question weighing on her mind. So, she just did. "How'd it happen?"

Channah looked at her lap. "Yosef was getting his car from a parking garage. A robber tried to take his goods, and Yosef fought back." She paused. "During the fight, the guy shot him."

Mimi had never known anyone who had been shot before. The

concept seemed so alien.

"It doesn't make sense." Channah kept her head down. "It's so unlike him. We always talked about what would happen if, God forbid, he was ever robbed." She stopped herself. "God forbid? I guess God didn't forbid it."

Mimi was stunned. That was the most sacrilegious thing she'd ever heard Channah say.

"They always tell you in a robbery don't resist. Let the bad guy take your goods. Your life is more important. Insurance will take care of anything that gets stolen. We talked about this." Channah spat out those last words, like she was arguing with a dead man. "Yosef had so much to live for. We were going to spend our lives together. Why would he risk it all for a stupid diamond?"

They sat a while longer, neither saying much, both lost in thought. At one point, Mimi remembered that, the day before, she had basically told Channah to dump Yosef. With all that happened since, Mimi had forgotten she'd said that. She hoped Channah had too.

BEFORE MIMI AND HER FATHER LEFT, they paid their respects to Bernard, his wife, and their five kids—three boys and two girls. She hadn't seen any of them since her mother's funeral.

Mimi hated being the relative who says, "I can't believe how big you've gotten," but that was the first thing that popped out of her mouth when she saw the children clustered together in the kitchen. They were polite if a bit standoffish, which Mimi understood; not many kids would be eager to chat with a cousin they hadn't seen in years.

Bernard's eldest son had just turned fifteen and was beginning to sprout the facial hair that he'd likely wear his whole life. Two years ago, Mimi was invited to his Bar Mitzvah and didn't go. She had boycotted most family functions after her religious relatives sat out of her wedding to a non-Jew. She figured, if they wouldn't go to her event, she wouldn't go to theirs.

Maybe it was time to put that behind her. Because sometimes stuff like this happened.

Bernard resembled an older, shorter, plumper version of his brother, with the same puffy cheeks but a bushier beard and eyebrows. As a child, he was a bit of a know-it-all, always lording his knowledge over his slower younger brother. He often came across as brusque and wore a chronic grimace instead of his brother's ready smile—yet even if he had one, he wouldn't be displaying it today.

"Uncle Max, I have so much to say to you." He had a large tear on the left side of his shirt, a sign he was in mourning. He pulled Mimi's father close. "My brother, he could be immature. He needed guidance sometimes. I tried to provide it. I know you did too."

Max bowed his head as Bernard spoke.

"Our father died when we were young," Bernard went on. "It is a terrible thing for a son to grow up without a father. In many ways, you filled that role. You were like a father to him."

Max looked up, his face stiff with sorrow. "Yosef was a lovely person. I am so sorry about this."

"There have been a lot of tears, Uncle Max." Bernard's voice broke. "There will be a lot more."

Max uttered the traditional words of comfort, "May God console you among the other mourners of Zion and Jerusalem."

As a rebellious adolescent, those religious homilies rang hollow to Mimi. Who were the mourners of Zion and Jerusalem, and what did they have to do with anything? Now, she understood those phrases better. They don't provide consolation. It's just that no one knows what to say. So, they say that.

As Mimi drove her father back to his house in Queens, the ride was mostly silent, until Max blurted from the darkness, "Did you hear what Bernard said? That I was like a father to Yosef." After that, he softly sobbed, all the way home.

CHAPTER FOUR

MIMI DROPPED HER FATHER OFF AND returned to her apartment in New Jersey. As usual, it was cold.

Mimi had lived in the small drab two-bedroom since she separated from her husband. It had been the cheapest she could find. She figured she'd soon graduate to something better. Now, she struggled to afford it there.

Leaving a complaint on the landlord's voice mail was, she knew, pointless. She fired up the space heater and fetched her favorite blue blanket from the closet. She stretched her sweater sleeves over her hands and put on her thinking music of choice, Edith Piaf. Mimi's mom was from Antwerp, Belgium, and listened to a lot of French music when she was growing up. After she died, Mimi played it as a kind of homage. She didn't understand the words, and didn't have to. It all sounded so melancholy; she could graft her own sadness on top of it.

The minute Mimi lay on her recliner, she started to cry. Yosef's death brought back memories of her mother's death from cancer two years ago. Her mom's illness was long and drawn-out, full of doctor appointments, chemotherapy treatments, hospital visits, shifting prognoses, and brief moments of hope that were quickly scuttled. When Mimi looked back, she realized it was hopeless the entire time.

Mimi always felt closer to her artistically inclined mother than her religious businessman father. After her death, she realized how little she knew her. Her mother wanted to be a painter, and taught art part-time at the local synagogue. Her family considered it just a sideline—until the *shiva,* when a parade of former students testified to how encouraging and inspiring she was. Mimi dreamt about her mom all the time.

Her mother's death kicked off a long downhill slide for Mimi. A little later, she saw an Amazon notification on her husband's phone announcing the delivery of a diamond bracelet. For a moment, she thought her husband had bought a gift to cheer her up after her mom's death. But she wondered: If he was in the market for diamonds, why didn't he ask her father? Besides, Mimi wasn't that into jewelry. Two days later, she spotted the bracelet—on a table at her best friend's house.

Just to be sure, she snapped a picture and asked her father to estimate the caratage. It matched the Amazon item perfectly.

Mimi later wondered whether it was smart to have ventured down that particular rabbit hole. Yes, it was always better to know the truth. That was one of her credos as a journalist. Maybe that little dalliance wouldn't have lasted. Maybe she shouldn't have cornered her husband with the evidence like she was doing a newspaper exposé. He did stammer and confess. It was her most successful investigation. And it had the worst result.

Amid all the turmoil in her life, everyone at the website swore they understood what she was going through. When she struggled to complete routine tasks or got in fights with the higher-ups, that only went so far. When her boss, a close friend and partner-in-crime when they'd sat in adjoining cubicles, called Mimi in her office for a long-faced parting of the ways, it wasn't unexpected. It felt like a sock to the jaw regardless.

As Mimi fought off the cold with a blue wool blanket, she struggled to understand where her life had gone wrong. In her twenties, she was focused and aggressive. She set out for a journalism job and a husband. By thirty, she had landed both.

She later realized, with help from her therapist, that her fast and furious younger self had been propelled largely by fear—fear of failure, fear of being alone, fear of not living up to the standards she had set for herself.

Now, with the life she had built in ruins, and her worst fears realized, Mimi was no longer sure what she wanted, only that it wasn't being unemployed, single, and stuck in a cold apartment, pondering all the losses in her life.

MIMI WAS, BY HER OWN ADMISSION, a crappy accountant. She could only do the job for twenty minutes before she lunged for the Internet.

In the days following Yosef's death, Mimi could barely focus on the mundane task of balancing her father's books. She challenged herself to make it interesting. Think like a journalist. Have the numbers tell a story.

Which she did. The story they told was an ugly one.

One afternoon, as Max returned from lunch, Mimi looked straight at him. "We need to talk."

Max groaned.

Mimi pulled her chair to her father's desk. She had written out what she planned to say. "Dad, I have some bad news." Her eyes stayed on her notes. "I'm extremely sorry to tell you this. Your business is going bust."

At this, she glanced at her father. He was sneaking a peek at his computer.

"I've double-checked the numbers. I've triple checked them. You owe thirty thousand dollars to the bank. You owe the landlord two months' rent, which means you're seriously in danger of eviction. You only make about two hundred dollars on each diamond, which is around a two percent margin. That's like keeping your money in a savings account. That might work if you made tons of sales. You're only making one or two a month. Plus, you have substantial expenses. There's rent, money for security, and, I hate to say it, my salary. At this rate, your business will barely last a year."

She looked at Max. He was picking lint off his shirt.

Her voice quickened. "I know how much your business means to you. However, if this continues, you're in serious danger of the bank pulling your credit and gaining control of your business. That would jeopardize your company assets, possibly your personal savings, even your home. Your best option is to wind things down in an orderly fashion." She had organized her findings into a five-page report, complete with charts and full-year financial projections, which she placed on his desk. "Here's a summary of my findings. I'm happy to go over them."

He didn't react.

"Any comment?" Mimi asked finally.

"*Nu*?" he said, adding a half-shrug, as if this discussion didn't merit a whole one.

Mimi was dumbfounded. She'd uncovered a real problem, and now her father had dismissed her work with some flippant Yiddish.

"That's it, Dad? *So what?*"

"The business has ups and downs," he said, waving away her concerns like they were a pesky fly. "We're having a few lean months. It's not the end of the world."

The father who had spent his entire life complaining about his business was now telling her it wasn't so bad.

"This is right after Christmas and just before Valentine's Day," Mimi said. "Those are the two main diamond-buying occasions."

"I'll admit the phone hasn't been ringing lately. Business is a little slow."

"If things are that slow, you shouldn't pay my salary."

"That's not an issue, *bubelah.*"

Her dad could usually stop her in her tracks by calling her *bubelah.* Sure enough, she tried not to blush.

"Dad, you need to take this seriously. This is a crisis."

"A couple of big sales will get me out of the hole. Sol and I said *mazal* on that one carat princess."

"Did he meet your price?"

"No, I met his."

"Did you make any money on the deal?"

He shrugged. Meaning no. "You have to keep inventory moving. Did I ever tell you the story about how Yeheskel got trained in the diamond business? His father told him, 'Yeheskel—'"

"Dad! I've heard that one already! You can't run your business like this."

Max's face morphed into a scowl. "I built this company. I've kept it going for forty-five years. What do you know about how to run this business?"

"I know you must pay your rent."

"Big deal. The landlord gets his precious check a few weeks late. He's a billionaire. I've been late with the rent before."

"How about the bank? They're okay waiting too?"

"I'm small potatoes for them. I've known the loan officer for years. We're old friends. He knows I'm good for everything."

"I don't know if we still live in that kind of world."

At this, Max's face curdled, and his eyebrows met in disapproval. "Look, Mimila," she knew when he said that, he was ending the discussion, "let me worry about the business. You worry about your job."

"Dad, this is my job! I'm your accountant!"

"Actually, since Channah is out," he said, half looking at her, half typing an email, "your job is answering the phones."

With Channah on leave, Mimi had taken on her reception duties, in addition to her own. It meant coming in five days a week, instead of three, and she found it hard work, harder than she expected. While Channah juggled everything with good humor, by the end of the first day, Mimi thought she'd go crazy if she answered one more phone call.

Mimi's breathing hastened, her muscles tightened, her head began to pound. She felt like a teenager, fighting with her father. This job was regressing her.

After the debacle at her last office, Mimi swore she'd never again argue with a supervisor. But this was her father. No one could push your buttons like your family. They put them there.

She stormed out of the office and spent a half hour angrily pacing up and down Forty-Seventh Street, surveying her options. She didn't have many. This job was keeping her afloat.

She and her father barely spoke the rest of the afternoon, except for a stilted "good night."

This was why people should never work with their family.

CHAPTER FIVE

ON THE FINAL NIGHT OF YOSEF'S *shiva*, Mimi visited again, with a fresh plate of egg salad. No nibbling this time.

After seven days, the crowds had dissipated, and the women's room was empty except for Channah, still in *shiva* limbo.

"If there's anything I can do, please let me know," Mimi told her. "I know that's the same stupid thing everybody says. Really, I want to help."

For a second, Channah appeared deep in thought. "There is one thing. But it's big. And kind of weird."

"What is it?"

"I'll tell you. Remember, you can say no." Channah surveyed the room. It was just the two of them. She dropped her voice. "Do you think there's something more to Yosef's murder?"

"Like what?"

"Maybe I've read too many mystery books. I don't think this was a random gang robbery. I think Yosef was set up."

Before coming, Mimi had consulted an online guide to comforting mourners. The advice boiled down to: Listen, be compassionate, and show understanding. Don't judge their comments.

Even so, Mimi couldn't help reacting to what Channah just said. "What makes you say that?"

"Yosef was very careful. He never carried goods with him, certainly not outside of Forty-Seventh Street. That's why this is so weird to me. The one time Yosef has a valuable diamond, he gets hit by crooks. Maybe someone tipped them off."

"It's possible. It could be coincidence."

"Sure, it could. That's not the only weird thing." She twisted her hair around her finger. "I never understood how Yosef had the money to buy that big pink diamond. He was usually pretty careful about who he dealt with. Toward the end, he got desperate to make something of himself. Maybe bad people helped him with it, like loan sharks or something. Some of the people on the fringes of the industry are really scary."

As Channah grew more and more worked up, Mimi worried she wasn't such a good consoler.

"Yosef acted so strange before he died," Channah continued. "Why, after all those arguments, did he all of a sudden decide to get married, out of the blue, in the middle of the day when I'm answering phones? He didn't even bother to get me an engagement ring. Not that I consider that the biggest deal in the world, but he did work in the diamond business."

That indeed was strange. Yosef was a strange guy.

"He also said that he had something to admit to me. He said he'd made a big mistake. He wouldn't tell me what it was. He said we'd discuss it at dinner. I have a weird feeling about everything."

Mimi didn't know what to say. The online guide didn't cover anything like this. "Did you tell these things to the police?"

"Of course I told them. You know how they are. They have a million cases to investigate. If they can solve something right away, they're happy."

Mimi put her arm around Channah and squeezed her tight. A twenty-five-year-old had just died. How could that ever make sense?

"If I had the money, I'd hire a private detective to investigate." Channah swerved toward Mimi. "I thought, maybe you could look into it. I don't know many people who were newspaper reporters for nine years."

That was what Mimi got for bragging. During their lunches, Mimi had regaled Channah with tales of her time at *The West Jersey Metro*.

She had worked at the newspaper for nearly a decade. While she loved reporting, she found working for a local paper—at a time when the industry was consolidating—endlessly frustrating. She spent the first two years on the graveyard shift, waiting all night for something big to happen. It never did. When she graduated to days, she spent time on the features desk, followed by the town council beat, where she covered zoning disputes, hoping they would turn into something interesting. They never did. While Mimi nabbed the occasional scoop, reporting that a town council president was stepping down will never land you farther than page A3.

She started asking Lewis, the longtime editor in chief, for more investigative assignments. He always told her to come back in six months. Six months later, he would tell her the same thing. Finally, at a heated meeting, he blurted, "Would you stop pestering me? You're not ready right now. Your ambition outstrips your ability." Mimi darted from his office before he could see her cry.

Shortly after that, Mimi left the newspaper. She told her coworkers it was because she was moving in with her fiancé, who lived an hour away from the paper, and didn't want a long commute. That was true. She also could have made it work if she really tried. She had grown frustrated and needed a change. She figured that working at a woman-oriented current events site would catapult her to meatier assignments.

At first, the new job was great, better paying and less stressful, in a luxurious New York City office stacked with amenities. (At the newspaper, they had even cut out coffee.)

Yet, she never warmed to the work, which mostly involved crafting headlines and editing quick takes on the news. Soon, the budget axe fell at her new job too, and the publication reinvented itself as a woman's lifestyle site. By the third week, she had exhausted every possible pun on the word *bake*.

With all the problems in the newspaper industry, her former colleagues told her she was lucky she left the paper when she did. Part of her believed she never should have quit. With time, she would have proven herself. Even to that jerk Lewis.

"Channah, I was a reporter who covered town council meetings. Boring stuff."

"You're right, Mimi. I shouldn't have asked."

"Even if I did investigate, how could I find out more than the police?"

"I don't know. I only asked because I have nowhere else to turn. It was a crazy thought. Sorry I brought it up." She turned her face to the floor.

Mimi hated to see Channah upset. After all her friend had been through, she couldn't bear to let her down. "I could try," she whispered.

"Are you sure?" Channah lifted her eyes. "Feel free to say no."

"I'll see what I can find out. Don't expect miracles. I'm pretty rusty."

"Whatever you can do, will be so helpful. You're very smart, Mimi.

You don't realize how smart you are." Channah reached over to give Mimi a hug. "I'm so lucky to have a friend like you."

As Channah gripped her, Mimi wondered what she'd gotten into, and whether she could get out of it.

WHEN MIMI GOT HOME, SHE LAY ON HER RECLINER with a glass of wine. Could she investigate something as big as Yosef's murder? It had been a long time since she'd done this kind of thing, and even then, it wasn't *this* kind of thing.

When she lost her job at the website, she hoped it would be an opportunity to get back into real journalism. In a year of freelancing, the only assignments she received were of the lifestyle variety she had long grown tired of.

It never occurred to her to write about Yosef's death. While it made her squirm to think about, it was a marketable idea. Editors loved crime stories! Even if there was nothing more to his murder, the gang aspect was juicy enough. The fact that Yosef was her cousin gave the story a personal angle. She could also provide insight into the diamond business in a way few others could. It might jumpstart her career. She could win an award. Editors loved awards! She fantasized posting on Facebook about her new honor.

She instantly scolded herself. *Awards? Facebook?* This was Yosef, her cousin. She'd held him as a baby. He was a good person, and a private one. Could she rebuild her career on his corpse?

As her old editor Lewis would say, "Journalists don't cover the sun shining." They chronicled the worst parts of life. Mimi could be sensitive about this, bring Yosef to life, and honor his memory.

In any case, Channah had asked her to do this. She had said yes. She had no choice.

She didn't know what to make of Channah's talk of loan sharks. Nothing Channah mentioned struck her as evidence of anything other than Yosef being a flaky guy.

One thing did strike her as odd: Yosef's explanation for why the buyer passed on his pink. "They knew the truth." *What did that mean?*

Mimi needed a new direction. This was new. She and her wineglass moved to the computer, where she sketched out the case, as well as descriptions of Yosef and Channah and the diamond game's rites and rituals. The words flowed. She was still typing two hours past her bedtime.

She could have gone all night.

It was the most creative and engaged she'd been in some time. She felt like she was living, instead of just surviving. There was no backing out. She was on this train.

CHAPTER SIX

THE NEXT MORNING, AS MIMI WAS GETTING DRESSED for work, Channah called, her voice like sandpaper. "Mimi, I want to apologize for putting you on the spot last night. If you don't want to investigate—"

"No, I want to do it. Though, before we start, understand that I may try to sell this story to a newspaper or a website. If you feel weird about that, let me know."

Channah took a second to answer. "Do what you need to," she murmured.

"Okay. I'll need your help with some things. I'll have to interview you. I want to know what you remember about Yosef's last days."

"I'll write down everything." She sounded like she'd been given a homework assignment. "When do you want to do this? Tomorrow night?"

This surprised Mimi. "Are you sure you want to do it so soon? Some of the questions may be personal."

"If it helps you find the truth, I'll do it."

For the past week, Mimi had pitied her friend. Now, she realized: *Channah is a strong person.*

"One more thing." Mimi cradled the phone in her neck. "Don't tell my father I'm doing this. He'll worry I'll get hurt."

"God, Mimi," Channah gasped. "You think that's possible?"

"It'll be fine. The crime reporters at my old newspaper never had any problems. You know my dad. He worries about everything."

Channah was silent for a second. "I need to tell you something else. Even though *shiva* week is over, I can't come back to work this week. Or the week after. And probably the week after that. I just *can't*. I—" Her voice cracked. "I'm not well."

"I understand completely."

"If your father wants to stop paying me, fine. He can even fire me."

They both knew he would never do either of those things.

"Do what's right for you," Mimi responded. "When my mother died, my old job gave me five days off. The first morning back, everyone offered their condolences, and, by the afternoon, they acted like I'd returned from vacation. I had just watched someone die, and they expected me to care about proper use of a semicolon.

"Come back when you're ready. Not a moment before. My father will understand."

"I'm sure he will," said Channah. "He's a very understanding man. Tell him not to worry about me. Really, I don't want him worrying."

WHEN MIMI GOT TO THE OFFICE and told her father, he did understand. And he did worry.

"It's so terrible." Max shook his head. "Anyway, this means you're back on reception."

Mimi hated sitting at the front desk. She had always taken comfort knowing Channah would be back soon. It was now clear; she might be stuck there for a while.

Mimi knew the conversation was over unless she said something. "Doing the phones doesn't give me much time for the books."

"I'll live." After last week's discussion, he'd probably be happy if she never did them again.

Mimi's hands balled into fists. "I didn't come here to answer phones."

"What do you want me to do, Mimi?" Max glowered. "Channah's out. I need you up front."

Given the tragedy they were all dealing with, Mimi wouldn't make a fuss. "Fine," she growled, and slunk back to reception. She just wished her father had at least asked. Instead, he declared, "You're on the phones," like she was twelve and it was her turn to do the dishes.

WHILE MIMI WAS NONE TOO HAPPY about sinking from journalist to receptionist, the investigation increased her excitement about work and life in general. Instead of spending her down time at the desk doing crossword puzzles, she leafed through trade magazines and eavesdropped on her father's dealings. Working in her father's company was no longer just a stopgap. It had a purpose.

She searched for information on Yosef, though it felt creepy Googling her cousin. She did the same for Channah, which felt even worse. No matter. There was little on either of them, and it was all in Hebrew and tied to religious schools.

She made a list of people to call. She needed a police source. She knew from her friends on the crime beat that cops couldn't release information about an investigation to reporters. However, if you schmoozed the right cop, in the right way . . .

The last time she chatted up sources she was a cute twenty-something fresh out of college. In her days on the town council beat, Mimi went to bars where local politicos gathered and brought coffee to their offices. She even dated a councilman's chief of staff—although in retrospect, they may have just been sleeping together. She was never sure.

Now, she was a divorced thirty-eight-year-old. Her social skills had atrophied during her marriage, and her year sitting home being depressed didn't help.

It shouldn't be too hard to get back in the swing. She hoped.

Channah had given Mimi the card of the investigating officer, Detective Michael Matthews. She dialed his number. As the phone rang, her heart pounded and her throat tickled. She was back in business. She was a reporter again.

He picked up. "Detective Matthews."

"Hi, Detective Matthews. My name is Mimi Rosen, I'm doing a story on the murder of Yosef Levine for—" She paused. If she had learned anything from her months trying to freelance, it was that people ignored reporters who didn't know if their piece would be published. "*The West Jersey Metro*. I am looking for more information on the case."

"If you give me your email, I can send you the official report." He pronounced it *re-pawt*.

"That would be great." She remembered her old editor's tip. "Information is currency," he'd say. "If you share things with sources, they will share them with you."

Mimi opened her notebook and clicked her pen. "I was hoping we could have an information exchange. Trade any tips."

"I'm pretty limited in what I can discuss with the press. I do hope you will share any information relevant to an ongoing homicide investigation."

"Of course," Mimi stuttered.

Time for her old editor's other trick. Sources talk more if you throw out specific scenarios. Sometimes even their denials tell you something.

"I hear the police think the murder was the result of a gang robbery."

"The perpetrator was likely a member of an SATG."

"SA—?"

"South American theft gang."

"I have reason to believe this wasn't just a simple theft. Yosef may have been set up."

"Uh-huh." Matthews sounded skeptical. "Why do you think that?"

"For one, Yosef said he would never resist a robbery."

There was a pause.

"And—?"

"Well, that's it."

"When you read the police report, you'll see that the surveillance video clearly shows the victim resisted the theft."

"Can I see that video?"

"It is presently evidence in a police investigation. If we decide to make it public, we'll let you know."

"What if I come to the station? Will you show it to me?"

"No."

"Why not?"

"This is a police precinct, not a movie house." He punctuated this with a curt clearing of his throat. "Anything else?"

"Yes. Yosef was selling a three-carat pink diamond. He said that someone didn't want it because they knew the truth." She paused. "I heard him say that."

Matthews could be heard shifting in his seat. "You think that's related to his murder?"

"I don't know. Do you?"

"I'll make a note of it." It sounded like he was shuffling papers.

Mimi had one last trick. "Maybe we can meet up sometime. I'll bring coffee." She slid into a high register, to add a little flirt to her voice.

"That's very nice of you. I think we're okay. We have coffee in the precinct. What did you say your name and newspaper was again?"

"Mimi Rosen. *The West Jersey Metro.*"

"And you're writing an article on this case?"

"I hope to, yes."

"When do you expect this article to appear?"

This caught Mimi off-guard. "I'm not sure," she stammered.

"I appreciate the call. Unfortunately, I don't have a lot of time to chat."

He said *chat* like it was the world's biggest waste of time.

He was patronizing her. She hated that.

"I'm just making sure you guys are really looking into this."

"Our investigation is continuing."

"So's mine!" Mimi hung up, feeling like she'd scored a point against Mr. Condescending. Until she realized she hadn't provided her email. Matthews couldn't send her the police report. She was too embarrassed to call back.

Mimi buried her face in her hands. Social skills, rusty.

CHAPTER SEVEN

THE NEXT DAY, MIMI BROUGHT HER CAR into work so she could drive to Channah's that night. Hunting for a parking space near Forty-Seventh Street, she initially avoided the garage one block over where Yosef was killed. She realized that she had to go there. She was writing about this.

The week before, the garage was a crime scene, cordoned off with yellow tape and guarded by police officers. A makeshift memorial sprung up on the street outside, with candles, prayer cards, and flowers circling a picture of Yosef's silly grin. Now all that was gone.

As Mimi drove on the garage's long grey entry ramp, she felt a sudden foreboding, like she was going down the entranceway to Hell. She quickly found a space, parked her car, and hurried through the garage, trying not to think about where she was.

As she walked to the elevator, she felt a chill. This was where Yosef was accosted. Where he fought back. Where he died.

The ground spun beneath her. For one terrifying second, Mimi feared she would collapse. She wobbled back to her car and leaned against it, one hand gripping the door handle, the other pressed against her front window, its coldness grounding her and providing comfort.

As she caught her breath, she saw the garage security guard, who just five minutes earlier she'd spotted napping in his glass booth, run toward her. "Are you okay?" he asked.

"I'm fine." She took a tentative step away from her car and surveyed her surroundings. Fluorescent lights hung from the ceiling. There were round pillars painted half-red, half-white, with a black stripe around the middle. A sign listed parking as fifty dollars a day, less on weekends. It was a garage, like any other. All the horror had been washed away.

The guard now stood to her left. He was about fifty, with thinning brown-and-grey hair and yellow teeth, and he sported a too-big blue blazer with a patch marked "Expert Security." "It looked like you were fainting or something."

"I got overwhelmed." She took a few woozy steps. "My cousin was killed here last week."

She watched the realization hit his face. "Oh yeah. That was a real tragic thing." He introduced himself as Jimmy and asked if she needed an escort to the elevator. Before Mimi could answer, he cupped her elbow and walked with her.

Mimi didn't shoo him away; he might know something. The dizziness dissipated and she snapped into reporter mode. "People here must be pretty shook up."

"Oh yeah. They've beefed up security like crazy. I used to only work nights. Now I'm doing shifts 'round the clock. The extra money is nice, but it's exhausting." He expelled a yawn.

They walked a little more.

"I heard there are questions about the murder."

"You got that right." Jimmy's eyes became circles. "My boss saw the video of the crime. Says there's weird stuff on it."

Mimi stopped and turned to him. "Like what?"

Jimmy's head darted back and forth like the place was bugged. "Before the guy was shot, he and the robber had a big argument. Like they knew each other. Who has a discussion with someone with a gun in his back? My boss says the robber didn't even steal his diamond. Just a piece of paper."

They started walking again.

"What kind of paper?"

"Beats me."

"Do you have a copy of the video?"

"Nope. Police got it."

That was the most important piece of evidence in the case, and Mimi had no way of seeing it.

They arrived at the elevator. Jimmy pressed the button, and they craned their heads upward, watching the numbers drop.

Mimi tried to restart the conversation. "Must have been a real shock hearing about it."

"Oh yeah. I'll never forget when my boss told me somebody got killed here. He said it happened right over there." He pointed his oversized sleeve toward a spot a few feet from the elevator.

There were no blood stains on that patch of floor, no markers, nothing distinguishing it from the rest of the parking lot. Mimi had just walked over it, oblivious. That was now holy ground, the place where a decent man died tragically at a young age.

Mimi tried to look at it forensically. It was close to the elevator. Was that significant? Did it have different lighting than the rest of the garage?

"Hold it," Jimmy rubbed his forehead. "I was wrong. It happened over there." He pointed to another spot further from the elevator. He pulled his hand back and crinkled his eyes. "Come to think of it, maybe it was in the back."

His words were interrupted by the metallic ding of the elevator. For the first time in her life, Mimi was happy to get in one.

"WELCOME TO MY PLACE." CHANNAH MOTIONED around the basement of her parents' compact brick house in Borough Park. "It's not much, but it's mine."

Channah was the second of eight kids, and, after years of sharing a room, she'd moved into her own space in the basement after her sister got married. It wasn't a remodeled basement, more of a basement basement, with a low ceiling, naked light bulbs, a persistent musty smell, and an oversized white boiler, which stood a little too close to her bed. Mimi heard water drip and couldn't figure out where from.

The few signs someone lived there included Channah's half-made bed, the brown and yellow rug lying next to it, and a wooden dresser topped with pictures—with a framed one of Yosef in front. A nightstand near the bed held a torn-open bag of Butterfingers and *The Jewish Guide to Grief and Acceptance*, the first chapter of which looked well-thumbed. Channah always said she couldn't wait to move out of her house once she got married, and Mimi now understood why.

Channah offered Mimi a chair, then sat cross-legged on her bed. Her hair was stuffed in a haphazard ponytail, and she was clad in baggy pink sweatpants and a grey sweatshirt. With no *shiva* to go to, Mimi guessed she'd dressed like that all day.

"How are you holding up?"

Channah released a gust of air that blew up her bangs. "I'm okay. It's just really hard. I miss him so much. I miss talking to him. I miss everything about him.

"I even miss hearing him go on about sports. He told me once he had read one hundred books about baseball. You could ask him about any player and he'd reel off every stat and every team he'd been on. He would go on and on it and it used to annoy me so much." Her leg dropped to the floor. "I'd give anything to hear that one more time."

At this, Mimi again remembered how she told Channah to dump Yosef. It again made her feel awful.

Channah pulled a tissue from her nightstand. "You don't need to hear me moping and crying any more. You heard that enough last week."

"Cry all you want. It's good to get it out."

Channah extended her arm toward the nightstand and plucked a Butterfinger from the bag. "Want one?"

Mimi shook her head no.

"I've been stress-eating. Or grief-eating. The point is, I'm eating a lot." She tore open the wrapper, tossed the candy in her mouth, and quickly swallowed it. "Just a week ago, I was worried about losing weight for my wedding."

The room fell silent, except for the mysterious drip.

"I used to stress-eat a lot during my divorce," Mimi said. "One time, I bought a cake and couldn't stop eating it, so I threw it in the trash. Then I got worried I would fish it out of the garbage, and I dumped coffee grounds on it."

Two weeks ago, Channah would have let loose a throaty laugh, bounced up and down on her seat, and offered her own humiliating story in return. Now, she just returned a thin smile.

"Let's get to the investigation." Channah fixed her posture. "I spoke to Bernard. He is open to letting you examine Yosef's books. He'll set something up with the probate lawyer. He says he won't do an interview. He thinks the whole thing is nuts."

Mimi nodded. "Yeah, he told me the same thing."

"That's how everyone is. I talk about this, and they look at me funny and pat me on the head like, poor Channah, it's the grief talking. They think I'm this depressed crazy person. I know there's something more to this. You do too, right, Mimi? I'm not crazy. Am I?"

"Of course not," Mimi said, taken aback.

"Then ask me questions."

Mimi dutifully opened her purse and took out her pen and notebook. "Let's start with Yosef's business. What can you tell me about it?"

"Not much. I knew he was struggling. Like every dealer, he whined all the time. Mostly, he didn't talk about business. He had two interests, Talmud and baseball." Channah's chin drooped. "And me, sometimes."

Mimi looked up from her notebook. "I remember how he'd look at you, Channah. You topped the list."

"That's nice of you to say, but he never wanted to get married." Channah sniffled and reached for a tissue.

Mimi thought about stopping the interview and going to the bed and comforting Channah. She decided to stay professional. "Let's talk about that. Yosef wouldn't get married until he made something of himself. Why was that so important to him?"

Channah dabbed her eyes. "I don't know. I told him a million times I didn't care."

"Couldn't someone have helped him? Like your father, or his brother?"

"He wanted to make it on his own. He believed that was the only fair thing, because not everyone has family in the business. Sometimes I thought he was being noble. Other times I thought, just ask your brother, don't be a *shmuck*." She laughed like she was talking about her silly fiancé, not her dead one.

"He bought that million-dollar pink diamond. Did you ever ask how he afforded that stone?"

"Of course I asked."

"What did he say?"

"Don't ask." Channah giggled, which gave Mimi permission to laugh, too.

"Did he have a partner?"

"I never heard of one. If a dealer wanted to work with someone on a multi-million-dollar stone, I don't think they'd choose Yosef."

"Yosef told you some strange things on the day he died. He said he had something to admit to you. That he'd made a mistake. Any idea what that was?"

"No. He said he'd explain everything to me that night. He never did, because—"

Channah started to tear up. She didn't finish the sentence, and Mimi didn't want her to.

"Did he mention anything else?"

"He said he wanted to quit the business."

"Really?" Mimi jotted this down. "Did he say why?"

"No. He just said, 'I wish I never got involved with that pink.' That's why I think it might be loan sharks or something."

"Did he say anything else?" Mimi tapped her pen against her notebook. "I need you to remember."

Channah thought a bit. "He said maybe we could run away together and live on a mountain."

"What did you say to that?"

"I said, 'what are we going to do, two Orthodox Jews from New York living on a mountain? We wouldn't last five minutes up there.' He was serious. He asked if I would love him no matter what, even if he had no income or spent his days studying *Talmud*."

"And you said yes?"

"Of course I said yes! Do you know how long I waited for him?" Her leg made lazy circles on the floor. "I didn't expect to marry a penniless religious scholar. Life follows the direction *Hashem* wants, not the way we want." Her eyes teared up and she grabbed another tissue. "Sorry I keep crying. You must have more questions."

All the remaining questions dealt with how Channah heard that Yosef had been killed. Mimi had little desire to ask that. "We've covered enough."

She moved to Channah's bed and gave her a hug. They talked a bit about Channah's plans to redecorate the basement. That had a sad corollary: She was now stuck there.

Mimi put her hand on her friend's shoulder. "I'll call tomorrow to check on you."

Channah blushed slightly. "I never thought I'd be the kind of person who needs to be checked on."

"It's because I care about you."

"Thank you, Mimi. You don't know how much this means to me, you investigating this. You are such a good friend."

Mimi's back grew taut. Channah had pinned so many hopes on her. Mimi wanted to tell her, "I don't know what I'm doing. Yesterday, I made a fool of myself talking to a cop." Instead, she took her hand and promised to do her best.

Channah offered to escort her out. Mimi said not to bother, and Channah didn't argue. As Mimi ascended the creaky white stairs that led out of the basement, she turned to wave good-bye to her friend. Channah didn't notice; she was planted on her bed, staring at the floor, chomping on a Butterfinger. As much as Mimi wanted to support her, she was happy to leave.

On her way out, Mimi popped into the Morgensterns' small yellow kitchen to say hello to Channah's parents, who she'd met at the *shiva*. Her short stout mother, sporting an apron and obvious brown wig, stood bent over the sink, rinsing lettuce; her father sat at the table, reading a newspaper, his white hair covered with a knitted yarmulke. A pot boiled on the stove. It smelled like carrots.

"Are you hungry?" her mother asked. "I can make you a plate of something."

"No thanks." Mimi demurred.

"I want to thank you for being such a good friend to my daughter," the father said. "Channah is pretty devastated right now. She's had a terrible year, what with all the anxiety about marrying Yosef, and now this." He put down the newspaper. "How'd it go down there?"

"Okay, I guess." She paused. "I feel terrible about something. Right before he died, I told Channah she shouldn't continue to see Yosef. I don't know if I should apologize or—"

The parents exchanged glances.

"Don't worry about it." Her father waved his hand. "We told her that a million times."

"Really?" Mimi shifted her weight. "Why?"

The mother shut off the water with a thud. Mimi had forgotten how awkward it was to ask intrusive questions of people you barely knew. She would have to get used to that again.

"Look." The father rustled his newspaper. "Yosef was a lovely person, and this is a huge loss. The truth is, we hoped that Channah would marry somebody who could support her more. Our eldest daughter married a Torah scholar who learns all day. They have four kids and have to rely on subsidies." While he didn't say it outright, some religious students lived on a mix of private donations and public assistance.

"We don't have all the money in the world. When our kids leave, they're on their own," he continued. "You know, Yosef asked us for her hand a month after he met her. We couldn't give him our blessing."

This shocked Mimi. Channah always complained about Yosef's hesitancy to get married. He actually wanted to do it right away.

"I'm in diamonds too," the father went on, "and it's not such an easy business these days, and he wasn't doing so hot at it. We told him, 'Yosef, you're perfectly nice. You just need to prove that you're a *mensch*.'"

"What did he say to that?"

"He said he understood, and he would do better. From what Channah told us, he was trying, but he wasn't the most ambitious guy in the world." His finger jabbed the air. "Listen, Channah doesn't know about all this. Don't mention it. It would devastate her."

"We're parents," the mother offered. "We worry about our children. We wanted to make sure she was—" Her hands fluttered. "All right."

"This is a terrible tragedy," the father offered. "Yosef was a sweet boy."

Everyone referred to Yosef as a boy. He was twenty-five.

THINGS ARE COMING TOGETHER, MIMI THOUGHT as she drove back to New Jersey. The Morgensterns had told Yosef he couldn't marry Channah unless he made something of himself. That may have spurred him to land that multi-million-dollar pink. Nobody understood how he did that. The day he died, Yosef wished he had never gotten involved with it.

Mimi felt like she was looking at a puzzle with a major piece missing. That piece was the pink. What was with that pink?

CHAPTER EIGHT

Max scrunched his eyes as he scrolled through an online trade publication. He uttered *"Oy."* Followed by another *"Oy."* Then a third *"Oy."*

Mimi peered at him. It had to be bad to get a triple *oy*.

"See this?" He pointed at his screen. "A lab in Antwerp just discovered over one hundred synthetic diamonds. And they weren't disclosed."

"What's the big deal? Aren't synthetic diamonds the same as cubic zirconia?"

"No, there is a lot of confusion about that," Max jumped in as if he'd been waiting all day to correct her. "Cubic zirconia looks like a diamond, but it's a complete imitation. A simulant, we call it. Synthetic, or lab-grown diamonds, are actual diamonds. They're just produced by machines, rather than by nature.

"The thing is, the lab-growns have less value. And it's hard to tell the difference between the synthetic and the natural. If you're dishonest, you can make money by passing off one as the other. Unfortunately, this world will never run out of crooks."

The wheels turned in Mimi's mind. "Do they make synthetic colored diamonds too?"

"Sure." He sounded like she had just asked the world's stupidest question. "For a long time, that's all they made. Green, yellows, pinks."

Pink. *Bingo*. Yosef said his buyer didn't want the pink diamond because they knew the truth. Maybe the pink was synthetic. It wasn't much to go on. It was all she had.

"How would you know if a diamond was lab-grown?"

"There are machines you can use. It's best to have experts look at them. The people at the USGR, they're the big *mavens* on that."

Ah yes. The big gem lab.

"Why are you interested in this?"

"I don't know. I might write about it."

"If you talk to the USGR, you should look up your old friend Paul Michelson. He's a big *macher* over there."

At first, Mimi didn't remember the name. In a flash, it all came back. "Pizzaface Paul?"

Paul Michelson also had parents in the business. When their families lived in the Riverdale section of the Bronx, he and Mimi were close friends, always playing together in a nearby park.

Then came junior high. With his Coke-bottle glasses, general clumsiness, and face flecked with acne, kids called him "Pizzaface Paul," and sometimes Mimi did too.

"I would feel weird getting in touch with him," Mimi said. "In seventh grade, there were rumors he had a crush on me."

"So?"

"I got teased at school about it. One time at recess, some bigger kids were picking on me. Paul jumped in and told them to cut it out."

Max lifted his eyebrows. "Shows he's a good guy."

"It does. Except, one kid punched him in the stomach. He doubled over and cried hysterically. I got worried I'd be made fun of even more. I just ran away. I never said thank you. His family moved soon after. I feel horrible about it."

"You were fourteen!" Max roared. "Call him up. I'm sure he'd be happy to speak to you."

So, Mimi called. Paul took a minute to remember who she was, but after some small talk, Mimi told him she was a reporter with a diamond-related question. He said she was welcome any time. They made an appointment for the next day at 3.

All right. Next stop, Pizzaface Paul.

THE NEXT DAY, MIMI WAS STANDING in the well-appointed USGR executive suite, checking in with Paul's executive assistant.

Wow. Pizzaface Paul has an executive assistant.

"He didn't tell me he about this appointment," the assistant scowled.

She wore a business suit and her hair was wrapped in a flawless bun. "He needs authorization for a meeting like this."

"Is everything okay?"

The assistant didn't answer but kept frowning as her fingers clicked the keys. "I'm the gatekeeper around here. If I don't keep track of everything in Paul's calendar, he gets all over the place."

"This isn't a formal meeting." Mimi smiled at her. "I'm an old friend."

The assistant's eyes didn't leave the screen. "He'll be right with you." She finally gazed at Mimi with a crooked smile. "I shouldn't complain. Paul is super easy to work for. He's a real distinguished gemologist."

A surge of pride ran through Mimi. Her childhood friend was a distinguished gemologist.

When Paul came out to greet her, Mimi felt a surge of something else. Pizzaface Paul had grown into a quite handsome man. His old goofy glasses had been replaced by efficient, chic wire frames. His hair was neat and short with some streaks of grey, which worked for him. He was about six feet tall, and his body looked lean and muscular. He still looked *nebbishy*. In a cute way.

Paul broke into a wide smile when he saw Mimi, and spun toward the executive assistant. "Sorry, Brenda, for not telling you about this. I was busy with a million things." He seemed as scattered as ever.

Brenda nodded silently.

Paul led Mimi into his office, which was wood-paneled and homey, with shelf after shelf of haphazardly stacked books on rocks and geology. He parked himself in front of a brown mahogany desk.

Mimi sat on his office couch and fished her notebook and recorder from her bag. "I hope I didn't get you in trouble with this appointment."

"It's fine," he laughed. "I deviated from procedure a bit by not notifying the higher-ups about this meeting. It can be a little corporate around here. I don't always follow the rules to the letter."

"You've changed a lot," Mimi blurted, and worried that was a stupid thing to say.

He chuckled. "I hope so. I haven't seen you in over twenty years."

Yep, pretty stupid. "What have you been up to since our playground days?"

"It's a long story." Paul played with a thick gold pen. "Being a bit of a geek, I always loved minerals and geology. I soon discovered there weren't many jobs for geologists that didn't exile you to the end of the earth. My parents helped me get a job here. I thought I'd only do it for a couple of months. It's been fifteen years.

"It's a good living. It allows me to be an instructor, scientist, and businessman all at once. It's interesting and fun, at least most days. That's about all you can hope for, right?"

Mimi gave a small laugh. "Yep."

"What are you doing with yourself?" He squinted at her. "You're a reporter?"

"Yeah." Mimi inhaled. "At the moment, I'm working for my dad. Just temporarily. It's a little difficult for journalists these days."

"I've heard." He rocked on his chair.

The conversation hit a lull. Mimi opened her notebook and pivoted to serious-journalist voice. "Speaking of which, I'm doing a freelance piece on synthetic diamonds."

He arched his eyebrow. "A fascinating topic."

"My first question is: How can you tell them apart from regular diamonds?"

"That's the million-dollar question. Every stone submitted to our lab undergoes a battery of tests—"

As he spoke, Paul's hands sketched pictures of the insides of gems. Mimi couldn't understand his talk about internal graining and spectro-something-something analysis, but he was a confident, natural teacher, if not without his clumsy moments. At one point he was so wrapped up in discussing surface inclusions, he knocked over a water bottle on his desk.

"He has a likeable earnestness," Mimi scribbled in her notebook. "An easy manner. Nice dimples." She surprised herself with that last one.

Mimi tried to stay on track. "Are there synthetics you can't identify?"

"We don't believe so." He twirled the gold pen. "Since lab-created diamonds are produced in a fundamentally different way than natural diamonds, they show different internal characteristics.

"To put it in layman's terms, if you split a robot in two, its insides would show a very specific pattern. I'm a human being. If you split me in two, it would be messy and asymmetrical. That's the evidence we look for."

Speaking of evidence, Mimi looked for signs that Paul was married. Not that she wanted to date him. She was just . . . curious. If working in this industry had taught her anything, it was to notice jewelry. He wasn't wearing a wedding ring. There was a picture of two kids. No wife, though. Jury was out.

"According to what you've said, most people couldn't tell if their diamond was lab-grown. Is it possible the diamond my ex-husband gave me was man-made?"

The ex-husband reference was meant as a hint; she hoped he'd follow it with a reference to his ex-wife. Instead, he talked about how synthetic detection was now standard practice throughout the industry.

"What about this?" Mimi broke in. "I know someone who recently acquired a three-carat pink radiant cut. How can he be sure that it's not synthetic?"

"First off, I would be surprised if any big diamond was synthetic. We rarely see man-made diamonds over three carats, because of issues with the crystal growth process." Like Mimi's dad, Paul was an endless source of facts about diamonds.

He flashed a conspiratorial smile. "If it was a big stone, we probably examined it. If you promise not to tell anyone, I can look it up in our database. Do you know how big it is?"

"Three point two carats."

"A nice big one," he grinned as he typed. "Three point two . . . pink . . . radiant cut." He waited a bit. "Computer's slow." He jiggled his mouse. "Yes, we did look at that stone—"

He stopped mid-sentence. His eyebrows shot up, and his face moved away from the screen like it smelled bad. His nose inched back toward the monitor; his eyes locked on the screen. As he studied his computer, Mimi studied him.

"Is there a problem?"

"No, there's—" He gaped at his screen. "I just received an important email. We did examine that stone, and it's not synthetic." He rose from his chair. "It was nice chatting." He darted to the door and swung it open.

Mimi didn't understand why this meeting, which had started out warm and friendly, was coming to an abrupt end. She scooped up her stuff and trudged out of the office.

Paul stood holding the door. "If you need anything else, give me a call." He handed off his card.

"It was great seeing you." She tried not to sound too needy.

"Same here." He disappeared back into his office with a slam of his door.

Mimi stood for a second, trying to understand what just happened, until she felt the executive assistant's eyes on her.

"Are you okay?" Brenda asked. "He didn't kick you out, did he?"

"He needed me to leave. He had an important email."

Brenda's mouth became a straight line. "That must have been some email."

Mimi headed to the door, weaving as she walked. That *was* strange.

It seemed even weirder the next day, when her father stopped by her desk.

"Do you know what happened with Paul Michelson?"

"We had a nice talk yesterday. Seems like a nice guy."

"I thought so too. I just got off the phone with someone who said the USGR fired him."

"For what?"

"It was an ethical thing. Apparently, he violated some lab rule."

Paul violated a rule? Mimi remembered how he was scolded for their interview. Did she just get him fired?

Holy crap.

CHAPTER NINE

ALL WEEKEND MIMI WONDERED whether Paul was let go for their unscheduled talk. That didn't seem like a fireable offense. But his secretary seemed mighty ticked.

On Monday, Mimi fingered Paul's business card with its office and mobile numbers. She dialed the mobile, guessing it was an office-supplied phone that would no longer work. When he picked up, Mimi realized she didn't know what to say.

"Hi, Paul. It's Mimi Rosen."

Paul mumbled, "Hi." He seemed as surprised to be talking to her as she was to him.

Next came a long awkward silence, and Mimi realized that she had to fill it. "You told me if I had any more questions to call you. That's why I'm, you know, calling."

"You realize I'm no longer with USGR?"

"I heard." She sucked in air through her teeth. "I'm sorry about that."

"I am, too."

That was an unexpectedly candid answer. Something told Mimi not to let this go. "You want to meet for coffee sometime?"

He muttered something that Mimi didn't quite catch until she realized he was asking her why.

"I want to learn more about gemology." She hoped that sounded sincere.

"That's fine," he said with a shrug in his voice. "If you're ever in Brooklyn Heights, I'd be happy to meet. My schedule is pretty open these days."

TWO DAYS LATER, THEY MET at a Brooklyn coffee shop. The minute Mimi saw Paul, her heart went out to him.

Last week, Mimi met a man in his element, confidently reclining on a leather chair. Now, she saw a far less secure guy trying to balance himself on a wobbly coffee shop stool.

He hadn't shaved, and, judging from the bags under his eyes, he hadn't slept either. During their interview, he looked natty and professorial in his tweed jacket and slacks. Today, he was dressed in a button-down shirt and jeans, and one of his shirt collars was unbuttoned and flapped as he spoke. While it might have been Mimi's imagination, in the last five days his grey-speckled hair seemed to have gotten greyer.

It brought Mimi back to when she lost her job. It felt like she was driving, and her car had swerved, and she didn't know where it was headed, only that she had lost control and it was scary.

She asked how he was doing.

"I've been better." No false fronts here.

Soon Mimi was back in compassionate listener mode as Paul lamented his lack of job prospects.

"There must be something out there for a guy with fifteen years of useless diamond knowledge." He stirred his coffee with a thin red straw.

"Paul, I was wondering, did you get fired because you didn't tell your secretary about our interview?" She took a small bite of her croissant.

"No." He laughed. "That's wasn't it." He bit his lip. "Have you heard anything about me in the industry?"

"The rumor is you were fired for something ethics-related." She ducked her head. "That's just gossip."

"I'm not supposed to talk about this, though you'll probably hear about it eventually, and I don't want you to think I'm some kind of crook. They accused me of taking a bribe to change a grade." He straightened his back. "I did not. That's totally untrue."

Of course, he would never admit to that. Still, Mimi found his denial comforting. "Why did they say that?"

"I have no idea. It was totally out of the blue. It happened last Friday. I went to lunch, and when I come back, my computer didn't work. I tried to call IT, and my phone didn't work.

"Arthur Tanner, who is the head of the lab, walked in my office, accompanied by the head of security and head of human resources. When I saw those guys, I knew it was trouble. It was like the two angels of death standing there."

Paul's shoulders hunched. "Tanner said they had evidence that I improperly bumped a diamond up several grades, and they believe I took a payoff. I told them over and over it was a lie. They didn't care. They said I had ten minutes to leave the premises. The director of security watched as I packed up my stuff. He walked me through the lab carrying a box of my things, in front of all my coworkers. It was totally humiliating."

"That's so crazy. Can't you sue or something?"

"I called my lawyer, and he said litigation is costly, and since they offered me a generous severance package, I might as well walk away. I can't go any period of time without a salary. I have pretty high child support."

Child support. He was divorced. Mimi was surprised how happy that made her. She would have been happier if the guy in question wasn't sitting before her, completely devastated.

"The thing is, the day before, I did find a likely case of bribery. With that pink you talked about."

Mimi perked up. "What do you mean?" A coffee grinder whirred from behind the counter.

"When I entered that diamond into the system, two reports popped up. One was from two years ago and said it had a weak color and clarity. The other was new and gave it the top color grade, fancy vivid, as well as a top clarity grade, VVS1. That's a huge difference in grades and values. Several million dollars difference."

"Maybe you found two different diamonds?"

"Two pink radiant cuts of the exact same size? Do you know how rare pink diamonds are? Colored diamonds are formed by geographic abnormalities, and you need the right amount of radiation at the earth's core to get that color."

Mimi would have to take his word on that.

"It was definitely the same stone. I immediately flagged the report to the Internal Controls department. Somebody took a bribe to upgrade that diamond. It wasn't me."

"Maybe the graders just disagreed." Mimi had finished her croissant and was picking at the crumbs.

"You don't understand. That stone should never have been graded twice. If we have a diamond already in the system, we flag it because it could be stolen. That should have received a suspected stolen gem report. Someone overrode that function. Only people in the executive office can do that. That's just Arthur Tanner and me."

He stopped his stirring. "God, I hope Arthur isn't involved in this. He lives and breathes USGR. He's a true believer. We've been like brothers."

"Didn't you say you reported the diamond to the Internal Controls department?"

"I did. They claimed they never received it. The whole thing is—" He screwed his face in frustration. "Crazy." He lifted himself from the stool. "I should go home."

"You don't want to talk more?"

"Not right now. I need to sit and think."

Then came that awkward moment when a man and a woman have to say good-bye. Mimi expected a handshake or one of those quick pseudo-hugs.

Instead, Paul said, "Great to see you." He put his hand on her shoulder, bent over, and gave her a firm peck on the cheek.

Mimi felt blood rush to her face, which she hoped he didn't notice. She tried not to read too much into his kiss; they *were* old friends. Though he'd come a long way from Pizzaface.

"Good luck." Mimi smiled at him.

"I'll need it." He discharged a dry nervous chuckle. He was doing that a lot. He didn't five days ago.

Paul looked so sad Mimi wanted to hug him. She also decided he was innocent. She left the coffee shop with a second mission: exonerate Paul.

During the ride home, it dawned on her: If what Paul said was true, then Yosef bribed someone at USGR. Her dear deceased cousin was a crook.

CHAPTER TEN

THERE'S A SAYING, "IN THE DIAMOND INDUSTRY, a secret is something you tell one person at a time." As Paul predicted, the entire business was gossiping about how he'd been fired for taking a bribe.

Mimi's father had no shortage of opinions on the matter. "The people at the USGR act like this is a limited problem." He pecked at his toasted bagel. "This goes further than one guy. I bet many people over there are taking payoffs. I see reports all the time that don't match the stone."

"Do you think USGR is lying about Paul?"

"No. They got him on *something*. It's a shame. If someone bribes a grader, they can buy a stone for cheap and make a huge profit on it. That hurts honest guys like me, because there's no way to compete with crooks. It's everything wrong with this business."

It did explain how hard-luck Yosef could afford a multi-million-dollar diamond. He bought an ugly stone, and bribed someone at USGR to upgrade it. It made sense, even if it wasn't an explanation Mimi particularly liked.

Max bit into a potato chip. It made a loud crunch. "Paul was always nice to me, and I was friendly with his parents. But any grader who took a bribe belongs in jail." His face contorted. "Yeech!"

That brought up a good point. Taking bribes was against the law. Why wasn't Paul prosecuted? Instead, he was let go with a generous severance package. Something didn't add up.

"Actually, Dad," Mimi ventured, "Paul told me he's completely innocent."

"What's he gonna say? 'I'm a crook!' Why are you talking to a guy in trouble like that?"

"I enjoyed meeting him, and I wanted his side of the story. Just because there are rumors, doesn't mean they're true."

"Nine times out of ten, they are. Do yourself a favor, Mimila. Don't get involved with a *ganef* like that. But it's your life. Do what you want."

That was Dad-speak for, "Do exactly as I say."

It was ironic. Max had always wanted her interested in a nice Jewish guy. Now she was, and he didn't want her talking to him.

THE NEWS ALSO HIT THE INDUSTRY WEBSITES. "Industry Meets on Possible USGR Bribery Scandal," one blared.

> Following reports that a high-ranking lab official at the U.S. Academy for Gemological Research (USGR) had resigned for allegedly taking bribes from clients, USGR officials tried to assuage trade concerns.
>
> Lab director Arthur Tanner declined to say if bribery was involved in the dismissal.
>
> "We have thousands of employees and, unfortunately, sometimes we have a bad apple. After a thorough internal investigation, we have determined that any problems were limited. The trade can rest assured the USGR will stay true to our mission of improving the image of the diamond and jewelry industry."

Mimi sneered at Tanner through the screen. He seemed the epitome of a corporate phony, grinning for the camera as he consigned Paul to the trash heap. She scoffed at his title—USGR lab director and chief excellence officer. He reminded her of the corporate higher-ups from her publishing days, who would utter noble-sounding paeans to journalism, and fire half the staff a month later.

All right, Arthur Tanner. We'll see who's the bad apple.

THAT AFTERNOON, MIMI CALLED THE USGR, saying she was from *The West Jersey Metro,* and arranged an interview with Arthur Tanner about synthetic diamonds.

At the office, she was greeted by the administrative assistant's now-familiar look of disapproval.

"Weren't you here the other day?" Brenda pecked at her keyboard. Still the gatekeeper.

"This is a more formal interview," Mimi said. "Is there a problem?"

Brenda stared at her computer. "No. It's fine." She gestured for Mimi to take a seat.

As Mimi waited, she snuck a glance at Paul's old office. The door was open, and the lights were off, with nothing on his desk but a shadow. His name had been taken down from the door. The USGR wanted to erase his existence. It made Mimi more determined to nail Tanner.

In person, Tanner looked smaller than his picture. His slicked-back dark hair had just a hint of silver on the side, and his teeth were so white they looked like Chiclets. He was wrapped in a brown designer suit that probably cost more than Mimi's monthly rent. He shook Mimi's hand so vigorously, she felt like she was being milked. They probably taught him that in business school.

Tanner's office was twice the size of Paul's. Instead of shelves stuffed with gem books, they were packed with neatly organized tomes on sales and management. On his desk sat a photo of a much younger Tanner, clad in army fatigues, a soldier in a long-ago war. His wall featured a framed poster of a sweaty runner with the caption, "Passion. To achieve, you must believe."

Tanner strutted to his desk and parked himself in the chair with real purpose, all while maintaining eye contact. He sat ramrod straight and seemed taller sitting down; maybe he had a booster seat.

"Hello, Mimi. How can I help you, Mimi?" He said her name twice. They probably taught him that in business school too.

"I'm eager to learn about synthetic diamonds."

"Fantastic. Great," he replied, as if her comment was so exciting it merited two positive adjectives. "Brenda told me you already spoke with our former lab director Paul Michelson. He must have told you the basics."

"He did. I figured, since he's no longer with the lab, I should get the opinion of its top executive."

Tanner flashed his full set of Chiclet-teeth. "Please proceed."

Mimi turned on her recorder, and asked Tanner the same questions she'd asked Paul, and received mostly the same answers. There was one difference. Tanner peppered his answers with a reference to USGR's mission of improving the image of the diamond and jewelry industry.

"Detecting synthetics is crucial, Mimi. Our mission demands it."

Mimi nodded politely and took desultory notes for about ten minutes, until it was time to ask Mr. Mission about the real news. "Turning to other lab business—" Mimi breathed out. "I understand the USGR fired an employee for bribery."

Tanner stiffened and slightly blanched. He might not have expected the question but didn't seem unprepared for it. "I'm glad you asked that, Mimi. We must be transparent about events at our lab. Transparency is one of our seventeen core values.

"We can't go into specifics regarding any particular employee. However, I am able to confirm to you that, after a thorough internal investigation, we let one high-ranking employee go for violations of our code of ethics. Since we've resolved that situation, the trade and general public can have full confidence in the integrity of the USGR and its commitment to its mission."

"God," Mimi scribbled in her notebook. "This guy talks in press releases."

At her old newspaper, the editor always inveighed against "the jukebox." Most high-level people, he'd say, spit out pre-planned answers to questions, like they're a jukebox. The trick was to get them off-script. You wanted to break the jukebox.

Mimi pressed on. "Can you specify what those violations were?"

"Unfortunately, I cannot go into any more detail. I can just assure you that the industry can have full confidence the USGR will remain committed to its mission." The jukebox.

During her newspaper days, Mimi learned that no one trusted internal probes. That was how organizations covered things up. If they really wanted the truth, they brought in outsiders.

"Wouldn't it give you more credibility if you enlisted an independent investigator?"

"No reason for that." He broke into a smile as tight as the knot on his tie. "Any investigation we conduct will uphold the integrity and reputation of the USGR." That didn't come close to answering the question. The box played on.

"Obviously, the executive you dismissed was the person I interviewed, Paul Michelson."

Tanner's jaw clenched. "Again, we cannot confirm or deny anything about a specific employee."

Mimi gripped her notebook. "The reason I'm asking is, some people feel that Mr. Michelson was fired unfairly. They think he was only let go because he discovered a pink diamond had been upgraded."

"Once again, we don't discuss specific employees." His nose wrinkled. "However, your information is incorrect." The last bit sounded rushed and off-message. The jukebox was teetering.

"People are saying that he discovered a pink diamond had two different reports."

"That is, again, incorrect." He tapped a pen on his desk. "Sometimes people take shots at us. That's what happens when you're the leader in your field. It's okay. We have a broad back. We won't waver from our mission."

"It isn't true that a three-carat pink radiant received two reports? Shouldn't that stone have been flagged as a suspected stolen gem?"

Tanner opened his mouth and began to answer. He stopped and his glare grew icier. "Did Paul tell you this?"

Mimi clasped her arms to her chest. "I cannot reveal my source."

"Those are insider terms only he would know. It *was* him, wasn't it?" His index finger pointed at her. "That's the only person it could be."

"I don't know why that's relevant."

"It's obvious. Paul sent you here to intimidate us. Well, it's not going to work." He was on offense now. He seemed to like that better.

"Getting back to our interview—"

"This conversation is over."

"I have more questions."

Tanner slapped his hand on the desk. "No more questions. No more interview. You are leaving. Good-bye." He sprang from his chair, marched to the door, and thrust it open with a theatrical flourish.

Mimi had never been kicked out of someone's office before. Her old editor would say that meant she was doing her job. As she packed up her recorder and scurried out the door under Tanner's stern gaze, she wasn't finding it that fun.

"Tell your friend Paul we won't take this stunt lying down," Tanner hissed as he slammed the door.

Mimi stood outside his office, trying to process what happened, when she again sensed the executive assistant looking at her.

"Is everything okay?" Brenda asked. "Did Arthur ask you to leave, too?"

Mimi looked at her shoes. "Pretty much."

Brenda gave her head a small, almost imperceptible shake. "That happens to you a lot."

LATER THAT AFTERNOON, as Mimi sat at her father's front desk, she worried about Tanner's implicit threat to Paul. But, the USGR had already fired him. What else could they do?

Regardless, she should let Paul know. She was looking for an excuse to call him anyway. He'd no doubt appreciate her honesty and assure her it was no big deal.

She was about to call when his number popped up on her phone. Which made her happy, until she heard the sharp, pointed sound of his voice.

"It's Paul Michelson." His full name. No time for pleasantries. "I have a question. Did you talk about me to Arthur Tanner?"

"What?" she sputtered. "Why do you ask?"

"My lawyer got a call from the USGR. They said a reporter came in, asking about me. When I got fired, I signed a strict non-disparagement clause. They are accusing me of trashing them to the press. They just threatened to pull my severance.

"The only journalist I spoke to was you. That was just a friendly talk. You didn't repeat what I said to anyone there. Right?"

The air around Mimi turned hot. She started to sweat. She heard herself say, "Of course not."

Paul didn't respond right away. "You sure you didn't bring it up to anyone at USGR? Even by accident?"

"Nope." Mimi was surprised how self-assured she sounded in her dishonesty.

"You're just writing about synthetics anyway," he said, in kind of a statement-question.

Mimi's right hand bounced a pen on her desk, as her left grew sweaty holding the phone. This was torture. "Yes."

Paul moaned. "I can't figure it out. I didn't give any interviews. My lawyer tells me they are making a big deal of this."

"Will they take away your severance?" Mimi gulped.

"I hope not. I'm barely making it as it is. I have a million bills to pay. I can't afford to go one week without my salary, never mind however long it will take for me to find a new job." He took a breath. "I'm going to call my attorney, tell him that they're full of it."

Before Mimi could say good-bye, he hung up.

CHAPTER ELEVEN

THE PROBATE LAWYER GRUNTED as he pulled the clear plastic storage tub from the conference room closet. He set it on the conference room table with a thud. He opened the top latch and sorted through a stack of papers before plucking out a large bound spiral notebook. He handed it to Mimi, sitting by herself at the table's head.

"Here you go," he said. "This is what Yosef called," he made finger quotes, "'his books.'"

Mimi stared at the notebook in disbelief. Yosef's books were actual *books*, old-fashioned ledgers that he had filled out by hand. Who knew they still sold those?

"How about the rest?" The tub was stuffed with photos, papers, all the scattered remnants of Yosef's quarter-century on Earth. "Can I look at that, too?"

"No," he answered quickly. "Bernard asked me to let you look at the ledger. I said yes as a favor. I can't let you see more than that. The police may go through this stuff. You shouldn't see it before they do."

Mimi said okay, and he closed the tub and left. Mimi scanned Yosef's ledger. It was filled not only with scrawl but Hebrew scrawl. She thought about taking a picture so Channah could translate, but there was so much writing over so many pages, she wouldn't know where to begin. She gave up and closed it.

Meanwhile, the tub sat at the other end of the table, beckoning. Mimi made sure no one was coming. She tiptoed over to it and opened its top latch. A book lying on top said "appointments." Mimi snatched it, closed the tub, and dashed back to her seat.

She held the book under the table, and rifled through it, her hands trembling. It didn't contain much, given it was a book for the year, and Yosef only made it ten days into February. It did have three notes for February tenth, the day he died.

The notes were all in Hebrew; Mimi couldn't make them out. She would need Channah for that. Mimi took out her phone to snap a picture. Before she could, the lawyer strode in the conference room. Mimi nearly jumped. She shoved the appointment book in her purse and tried not to act guilty.

"Find anything interesting?" the lawyer asked.

"Not really. I couldn't make heads or tails of it."

He laughed. "Me neither. And that's my job." He stood there. "I guess that's it."

That was Mimi's not-so-subtle cue to leave. She thanked the lawyer and left. It was only after she exited the building that she remembered she had the appointment book in her purse.

Mimi emailed snapshots of the appointment book to Channah, who called her soon afterward.

"Wow, Mimi. How did you get this?"

"I saw it when I looked at Yosef's books." That was true. Kind of.

"Before Yosef died, he had a bunch of meetings. He kept saying how important they were. He never told me what they were about or who they were with. They're all here. Yosef was always meticulous about keeping track of his appointments.

"The meeting in the morning was with Rev. Hirshhorn. That's his rabbi. At 2 PM, he met with his brother, Bernard. At noon, it says 'DG.'"

"Who's 'DG'?"

"Not sure."

"Why did he have so many meetings?"

"Beats me. I'm surprised he met with Rabbi Hirshhorn. Yosef wouldn't take up a rabbi's time unless it was important."

"He did Yosef's funeral, right? Do you think he'll talk to me? He seems intimidating."

"Oh yeah," Channah laughed.

"Maybe we can talk to him together." She was hoping to lure her friend out of the house.

"No way. I'm scared to meet a man like that." Left unsaid: Channah, a religious woman, wouldn't feel right questioning a prominent rabbi. But Mimi could.

MIMI CALLED RABBI HIRSHHORN'S OFFICE LATER that morning, said she was doing an article on Yosef's murder, and booked an appointment for that afternoon. It was an unseasonably warm mid-February day, and Mimi was dressed in a light coat and short-sleeve blouse. The street around the synagogue was strewn with litter and mostly empty, except for one lone Hasidic man who followed her out of the subway. As Mimi entered the worn wooden synagogue, she thought her father would be happy she was meeting a rabbi.

Like his sanctuary, Rabbi Hirshhorn's study was brown, musty, and cramped. Against each wall were wooden bookshelves which held old editions of ancient texts. Something was off about his desk, though it took Mimi a moment to realize what: it held no computer.

As Mimi entered, she didn't offer her hand for shaking. He wouldn't do it, because of *Negiah*, the doctrine that restricts touching between the sexes.

"Please, Miss," he barked, "leave the door open."

Of course. They were a man and woman who weren't married meeting alone in the same room. Also, *Negiah*.

Rabbi Hirshhorn sat parked behind his desk, a bearded mountain. His face was stern and unsmiling, with two bushy black-grey eyebrows sitting atop it like watchful caterpillars. Mimi understood why Channah was scared to speak with him. Face to face, he was as imposing as he was behind the pulpit.

Mimi peeled off her coat and sat on the tattered brown chair that faced his desk. She whipped out her notebook and smiled at him.

His face jerked away. He pointed his eyes at a bookcase. "What can I help you with?"

"I'm writing an article on the murder of Yosef Levine."

"That's right." He stroked his long white beard but stayed otherwise still. "Being a rabbi, you witness many life events. I still feel the pain of that, like a fresh wound." He put his finger to his chin. "What is the nature of your article?"

"I want to find out more about Yosef."

"The eulogy I delivered at his funeral should give you some insight. I can provide you with a copy."

"You don't need to. I was at his funeral."

"What else can I help you with?"

"I know you met with Yosef right before he died."

"We talked on the day he passed away." The heavy breathing restarted, the only sound in what seemed like an endless silence.

"What did you speak about?"

"Unfortunately, I cannot say." He twirled his beard around his finger, like it was a piece of cotton candy. "What parishioners tell me is confidential."

"This person is no longer with us."

"To the contrary. He may not be here in the flesh. He is still with us in spirit. My responsibilities to him remain the same."

"Did he mention the pink diamond he was selling?"

One of the caterpillar-brows bounced upward, and he took a sharp, loud intake of breath. "Again, I cannot say."

Mimi scribbled in her notebook, "By the way he's reacted, that's a yes." She clutched her pen. "Can you tell me anything about what you discussed? Please. I cared about Yosef. I'm sure you did too."

"I can tell you in general terms what parishioners come to talk to me about. For the most part, it is problems with family and business—usually a question of ethics or conscience."

When Mimi watched TV detective shows, witnesses poured out important details with minimal prompting. She could only fish for morsels from a curt Jewish Buddha.

"Anything else? This is important."

"I'm sorry, miss. I've said all I'm able. Maybe you should talk to David Garstein at the Consolidated Diamond Bourse on Forty-Seventh Street. Yosef spoke with him after he met with me."

David Garstein. That explains who "DG" is.

The rabbi's face turned from the bookcase toward a map of Israel on the wall. Mimi always observed people's body language. His was terrible, particularly his eye contact. He hadn't looked at her once. That had to be more than a quirk. Time to break the jukebox.

"If you don't mind me saying, Rabbi, you've never looked at me the whole time I've been here. That indicates you have something to hide. I'd like to know what it is."

His face reddened and he emitted a growl that sounded like the roar of the ocean. "I'm not looking at you because you are not dressed modestly." The words spilled out of him in a river of rage. "Don't you know how to dress in front of a *frum* person?"

Mimi looked at her blouse, which showed a peek of her breasts. Common for Manhattan. Radical for here. She grabbed her pocketbook and covered her neckline. "Sorry. I wasn't aware."

"You are now." He finally faced her.

"I didn't do it deliberately. I'm not dressed *that* immodestly. I'm only showing a little cleavage."

"I'd rather not discuss it."

"Of course." Mimi stood up and hurriedly put on her coat. "I didn't mean to offend you, Rabbi. I was raised Observant."

"And you're not now?"

"No."

"You're not winning me over."

Mimi quickly thanked him for his time, mumbled goodbye, and slunk out of the office, happy to be free. Her father would not be happy about this, at all.

After Mimi left the 18th century *shul* for the 21st century sidewalk, she spotted the same Hasidic man who had trailed her out of the subway standing across the street. He was a tall man in his late twenties or early thirties, watching her exit the synagogue as he leaned on a mailbox in the middle of an otherwise empty block. She looked back at him, and he fixed his stare at her. His gaze was so fiery and intense, his eyes so hooded in anger, it was like he hated her, like he wanted to hurt her. It unnerved her enough that she jerked her head away and hurried to the subway.

Mimi knew something about the guy didn't make sense, though she only figured it out on the subway back to Forty-Seventh Street. The rabbi had acted like he'd rather die than look at her low-cut outfit. The Hasidic guy was just as religious. Yet, he was staring right at her.

CHAPTER TWELVE

THE NEXT MORNING, MIMI CALLED CHANNAH to find out how she was doing. Channah said she was fine. It was obvious she wasn't.

"You sure?" Mimi asked.

"Yesterday was a hard day."

"What happened?"

"Sometimes I can go through life and not think about what happened. Other times, it just paralyzes me, and I can't do anything but lie in bed and cry. Yesterday was one of those days."

Mimi strove to say something that wasn't a cliché she'd uttered countless times.

Instead, Channah brought up what she really wanted to talk about, the investigation. "How did your meeting with Rabbi Hirshhorn go?"

"Okay." Mimi felt no need to regale her with her religious *faux pas*. She wanted to forget them. "He can be a scary guy."

"Definitely. Yosef told me he used to breathe so heavy, as kids they called him Darth Rabbi." She giggled at this. It was the first time Mimi really heard her laugh since Yosef died. "Did he tell you anything?"

Mimi chewed her lower lip. Channah would be devastated to learn that Yosef bribed a grader. At some point, Mimi might have to tell her. But not today. She wanted to wait until she was sure.

"He told me what 'DG' stands for." Mimi checked her notes. "David Garstein, head of the Consolidated Diamond Bourse. Yosef met with him after the rabbi. Do you know what the Consolidated Bourse is?"

"The CDB is where all the dealers get together to trade. They call it 'the club.'"

Ah yes. "The Club." That Mimi knew.

"Garstein is the club president. Yosef talked with him all the time."

Mimi jotted this down. "Interesting. What you do know about David Garstein?"

"Just that he's Israeli. And your father hates him."

"Why?"

"Don't know. He always calls him 'that shmuck Garstein.'"

WHEN MIMI WAS GROWING UP, the Consolidated Diamond Bourse of New York was the industry's throbbing heart, the place where everyone came to do business and hear the latest gossip. Mimi's father talked about "the club" constantly; it was its own world, with its own restaurant, synagogue, and legal system—disputes between members were settled through binding arbitrations, and Mimi's father followed the latest judgments like other men tallied box scores. Max took Mimi there once as a little girl; he needed a special dispensation as women weren't allowed on the club floor. She remembered it as large and crowded, with so many people arguing and joking and brushing against each other, it was overwhelming and scary. In retrospect, it was vital and very alive.

When Mimi told her father she was planning to visit, he scoffed. "Don't bother. That place is halfway to dead. Even I quit last year. Why are you going there anyway?"

"I'm doing an article on synthetics, and I figured it might be interesting to interview David Garstein—"

"*Oy.* Not that *shmuck* Garstein."

"What do you have against him?"

"He's your typical slimy politician. When he was running for club president, he kept going on about how he would bring new this, new that. Why does everything have to be new all the time? Old things aren't always bad. I'm old. I'm not bad.

"He even hired a professional campaign manager to get him elected. I'll never forget, on Election Day, he gave everyone embossed umbrellas. I ended up throwing mine out because I couldn't stand to see his name anymore. Which killed me. It was a nice umbrella."

WHEN MIMI ARRIVED AT THE CONSOLIDATED DIAMOND BOURSE, the

club floor seemed, if not halfway-to-dead, pretty close to it.

The trading area was a long narrow white-walled room with twenty tables on each side and a well-worn red carpet in the middle. It could in theory hold hundreds, but Mimi only saw about twenty-five people there—all men, though its rule against women had long been lifted. The one woman worked the diamond weighing station at the back of the hall; she looked bored and thumbed her phone. A few dealers paced up and down the aisles while talking on their mobiles in frenzied Yiddish. The club's trading tables, meant for buying and selling diamonds, were empty or used for chess games.

Mimi arrived at the club's executive offices and gave her name to the young blonde receptionist, who said President Garstein—that was what she called him, President Garstein—would be right with her. Mimi took a seat and waited for the next half hour, reading and re-reading the sole issue of an industry trade magazine that lay on a nearby table.

Every few minutes, the secretary seemed to remember Mimi was there, and assured her, "He'll be right with you." Mimi could hear Garstein through the door screaming through a series of phone calls. The racket didn't faze the secretary or other office workers—they seemed to have tuned it out long ago.

Eventually, Mimi was summoned to Garstein's office. It was a nice office—nicer, even than Tanner's—too nice for the head of a halfway-to-dead organization. There were Herman Miller chairs in front of his desk and a high-back leather chair behind it, large windows that offered a panoramic view of Fifth Avenue, and a spotless, endless yellow rug. The wall behind his desk was covered with pictures of Garstein with local politicians, as they visited the club in search of votes, money, or both.

The industry's bright young hope was standing at his glass desk with his hands thrust in his pockets and a grin plastered on his face. He was in his early 40s, tall and rail-thin, with slicked-back black hair that fell to his shoulders. He was tieless and dressed in a tight-fighting brown suit that was so shiny it dared you to ignore it. She could picture him as a real politician—he looked slick enough—if not for his thick Israeli accent. He muttered a perfunctory apology for his lateness and barked at the secretary to bring him a Coke.

"You're Max Rosen's daughter, right?"

"Yes." Mimi took a seat.

He fell into his chair, his hair glistening in the light. "How is your father? Is he all right?"

Mimi stopped setting up her voice recorder. "What do you mean?"

He swiveled his chair. "Last year, he told me he was quitting the club because the bathrooms weren't clean enough."

That sounded like her dad. Nothing bugged him more than dirty toilets.

Mimi snickered. "He can be quite particular about that kind of thing."

"Everyone in this club is particular about everything. I walk around, one member tells me the temperature is too cold. The next minute, another says it's too hot.

"Is that a reason to quit a club that he's been a member of for forty years, because the toilets are dirty? What's so terrible about them? I use them all the time."

The secretary arrived with his soda, and Garstein responded with a mumble that barely qualified as a "thank you." His eyes trailed her figure out the door.

"We talked about it, but he wouldn't change his mind." Garstein took a swig of Coke. "He can be quite difficult."

"You don't have to tell me," Mimi laughed.

"Maybe he can't afford the dues. The old guys have it tough these days."

Mimi was eager to leave this topic. "I'm writing an article on the murder of Yosef Levine."

"Oh, yes." His face took on a look of considered sadness, which morphed into considered determination. "Those South American gangs are a plague upon our business. Immediately following this terrible event, I called the police commissioner, who I have known for many years." He pointed his Rolex-studded arm to a framed portrait with the police commissioner, which was smaller than his picture with the mayor but larger than his picture with the city council president. "I made it clear to him, we need a lot more policemen on our block." His finger sliced the air. "I promise, I will not rest until everyone on Forty-Seventh Street can do business in complete safety." With that, his finger came to a rest, pointed at the ceiling. He sat breathing hard, as if waiting for applause.

"Still—" his finger went back to work, "—as many improvements as my administration has made, you can't stop everything. At the end of the day, our industry is safe and getting safer. That's the message I want to get out."

The interview had just started, and he had already given her three plays of the jukebox.

"I understand all that." Mimi flipped open her notebook. "I'm interested in a different angle. I know that you met with Yosef the day he died."

Garstein shot upright on his chair. "Who told you that?"

"I can't say."

"I guess people like to talk." His nostrils flared. "It's true. I met with Yosef. It was right before he passed away." He took a swig of Coke.

"Can you tell me what you talked about?"

"Unfortunately, I cannot. I need to maintain strict confidentiality when members come to me."

This amused Mimi. "You're not a rabbi."

"People come to me with problems all day. Sometimes I feel like one."

"Yosef was murdered. It's possible that whatever he talked to you about had some relation to that."

"I don't think so. He wasn't worried about his safety or gangs or anything like that. He came to me with a business problem."

"Did that business problem involve the pink diamond he was trying to sell?"

His grip on the Coke can tightened. "No, that wasn't it. He owed people money. He wanted me to help negotiate a settlement." He reclined on his high-back chair, seeming pleased with his answer.

Garstein had just gone from safeguarding Yosef's privacy to completely violating it. Some great politician. He couldn't even lie convincingly. Time to break the jukebox.

Mimi leaned forward and went for it. "I have learned that Yosef's pink diamond had been upgraded by the USGR. He talked to you about that. Right?" Mimi wasn't certain about either of those things but uttered them with her unblinking reporter face.

Garstein stared at her like he'd just noticed someone else was in the room. "You've done your homework. Let's just say Yosef wanted my advice. I told him, 'if this really bothers you, the only thing to do is call the USGR. Let them know what happened. They'll take care of it.'"

"Did he call them?"

"Sure. Right when he was sitting here. He phoned Arthur Tanner and left a message. He asked to meet with him that afternoon."

Tanner hadn't mentioned a call from Yosef. He didn't mention much. Mimi scribbled a note to ask Tanner about that, if he ever deigned to talk to her again.

"What happened? Did they meet?"

"I believe so. Right afterward, the USGR fired the bad apple. That shows they got the message. They did it in a quiet way, which is how to do it. The industry and the consumer must have confidence in the USGR. They safeguard the image of our industry. That's their mission."

Garstein seemed unsteady at the beginning of this answer. When he arrived at the talking points about the USGR, he glommed onto them like a life raft. This jukebox couldn't be easily broken.

"I thought you were writing about Yosef's murder. What does that have to do with the USGR?"

"Do you think it's a coincidence that Yosef had this issue right before he died?"

"Of course it is. It's not like the stupid South Americans know anything about certificates. A report may have been changed, it's true. I'm not happy about it. It's not worth writing a story about."

"Why not?"

"These things happen. Luckily, the USGR caught it. Any problems were limited. One guy changed one grade. Big deal."

Mimi wriggled in her seat. "I've spoken with people who think this is a big deal. They believe there is a bigger problem at the USGR, beyond the—you know—one bad apple."

"They have no proof of that. Do you?"

"No, but there's a feeling—"

"So what? Some people believe a dumb thing. You're going to write that in an article?"

"There's a perception—"

"I know what's happening in this industry. You don't. People in this business turn everything into a crisis. There's a joke. A father says, 'my baby will be a diamond dealer. He's constantly crying.'"

Mimi laughed, even as she noticed the gender pronoun.

"I don't want to tell you what to do. But don't write about this. If this comes out in the newspapers, that will kill consumer confidence, and that hurts all our businesses. Mine, your father's, everybody's."

Garstein steepled his fingers in front of his face. "Diamonds are a symbolic item. You can't eat them. They have little practical use, aside from being beautiful. People want diamonds for what they represent, love, commitment, and glamour. We often say that when a woman gets a diamond, she's not excited because she got a ring. She's excited because she's getting a husband.

"That's the diamond dream. That's what built our industry. None of that works if consumers don't have faith in the product. If you write an article saying there's a problem with grading reports, people will panic. They'll look at their diamond not as a symbol of love. They'll say 'oh my God. Do I have to get my report checked?' You'll break the spell. You'll kill the magic.

"In the end, this business is a family. Sometimes, in a family, people do things we don't like. That happened at the USGR. They took care of it. They got rid of the guy. I wouldn't mind if they took him out and shot him."

Mimi bristled.

"The important thing is that we stick together and consumers continue to buy diamonds. That's how we'll prosper. That's how your father built a great business."

Just a few minutes ago, he suggested her father was going bankrupt.

"The things you want to write about, murder and bribery, it's all negative. It hurts the industry. Can't you write something upbeat? Maybe write a story about David Garstein, the young Turk reinvigorating Forty-Seventh Street. That's what people want to read. Not another depressing story. That puts people in a bad mood."

"If bad things are happening, shouldn't we shine a light on them? Don't people have a right to know?"

"You're very stubborn." He looked her up and down, like he was examining a new car. "You're attractive, though you wear no wedding ring. You might be too feisty. That's okay in small doses. Too much, it scares men away." He took another Coke swig. "We can work on that. We should go out sometime. I can show you a good time. David Garstein knows how treat a girl."

Mimi couldn't believe he'd just called her a girl, but that was only the third or fourth most offensive thing he'd just said. She could only respond with a few shocked syllables. *Didn't the CDB have an HR department?*

She tried to get back on track. "About Yosef—"

"We'll talk about that when we go out."

Mimi didn't know what was worse, that he was asking her out, or that he was doing it while discussing a murder. She wanted to tell him where he could stick his consumer confidence and his Coke can and everything else.

She needed information from this man. He clearly knew more than he was telling. Yet, he was only interested in one thing, and that thing wasn't Yosef.

When Mimi worked at the newspaper, she often received unwanted attention from sources. Most of the time, she extricated herself with a polite smile or mention of a boyfriend. With Garstein, she thought of only one thing to say.

"Sure. I'll go out with you."

Mimi stood on the sidewalk, disgusted with herself. She hadn't gone out with anyone in years. She would have to wade back into the dating pool eventually. This wasn't how she wanted to do it.

There was so much she wanted to ask Garstein, so much she should have pressed him on. He had gotten her off track by hitting on her. Maybe he was cleverer than she thought.

There was one bright spot. Garstein had confirmed that Yosef talked to him about the pink being upgraded. That proved she was on the right track. She could pry more out of him when they went out. She sauntered down the street, feeling giddy.

Until she saw him. The Hasidic guy with the fiery eyes. He was standing across the street with his hands interlocked at his waist, watching her leave the club with the same intense concentration as before. She craned her neck at him, and they made brief eye contact. She pulled her phone from her purse. If this guy was tracking her, she wanted a picture.

A truck barreled down the road, blocking her view. When it passed, he was gone.

CHAPTER THIRTEEN

CHANNAH CALLED MIMI THE NEXT MORNING to say she had arranged an interview with Yosef's brother, Bernard.

"He finally agreed, huh?" Mimi asked.

"It wasn't easy. He keeps telling me the whole thing is crazy. I guess I wore him down."

"He works for a big company, right?"

"Yeah. Dynasty Diamonds. One of the biggest." Channah paused, "What will you ask him?"

Mimi had already begun formulating questions in her mind. "According to the appointment book, he and Yosef spoke on the day he died. I'd like to know what they talked about. I'm also interested in who's getting the proceeds from the pink."

"I don't know. Not me, that's for sure." Channah laughed. "His immediate family, I guess. Which is basically Bernard."

"If this was a detective show, we would look at who stands to profit from this death. And that would be—"

"What are you suggesting, Mimi? You think Bernard—" Channah produced a sound of guttural disgust. "How can you say that? He's your family."

"I'm not accusing him of anything. I was just wondering."

"Bernard is rich. He doesn't need the money. He's been great to me through this whole thing."

Mimi knew when to back down. "You're right. That's probably a bad question to ask."

Mimi sighed. It was a bad question to ask, particularly to a cousin. That was one of the hard parts of being a journalist. She was duty-bound to ask it anyway.

DYNASTY DIAMONDS WAS LARGE, MODERN, AND reeked of money; one might mistake it for a non-diamond company, if not for the picture of the Grand Rebbe in the hall and the young Orthodox woman at reception. As Mimi walked through the halls, phones rang and people scurried in and out of offices, even though it was after hours. This was a real business, a true place of commerce. It made her father's company seem like a glorified retirement home.

The receptionist led Mimi into an empty conference room and handed her a bottle of water. Mimi sat for a few uneasy minutes sipping the water until her cousin made his entrance.

Bernard parked himself at the head of the table and leaned back, hiking his knee to table level. Mimi again gave her condolences. Bernard asked about her dad and sisters, and added, "How's your husband?"

This surprised Mimi. Bernard had only met her ex once, at her mother's funeral.

"We got divorced," Mimi replied. "A year ago." She couldn't resist adding the last part. Obviously, her life wasn't her cousin's main concern.

"As long as we're on the subject," Bernard fidgeted a bit, "I hear you're upset that my family didn't attend your wedding. Please understand that we couldn't."

Actually, from everything Mimi understood, he *could*. He just chose not to. She appreciated him at least acknowledging her feelings. Perhaps this tragedy had brought something out in Bernard. She sensed something different in him, something fragile that wasn't there before.

The receptionist entered, asking if they needed anything else. Bernard requested "a thing of peanuts" and sent her off.

"Channah says you want to write an article about Yosef. She thinks you're an impressive investigative journalist."

"That's nice of her to say." Mimi waved away the compliment. This was why it was good to be friends with Channah. Detective Matthews treated Mimi as a joke. Her father considered her the receptionist. Channah thought she was an impressive investigative reporter. Even Mimi wasn't sure how true that was.

"What kind of article are you writing?"

"I'm sure you've heard Channah's theories."

His eyes turned skyward. "Our friend has a bit of an overactive imagination. I talk to the police pretty regularly, and they're convinced it was a standard robbery by a South American theft gang. Do you have any evidence otherwise?"

"Not really."

His eyes narrowed. "Why are you doing this? To humor her?"

This question brought Mimi up short. It was a good one.

"No, I—" Mimi doodled on her notepad. "It could be an interesting article."

"My brother was killed by an animal. That's not big entertainment."

Mimi stopped drawing. "Of course I'd be sensitive about anything I write. Yosef was my family."

"Yes. You're also a journalist. Plenty of journalists have screwed their families."

Before Mimi could respond, the receptionist returned with a bowl full of peanuts. Bernard scooped up a fistful while glancing at his phone. "I have an overseas call in ten minutes. What can I tell you?" He gazed at Mimi like she was an exotic animal.

"You met with Yosef the day he died. What did you talk about?"

"His engagement. He wanted my blessing."

"What did you say?"

"*Mazal tov*, of course! I didn't know Channah then. Turns out she's a terrific girl. She would have been good for him."

"Was he acting any different?"

"My brother, may he rest in peace, was always a little different. He seemed happy. Eager to start his new life."

"Did he mention quitting the diamond business? He told that to Channah."

"No, but I don't find that shocking. He was never really in it." He popped some peanuts in his mouth. "Business-wise, Yosef and I didn't intersect much. I know he was having serious problems. My brother's heart was in the right place. I was never sure about his head."

"How so?"

"He wanted to do business on his own, be a small dealer, trade a little here and there. I explained that doesn't work anymore. All the little *pishers* are going out of business."

Mimi blanched. Her father was one of those *pishers*. Bernard may not have meant to insult her dad. Yet, he just did.

"A few might make it," Mimi offered, hoping for reassurance.

"The business has changed. How much do you know about the history of the industry?"

"A little. I can always learn more."

"The business used to be run by a cartel. Vanderklef. In the old days, they controlled just about every diamond. When the market turned slow, they'd stockpile them in a vault to keep prices up, which protected everyone's investment in their inventory. And they did tons of advertising. They're the reason brides get engagement rings.

"In those days, you had one big company pushing tons of diamonds onto the market. Since diamonds aren't cheap, you needed a lot of companies to share the burden of carrying those goods. That's why there are so many dealers on Forty-Seventh Street. You had all these little guys that just passed diamonds from one hand to another.

"Around the late nineties, the antitrust people started cracking down. When Vanderklef declared the monopoly over, it felt like my father died again. It turned the industry upside down. Today, with computers, everything is more transparent. There's no longer room for middlemen that just trade diamonds back and forth. The industry is consolidating. The big fish are swallowing the little ones.

"I explained this to Yosef. I even tried to get him a position here. Believe me, I was doing him a favor because he didn't exactly possess a sought-after skill set. Unfortunately, my dear brother had this *verkakte* notion he would make it on his own, that he shouldn't rely on his family. I only work here because of my father-in-law. Family is what this business is all about." He downed a peanut. "Yosef could be a little headstrong. It probably killed him."

Mimi looked up from her notes. "What do you mean?"

"He listed that big pink diamond on an online network. He thought it would turn him into a big respected dealer. I warned him to be careful. You don't want the whole world knowing you have a valuable stone like that. The crooks pay attention to that stuff. They have back doors into those sites. They know how to track people down. He made himself a sitting duck."

Mimi's father convinced Yosef to list that diamond online. Now his brother was saying that led to his death.

Bernard's phone buzzed. He picked up. "Yeah."

Mimi could hear agitated squawking from the other end.

"What's his offer?" Bernard groused.

More squawking.

"I'm sick of playing games with this guy. He thinks he can steal everything. Tell him that's our offer. If he wants cheaper diamonds, he can dig 'em out of the ground himself."

More quick barks. Bernard uttered, "Yeah, bye," and put his phone down.

His eyes returned to Mimi. "Sorry. I've been gone a week, and I'm catching up with a million things. Anything else?"

"That pink diamond was found to be worth over four million dollars. How could Yosef afford it?"

"I couldn't tell you. As you probably saw, his books are a mess."

"Did he buy it with a partner?"

"If he did, it was a silent partner, so silent he hasn't spoken up yet. That's a pretty valuable diamond. If anyone had a stake in it, they would have claimed ownership by now. As far as we can determine, Yosef owned that diamond outright, and the transaction was done off the books. In cash."

"That was a four-million-dollar stone. How'd Yosef get that much money?"

Bernard gave a full-body shrug, using his shoulders, head, and eyebrows. "I wish I could call him up and ask him."

"There's one possible explanation. Yosef could have bought it for cheap and paid someone off to give it a better grade."

Bernard looked surprised. "What do you mean?"

"I've found information that Yosef bribed someone at the USGR to improve the grade of the stone."

He scowled. "Look, it's no secret that the USGR has a problem over there. They just fired a guy for getting paid under the table. But I can't imagine my brother doing something like that."

"I found it hard to believe, too. He talked about it with people before he died."

Bernard looked at her skeptically. "He did? You know that for a fact?"

Her shirt began to stick to her back. "I believe so."

His lips formed a semicircle. "He didn't mention that to me. I'd like to see proof before we jump to that conclusion."

Bernard's phone buzzed and he again picked up. "What now?"

More squawking.

"That's a better offer, but still unacceptable." He paused. "If we're talking about a measly half a million-dollar difference, tell him fine. I don't have all night to deal with this nonsense."

The squawking stopped.

"Be well," Bernard said and hung up.

Mimi was getting a weird feeling about her cousin. He was never big on social niceties. But who conducts business during an interview about his brother's murder? He'd just dismissed a half million dollars as "measly"; that morning, Mimi dodged a collection call seeking two hundred bucks.

"Anything else?" He snuck a glance at the door.

Time for the big question. "What's going to happen to that pink diamond?"

"As Yosef didn't have any kind of will, we're working all that out with the probate attorney. His only valuable asset seemed to be that diamond."

"Who will get that?"

His nose twitched. "I can't say."

"Won't it go to the surviving family? That's what normally happens without a will."

"Again, that's not something I want to discuss."

"Any reason?"

"Of course there's a reason. I don't wish to share it."

What is he hiding? Time to break the jukebox.

"Bernard, I am trying to be respectful. We are talking about a four-million-dollar diamond here. I don't understand why you won't answer my questions about it."

Bernard produced a long sigh. He wiped his hands, letting peanut dust fly.

"If you must know, since Yosef loved sports, as well as children, the money from that stone will fund an athletic scholarship for underprivileged kids. It's our attempt to make something positive come out of this tragedy."

Mimi turned pale.

"I don't want that in print because I'll have a million *shnorrers* knocking on my door with their hands out. When it's up and running, everyone will know. I will show you the receipts if you don't believe me."

Mimi felt like a deflated balloon. "That's not necessary."

Bernard checked his phone. "I have to go." He rose from his chair. "It was nice to see you. Please give my regards to your family. And feel free to contact me with any questions. I hope you understand this isn't my favorite subject to talk about. My rabbi says the world of diamonds is a world of illusion. That's where I want to live right now. The real world is too painful." He walked to the door. "How is Channah doing?"

"She's having a tough time."

"She's not the only one." The corners of his eyes turned red, and sadness seemed etched on every inch of his face.

She wanted to say something to comfort him but didn't get a chance. Bernard had already zipped out the door and was yelling at someone about diamonds.

THAT NIGHT MIMI COULDN'T SLEEP. As she lay in bed, she looked at her investigation with cold hard eyes. For all the interviewing she'd done, she'd only discovered a bunch of disconnected scraps that didn't really fit together. Plus, she kept making mistakes. In just a week, she'd gotten an old friend in trouble, agreed to a date with a creep, and offended a rabbi.

Perhaps she *was* in over her head. Maybe her old editor Lewis was right: Her ambition did outstrip her ability. She might not be ready for this. She might never be.

She remembered how, a day before she left the paper, Lewis called her in his office for a one-on-one. The crusty old bastard rarely did that.

"Sit down, kid." He called everyone "kid."

Mimi originally found it endearing, until she realized he only did it to women.

"I know you think I never gave you a chance."

Of course he knew that; she complained about it in her exit interview. Since Mimi was out the door, there was no point in holding her tongue, not that she was good at that anyway. "Do you deny that?"

"I don't know, kid. You've got potential." Tobacco wafted off him; he must have just come in from a smoke. "You're just missing the one quality great reporters have."

What's that? A penis?

"Patience." He rested his hands on his chest. "You're aggressive. That's good in a journalist. You just don't know your limitations. The minute you got here you kept asking for more more more. And you weren't ready."

Mimi scowled. *Did he call her in just to insult her once again?*

"Look, reporting is a pain. I did it for years. I'd much rather do this, yell at people all day.

"One thing I've learned: Like a coin, every story has two sides. Sometimes more than that. It can be difficult figuring out who to trust. Your BS meter needs to be constantly running. You gotta keep digging until you find the truth. That's where the patience comes in."

Why is he telling me this? I'm leaving the newspaper anyway.

He leaned over his desk. "Honestly, it's a shame that you're leaving to do this website stuff." He didn't use the word *woman's* website. That seemed to be the inference. "The way the newspaper business is, I can't blame you. I do think you could be a great reporter someday. You just need to have a little more confidence, develop a thicker skin, and stop trying to do everything at once. It'll take time. And patience. Good luck." He thrust his hairy arm over the desk.

Feeling insulted, Mimi gave it a weak shake and left. Thinking back years later, she realized he'd paid her a tremendous compliment. He said she had the potential to be a great reporter. He wouldn't say that if he didn't mean it.

O.K., Lewis, I'll show you I have both reporting chops and patience. I'll give this more time. She found something comforting in that and drifted off to sleep.

WHEN MIMI ARRIVED AT HER FATHER'S OFFICE the next morning, Max said a note had been slipped under the door for her. He handed her a plain white envelope that was, sure enough, addressed to Mimi Rosen.

"I guess you're making friends," he grinned.

Mimi ripped it open to see a white paper with only two lines of type on it. "If you want to know what is going on at the USGR, go to the Diamond News Forum. Read the posts by the USGR Avenger."

Mimi's mind and heart raced. "Who dropped this off?"

"Not sure. I think it was a Hasidic guy."

"A Hasidic guy? Are you sure?"

"I think so. What's the big deal about a Hasidic guy? Forty-Seventh Street is full of them."

Mimi spent the day examining the note. She Googled the typeface and held it up to the light. It was just black type on white paper, yielding no secrets.

When she came home, she booted up her computer and went to the Diamond News forum.

She didn't leave her chair for five hours.

CHAPTER FOURTEEN

IT DIDN'T TAKE MIMI LONG TO FIND THE USGR AVENGER. He posted on the Diamond News forum all day every day, always about the USGR.

"The USGR acts like just because they got rid of one person, they got rid of their problem," he wrote in a typical post. "That is a COMPLETE LIE! The problems over there go far deeper than that!!"

He was agreeing with Mimi's father. She leaned in, intrigued.

"If they really want the truth, why didn't they bring in outsiders to investigate?"

Even better, Mimi thought. *He agrees with me.*

He published dozens of posts a day. It didn't seem like he ever slept. He seemed obsessed. And angry. And paranoid. Anyone who disagreed with him got branded a USGR lackey.

His posts appeared composed with a red face and gritted teeth and were riddled with proofreading errors; the editor in Mimi went into conniptions with each new grammatical atrocity. He seemed in love with exclamation points and his caps lock. That was how Mimi pictured him, a walking caps lock.

Who was he? A rogue grader? A disgruntled former employee? And what was he avenging? The other posters were just as curious. He always dodged the question. "What do you think? I want a target on my back? That the USGR should try and wipe me out?

"The USGR will do anything to keep their secrets!" he declared. "I know for a fact, they once killed somebody."

Mimi stared at the screen, her jaw dangling. She had to meet this guy and find out what he knew.

But, how? She didn't know who he was. The only clue she could make out was he was probably Jewish, as he frequently told antagonists to kiss his *tuchus*.

"I have information that will rock the USGR to its core," he proclaimed. "It will make a splash so loud people will hear it from miles away. I just need the right vehicle."

Mimi decided she would be that vehicle.

MIMI STAYED UP UNTIL TWO IN the morning reading the USGR Avenger's posts. The next morning she wasn't tired. Her adrenaline flowed as she strategized how to reach out to him.

She was a little nervous about reaching out to someone who came across as unbalanced. Yet, at her old newspaper, cranks and crazies often made the best sources. One elderly man had a seemingly endless amount of time to dig up dirt on local politicians. He would pass tidbits to Mimi during marathon two-hour phone calls, while his parrots squawked in the background.

Before noon, she sent the Avenger a private forum message. "I'm a journalist from a newspaper investigating the scandal at USGR. I want to hear your proof of the corruption there. This could be the diamond industry's Watergate. Call it 'certifigate.'"

He replied within minutes. "Don't think I'm going to fall for that one. You DESPICABLE USGR SPIES have to be way smarter to find me!!"

About what Mimi expected. She pounded out her response with fury. "No, I'm for real. I want to break this story open. By coming on the forum, you've taken an important step. Now take another."

No response. If he was Jewish, time for the big gun. Guilt.

"If you truly want to expose the USGR, do something about it. Otherwise, you're aiding and abetting corruption. WHY ARE YOU WAITING?"

Now Mimi was riding the caps lock. It was contagious.

He didn't respond.

She had just about given up until two days later when she received a message. Subject line: "Let's talk."

Mimi quickly wrote back saying she wrote for *The West Jersey Metro*, had heard about the problems at USGR, and considered this a hot story. She just needed proof.

"Yes," the Avenger replied. "The evidence I've collected will turn the ENTIRE industry UPSIDE DOWN like nothing has ever been turned upside DOWN!! That said, I must protect my identity. I refuse to talk to you unless you pass certain tests. These tests will be of my choosing and are NOT OPTIONAL!!!"

He asked about her background. Mimi was reluctant to give her name, but she had no choice. She attached scans of her newspaper stories, hoping he wouldn't notice they were a decade old.

He didn't. He stayed skeptical regardless. "Even if you're legit, it's possible you're being used by the bad guys." He made her swear that she didn't have friends or family at USGR, which was true; Paul no longer worked at USGR, and she wasn't sure he was her friend.

Didn't matter. "I'm not convinced. You might call me crazy. I just think I'm careful."

No, you're crazy, Mimi sighed.

During their fifth back-and-forth, Mimi had a brainstorm. "Here's proof I want to get to the bottom of this. I asked Arthur Tanner tough questions about bribery at the USGR and he kicked me out of his office."

"Really?" The Avenger replied with unprecedented speed. "The great all-powerful Tanner made you leave his office?! LMAO!!"

"Yep. Kicked me out. I'll attach a recording of the interview."

She sent him an audio file of their conversation about Paul, up to the point where Tanner not-so-politely asked her to leave.

"Wow," he declared a few hours later. "I loved that interview. You got kicked out of Tanner's office because you stuck it to him. THAT'S GREAT!! I must have listened to that a million times. ROFL!"

Mimi's uncomfortable moment was now the Avenger's favorite podcast.

He asked for her number. A minute later, he called. The number was, not surprisingly, blocked.

"This is the Avenger."

"Hi, Mr. Avenger." She wasn't sure how else to respond to that.

"I've decided to take a risk. This information needs to get out. What's happening is hurting honest people in this business. The wrongdoers need to be exposed."

Without the exclamation points and caps lock, the Avenger seemed normal—at least for someone who called himself the USGR Avenger.

"Once I heard Tanner kick you out of his office, I knew you wouldn't back down, even against the mighty USGR." He pronounced USGR with a space between each letter, like it was the KGB. "I gotta meet you."

Two days ago, she was begging for his attention. Now, he couldn't wait to get together.

"We shouldn't talk in public. Spies might overhear. Why don't you stop by my office tonight? I'm at 460 Fifth. Room 1010."

Room 1010. The person Mimi had spent the last three days looking for was located one floor up from her.

At 7 PM, WHEN THE ONLY people IN THE HALLS were the night cleanup crew, Mimi ventured to Room 1010.

Part of her felt proud. She had set out to meet the USGR Avenger, and now she was. Maybe if Woodward and Bernstein started today, they'd trawl web boards.

Another part of her was terrified. She didn't know this guy. Yes, she was meeting him in a well-protected office building. She should still take precautions. She texted Channah, "I'm meeting new source, rm 1010. Says has big info."

She came to the door. It read, "Larry Greenbaum Diamonds." She took a deep breath and rang the buzzer.

"Mr. Avenger," she called out. "It's Mimi."

He opened the door. After so much build-up, she was expecting . . . she didn't know what. As on the phone, the Avenger was remarkably unremarkable. He reminded Mimi of a grizzled ex-hippie. Short and doughy, he sported glasses, an unruly beard, and a big mop of black and white curly hair. He was wearing jeans and chewing a toothpick. The top of his black button-down shirt was open, with more than a few grey hairs peeking out. He buzzed her through the standard security double-door and welcomed her into his office.

"Hello, Mimi from *The West Jersey Metro*." He closed the second door after her. "Come in, Mimi from *The West Jersey Metro*."

Like her father's office, Larry's seemed a one-man show, if smaller and even more chaotic, with so many papers piled on his island of a desk it was a wonder the place didn't burst into flames.

Mimi tried to put him at ease with a handshake and a wide smile. "Nice to finally meet you."

"Likewise." He bit down hard on his toothpick. "Now, tell me who the hell you are." He wasn't smiling. And he'd pulled out a gun.

CHAPTER FIFTEEN

MIMI STARED AT THE PISTOL. SHE had never seen a gun up close before. It was ugly and dark. And pointed at her.

She lifted her hands and backed away. She flashed on Sol's rules for robberies. Keep calm. Don't make sudden movements. Don't even raise your hands. *Crap*.

"Sorry," Mimi blurted.

"What?"

"I put my hands up. I'm not supposed to do that. Should I put them down?"

"No!" growled the Avenger.

"Okay. And sorry for talking."

"What?" he barked.

"I just remembered; I shouldn't do that either."

"Would you shut up!" he screamed. "Tell the truth. That audio of you and Tanner sounded convincing. It was a complete fake!"

"No, it wasn't! How could I fake that?"

"You tell me," he sneered. "You said you worked for *The West Jersey Metro*. I believed you. This afternoon, I thought to do some checking. I called the newspaper and they said you didn't work there. You're not a real reporter, are you?"

Mimi's heart was thumping so hard she could feel it. She was shaking. So was he.

"I don't work there now." She tried to make her voice sound authoritative. It came out a quiver. "I hope to sell this to them freelance. I worked there six years ago. I sent you clips. I couldn't fake those."

His breathing made a labored painful-sounding wheeze.

"Maybe you used Photoshop."

"I don't know Photoshop!"

"Prove it!"

"How can I prove I don't know something?"

Larry stroked his mostly white beard, as the hand with the gun fell to his side. That didn't make Mimi's heart pound any less.

Suddenly, the sneer returned. "How do you know so much about the industry? You knew what was going on at the USGR, you knew about the message board. Only industry people are allowed on that board. How do I know you're not working for the USGR?"

"I don't work there. I work for my father's diamond company!"

"Where?"

"Downstairs."

"Prove it. Let me see your building ID."

"I don't have a building ID!" The tears she'd been holding back burst through. "I'm just working for my father on a temporary basis. I intend to go back to journalism. Getting an ID was a psychological leap I wasn't ready to take." She started sobbing full force.

"Don't cry." Fear crossed his face. "Want a tissue?" He had morphed from a scary guy holding a gun to a clueless man dealing with a crying woman.

"Yes," she sobbed.

He opened a desk drawer with his non-gun-holding hand and felt around. He ripped out a tissue and handed it to her. The weapon was now all the way by his side.

"I didn't expect you to start crying." He sounded hurt.

"What do you expect when you point a gun at someone?" She wiped her eyes.

"I don't know! It's not like I do this all the time! I just wanted to find out what was going on."

"I told you everything. I work in the building, for my father, Max Rosen."

His face brightened. "You're Max's daughter? He's a good guy. If you're related to him, you must be okay. You should have said so."

He laid the gun on his desk and wagged his finger at her. "I'm gonna trust you. Though, let me warn you: You should get a building ID. It saves you time in the morning."

Mimi was out of danger but couldn't stop shaking.

"Sorry I scared you. I would never shoot anyone. The gun isn't loaded. I don't even have bullets." He toyed with his glasses. "Can I get you a glass of water or something? More tissues?"

Mimi asked for—and got—all of those things. Larry stashed the gun away in his safe, shutting it with a thud.

She sat taking measured sips of water. Her pulse hadn't stopped thumping, and her underarms felt like wet sponges. She considered leaving and going to the police. She felt obligated to stay. She owed it to Channah. She owed it to herself.

Larry plopped himself onto a fake leather chair with the stuffing coming out on top. Amid the mess of papers, boxes, loupes, and tweezers stood a yellowed picture of a younger, happier Larry, smiling and holding a little girl. Next to that, towering over everything, was a big brown bottle of Johnnie Walker scotch.

Larry grabbed the bottle and poured a glass of scotch filled to the rim, "because he had company," he said. Judging by the papers on his desk with brown circles on them, this was not his first dinnertime scotch.

He handed the glass to Mimi. "Have some. It'll calm you down."

"I'm fine." She wasn't, though nothing could settle her nerves right now. She put the glass to the side. She needed to get the info and get out. "Let's talk about the USGR. You said you have evidence of bribery."

Larry lit a cigarette and took a dramatic puff. Smoke filled the air. Mimi weighed asking him to put it out. When a guy has just put away his gun, you don't rock the boat.

"Let me show you my treasure trove." He grinned as he rolled his chair to a rust-covered filing cabinet, opened the top drawer, and, after a few seconds of swear-laden rifling, yanked an overstuffed yellow folder from the top drawer. It was held together by a dirty brown rubber band and had "evidence" written on it, underlined with exclamation points.

Larry wheeled himself back to the desk and opened the folder like it really held treasure. It was packed with old photocopies of reports; each had a grainy picture of a diamond attached. He pushed it toward Mimi. She glanced at it, not sure what to make of it, or of him.

"I'll give you some background." Larry lifted his cigarette from the ashtray and crossed his leg to his knee, revealing a pink gap between his sock and pant leg. "For many years, my late father made a nice living in this business. He devoted his life to it. He believed in making it better."

Larry removed his glasses and rubbed his sunken eyes, which made him look both younger and sadder. "He served on all the industry committees. He was even an arbitrator."

Diamond club arbitrators were considered the most judicious people in the industry since they refereed disputes between their fellow dealers. Max served as an arbitrator for a decade. He was proud of that.

"One time he was complaining to a friend how the USGR gave him a certain grade on a stone. Like all dealers do. The guy told him, 'if you submit it through a certain dealer, it will get a better grade.' My father figured what the hell. He approached the dealer and asked him to submit the diamond. The guy winked at him, sent the stone into the lab, and, sure enough, it received a better grade. He submitted another diamond through the guy, and it got two grades higher than normal. The dealer went to him with a big smile and said, 'just keep doing this, add a percentage for the grader plus a cut for me, and we'll be good.' My father was appalled. He said this was immoral. The dealer said to him, 'I live in a big house. You live in a little house. Work with me, you can live in a big house too.'"

As Larry spoke, the ash hung from his cigarette like a bent finger.

"Now my father could have kept submitting through this guy to get better grades. He could have made a lot of money that way. He didn't. He was a good man. He knew what was going on was wrong." Larry took a puff on the cigarette, and the ash tumbled onto his pants. "He confronted the people at USGR. They had this big meeting at a midtown hotel. He told them, 'you have a problem at your lab.' All the big guys were there in their fancy suits, including that *putz* Tanner. They all said there's no problem, sometimes graders disagree. Their typical lies. My father knew better. He wasn't the type to let things go. He made a lot of enemies that day.

"I admired my father. He came to this country from Belgium with nothing and built his business out of sheer willpower, just working crazy hours and taking chances and being smart. He was a *mensch*. That's the hardest thing in life to be." Larry put down his cigarette and sipped his drink. "There's a saying in Yiddish. 'When we compare ourselves to our fathers, we realize how small we are.'" Through the smoke, Mimi saw Larry's cheeks puff out and turn pink. He was choked up. Maybe because she was exhausted by all the crazy events, Mimi got *verklempt* as well.

"In the end, nothing was done." Larry banged the glass on the table.

"The USGR started taking its revenge, giving my father lousy grades on all his stones. Every. Single. Time. They never gave the poor guy a break."

He picked up the pile of reports, waving them in front of Mimi. "Look at these diamonds. Look at these reports. They don't go together!" He was now bouncing in his seat, saliva flying from his lips. "Here's the worst part. A few months later, my father saw the dealer on the street. The guy came up to him and said, 'I hope you like your little house.' That proves it was totally deliberate!

"You know how important the USGR is. Getting those bad grades destroyed my father's business. And his business was his life, so it destroyed him as well. He developed a drinking problem. He died two years later." Larry drained the last remnants of scotch from his glass and stared at its bottom.

Mimi tried to reel him back to the present. "Where does that leave us now?"

Larry looked up, and his eyes shone with a sudden burst of energy. "I'm out to make the USGR pay for what they've done. Fortunately, I found that message board. I've become the king of it.

"My business is basically over. I'm divorced. I've got a daughter who doesn't talk to me. My life is basically shit. This is it for me. I want to expose what the USGR has done, and what they keep doing. And when Tanner and the rest finally get what's coming to them, I'll toast my old man up in Heaven." He took a final puff of his cigarette and snuffed it out in the ashtray with a confident poke.

Larry obviously had issues. Mimi felt for him.

"Yeah, divorce can be tough," she found herself saying. "I'm divorced too."

"You're single?" He lifted his eyebrow, sat up straight, and gave his shirt a few quick tucks. "Want to go for a drink after?"

Did he just ask her out? A few minutes ago, he had pulled a gun on her. Not exactly a turn-on. She needed to wrap this up; she couldn't spend all night listening to a guy half-drunkenly hit on her and proclaim himself king of a message board.

"I can't, Larry. Let's get to the point. Where is your evidence of bribery?"

"I showed it to you."

"When?"

"Just now. Those reports."

"They're not evidence."

"Of course they are!" He waved a report in the air. "This stone is clearly a G. It got a J! Three grades difference!" He slapped it on the desk, and grabbed another, glanced at it, and thrust it in front of her. "They gave an I2 to a stone that's clearly an SI! All out of vindictiveness! Only a corrupt organization would do that."

"That doesn't prove anything. You can't judge the quality of diamonds from those photos. Those reports are, what? Four or five years old?"

"Six or seven." He stuck out his lower lip. "How about what that dealer said to my father?"

"We only have the word of your father that he said that, and he's no longer with us. It doesn't mean a man's guilty because he said something about a house. Can I talk to that dealer?"

Larry frowned. "He's dead, too."

"To write an article, you need proof. Like a record of someone being bribed. Or someone admitting they took a payoff."

"How could I get that?"

"You said you had it on the message board."

Larry folded his arms. "I may have exaggerated a bit."

Mimi pored over her notes, trying to salvage this awful night. "Didn't you say on the board that the USGR killed somebody?"

"I told you. They killed my father."

"They didn't literally kill your father, Larry."

"They didn't help!" His mouth flattened. "Granted, there were other issues."

Mimi's head began to pound. "You don't have anything more than these reports?"

Larry looked away, like a little boy who's been caught. "Not really. You gotta admit these reports are very good evidence."

"No, they're not. Any reporter would tell you the same thing."

"Does that mean nothing's gonna happen?" He looked ready to cry.

Mimi felt the same way. After all this, she only had "very good evidence" that wasn't good at all.

Mimi stuffed her notebook in her purse, zipped it closed, and stood up. "If you hear anything else, call me."

"All right." Larry gripped his desk and hoisted himself to his feet. "Sorry about pulling the gun on you."

"It's fine," Mimi replied, even though it wasn't. She could smell the scotch on his breath. "Let me know if you discover anything. Like, something about that pink diamond I brought up to Tanner."

Larry pepped up. "I know the guy who originally owned that stone."

"You do?"

"Yeah. He once tried to sell it to me. I remember, it had a terrible cert."

"Does your friend have a copy of the original report?"

"He's the kind of guy who keeps records of everything. I can ask him."

"Can you give me his number?"

"No. Let me reach out to him. He's a little paranoid." That was one of the least self-aware sentences Mimi had ever heard.

"Larry, if you can prove that pink diamond had two very different reports, that would be huge. That would prove something really is wrong over there."

"I'll call him first thing tomorrow." Larry broke into a lopsided grin.

That wasn't the story Mimi was planning to write. She was swept up in the moment.

"Please do. Not only would that show what's going on at the USGR, it would prove Paul Michelson is innocent."

Larry's smile faltered, and he sat down. "Yeah, I don't think that's gonna happen." He poured himself some scotch and brought the glass to his lips. "Paul Michelson's as corrupt as the rest of them. Don't you know?"

CHAPTER SIXTEEN

MIMI HAD A TOUGH TIME SLEEPING after meeting Larry. The next morning she hit the snooze button three times before she was finally awakened by a call from Channah.

The minute Mimi picked up, she heard Channah say, "What happened?"

"What do you mean?" Mimi stammered.

"You sent me a text that you were meeting with someone with good info." Channah paused. "Remember?"

Given everything, that text had slipped Mimi's mind. She longed to tell Channah about her crazy night. That would mean relaying her theory about Yosef, and she wasn't ready to do that, not yet.

"It's a long story. How about I come to your house in a few days and fill you in?"

"That would be great!" Channah's voice rose. "I'm so curious to find out what you've learned!"

After they hung up, Mimi pulled the sheets over her, wrapped the pillow around her head, and curled into a ball. She shouldn't have agreed to that.

MEANWHILE, THE MAN MIMI ONCE SCHEMED to get ahold of was not leaving her alone. And it was annoying.

Larry's calls started that morning. He first phoned to say he'd emailed the original owner of the pink, asking for the report. He rang back the next hour, furious; the dealer had refused. A half hour later, she heard from him again.

"I called the stupid jerk that has the report and he hung up on me," he fumed. "What the hell's the matter with him anyway? Doesn't he understand what's at stake here? This trade's full of pathetic sheep."

He called more that afternoon, sounding a little drunk, declaring he wouldn't give up until he got that cert. "This is about the integrity of the entire industry, even that coward dealer has to realize that." An hour after that he called to ask if Mimi saw what Tanner said in that trade publication, what a first-class *shmuck*.

Mimi was supposed to answer the phone for her father. Instead, she spent the day fielding calls from Larry.

The next day, he called even more. Each time he started off railing about the USGR and got so worked up Mimi could almost feel the spittle coming through the phone. In one call, he started talking about the USGR and ended up in a long diatribe on the sad state of professional sports. At times, he just seemed lonely. While Mimi felt bad for him, she wasn't his therapist.

She was also starting to doubt him. He'd announced on the message board he possessed hard evidence of bribery. He later told her that was an exaggeration. It was basically a lie. Last night, he said he'd get the second report. He hadn't delivered that either. Maybe he made that up too.

He was also taking up way too much of her time. Mimi remembered her old source at the newspaper, the parrot-keeper. When his calls yielded diminishing returns, she stopped taking them. She'd have to say good-bye to Larry too.

ON THE DIAMOND NEWS FORUM, LARRY was as active as ever, beating his chest that he was about to release "UNBELIEVABLE evidence in the press that a major stone has been upgraded. This will finally end the USGR's reign of tyranny. It will be the biggest DOWNFALL since the HOLY ROMAN EMPIRE!!!"

Mimi knew he didn't have that info yet—and he might not get it.

The other posters seemed to be growing as skeptical as Mimi and just as tired of him. "Come on, Avenger, let's see the evidence already," wrote one. "You've been promising it for weeks now. Put up or shut up."

The Avenger wasn't the type to respond well to criticism—or shut up. He slammed anyone who doubted him as a pawn of his nemesis. "I know a paid USGR troll when I see one!!! LOL!"

This just made the doubters further inflamed. "I'm starting to think you're full of it," wrote one.

Mimi was already there.

The site's moderators were losing patience too; they issued a "Special Forum Announcement" that the USGR had threatened to sue, so posters now needed backup for their assertions.

"Oh, you'll get it," the Avenger fired back minutes later. "I'm gonna BLOW the USGR to BITS and you'll see the carnage all over Forty-Seventh Street."

The more posters challenged the Avenger, the more he lashed out. Soon, his caps lock and exclamation point keys were working overtime, and he had introduced profanity into the mix—the online equivalent of pointing a gun at someone.

Which again drew the moderators, who sounded sick of him dominating their forum. They warned him to cease cursing or he'd be prevented from posting. Mimi watched with horrified fascination. She knew what would happen next.

"You think I care about this puny little message board?" the Avenger proclaimed. "I have evidence of MAJOR corruption. If you don't want me saying that, you can go—" That was followed by a word guaranteed to get him banned.

When the axe came down, nobody spoke up for him.

The king had fallen.

Mimi had been letting Larry's calls go to voice mail. After he was kicked off the forum, she needed to talk to him. Maybe the USGR Avenger didn't care about being banned. Larry did. That "puny little message board" was his life.

Sure enough, when they spoke, Larry sounded depressed and quite drunk. It was mid-afternoon.

"I thought more people would stick up for me," he sulked. "I swore a few times. Big deal."

He railed about how plenty of people cursed on that board and that none had been reprimanded, never mind tossed off. Whether or not he'd admit it, as with his father, there were other issues, too.

The message board had even erased his old posts, he said, proving this was the work of the USGR. "Ever since I started talking about that pink radiant, they've been tracking me. They've tapped my phone. I think they listen to my calls."

Mimi knew what it was like to feel paranoid but couldn't let that go. "They're monitoring you?"

"I can feel it. Last night, someone broke into my office and rummaged through my stuff. This morning, my office was a total mess."

"Larry, when I was in your office, it was a pigsty."

"They made it *messier*. Seriously, someone is after me. I'm not crazy."

Mimi remembered her old editor chuckling that when a source says they're not crazy, that's a clear sign they are.

"How 'bout this? My daughter's training to be a cop. How about you and her go to my friend's office? She'll say the police are investigating this, and you can grab the report."

"That's ridiculous."

"It would work!" he protested. "Don't worry, I'll think of something. I got some great plans. I'm going to set up a dead man's switch."

"A what?"

"A dead man's switch. It's like an insurance policy. That means if someone kills me, all my information gets sent to the authorities."

"I don't think you need that, Larry."

"Yes, I do. This is war. Hey A-holes bugging this call, I'm not giving in without a fight. It's either you or me going down, and it ain't gonna be me."

Mimi had been tuning out Larry's rants. Now, she sensed a new, more desperate tone. "Larry, don't take this the wrong way. You need to take it easy."

"Oh, what?" His voice shook. "You're abandoning me now? Have they gotten to you too?"

She remembered he once asked her out.

"No, Larry, we're working on this together. I'm your friend." Mimi wasn't sure how the word *friend* would be received. He didn't respond, though she heard his heavy breathing. "It's because we're friends that I think you should maybe talk to someone." She approached the next sentence carefully. "Like a doctor."

"What? You think I'm nuts?"

"Of course not. I've talked to doctors about my problems before. It's no big deal. You need it. You shouldn't be drunk now. It's three in the afternoon."

"Don't tell me how to run my life!" he exploded. "I'm gonna bust this USGR thing wide open, and you and all the other stooges will just have to sit and watch the fireworks. And I'll do it with a real journalist, not some crappy freelancer! If you're so good, why are you working for your father's diamond company?"

This wounded Mimi, more than she would have thought. She tried to stay calm. "Larry, I'm trying to help–"

No matter. He hung up.

THE NEXT AFTERNOON, MIMI HEARD SIRENS and saw police cars gathered outside the building.

"Just got awful news," her father said. "Some dealer upstairs shot himself." He shook his head and uttered an obligatory "terrible."

That instant, Mimi knew he was talking about Larry. And he hadn't shot himself.

CHAPTER SEVENTEEN

MIMI RAN OUT THE DOOR. SHE didn't have the patience to wait for the elevator, so she raced up the back steps, the clopping of her shoes filling the stairway. When she burst onto the next floor, she heard the steady murmur of police walkie-talkies and saw Larry's office cordoned off with yellow tape.

Mimi froze. Part of her wanted to cry. Part of her wanted to throw up. Another part said stay away. This was getting too ugly, too insane.

It was too late. She couldn't turn back. She walked to Larry's office, dragging herself further into this nightmare.

She approached the jacket-and-tie-wearing police officer standing outside Larry's office, looking at his phone.

"Hi." She tried to catch his attention. "Can I speak to the person investigating this?"

"That would be me, ma'am. Detective Matthews." *Crap.* The same cop she tangled with last week. He looked like she'd imagined: middle-aged, bulky stomach, bulky head, bulldog face, no smile, coffee breath.

"I'm Mimi Rosen, a reporter." She was still catching her breath from her sprint upstairs.

He pointed his blue eyes at her. "That's right. We talked before. You said you were from *The West Jersey Metro.*"

She nodded. "Good memory."

"I don't remember every reporter I speak with. I remember you. You shared your theory about the murder of Yosef Levine." His mouth broke into a mirthless smirk. "What can I help you with?"

"I heard Larry Greenbaum died." Mimi's voice trembled. "He was my friend."

"Sorry for your loss." It sounded like the millionth time he'd said that.

"They're saying he committed suicide."

Matthews folded his arms to his chest, forming an impressive barricade. "We obviously can't comment on an ongoing investigation."

"I hope you look into this. I believe Larry was murdered."

Matthews shot back an incredulous stare. "Why do you say that?"

"Larry was a big poster on a diamond industry message board. He was kind of the king of it."

"Okay." Matthews appeared as unimpressed by that as she was.

"On this message board, he said he had proof of bribery at the USGR."

Matthews took out a pen and flipped open his notepad. "USGR. That's the diamond lab?"

Mimi nodded. Matthews scrawled in his notebook, and she took that as permission to keep talking.

"He said he had a report that showed clear evidence of a diamond being upgraded. He planned to give it to me for an article."

"And did he?"

"No."

"Why not?"

"He never got it."

Matthews stopped writing. "Didn't he say he had it?"

"He exaggerated sometimes," Mimi said softly.

"Who has this report now?"

"I don't know."

Mimi heard a rumbling, from deep in Matthews' throat.

"Are you sure this report exists?"

Mimi shifted her weight from one foot to the other. "Not really."

"O.K." He returned his eyes to his notebook. "Can you show me these forum posts?"

"No. The message board took them down after they banned him."

"He was banned?" Matthews squinted at her. "Didn't you say he was king of the board?"

Mimi looked down. "He was deposed."

If it's possible for a face to sigh, that was what Matthews' did. This wasn't working. Time for a gear switch.

"Here's something. Larry believed his phone was tapped and his office was broken into."

Matthews' pen started moving again. "When did he say that?"

"Yesterday."

"What was your response to that?"

Mimi hesitated. "I said he should seek psychological help."

Matthews' eyebrows shot up. "You thought he had emotional problems?"

"A little. He was clearly depressed. And paranoid. And obsessive. He had a drinking problem. And anger issues. He might have been delusional. Aside from that, he was fine."

Creases appeared in Matthews' rock of a forehead.

Time for another gear switch. "How about this? Larry told me his gun didn't have any bullets. So how could he shoot himself?"

"He talked to you about his gun?" Matthews' pen went to work again.

"Yes."

"What did he say?"

"First, he apologized for pointing it at me."

"Hold it. He pointed his gun at you? In a threatening manner?"

"Well, yeah. How else would you a point a gun at somebody?" Mimi let out a sorry little laugh.

Matthews didn't laugh with her. "Threatening someone with a firearm is no joking matter." His jowls emitted tremors of disapproval.

"It was only for a few minutes. Afterward, he apologized. I figured, no harm done." Her hands flitted around in the air.

"I would never downplay someone threatening you with a deadly weapon. That's a felony. Don't you think you should have reported that to the police?"

"We were meeting about a story, and, you know, these things happen."

"No, they don't. I can tell you, that is very unusual. Why did he threaten you?"

"It was all a misunderstanding. He was mad because I said I worked for *The West Jersey Metro* and—" The minute that flew out of Mimi's mouth, she realized that was a stupid thing to say.

Too late. Matthews finished her sentence. "—and you don't." He jerked his head forward. "You realize you told me the same thing?"

Mimi felt her antiperspirant fail.

"In fact," he continued, "if you wonder why I am acting skeptical, it's because I found our last conversation rather strange. I decided to call *The West Jersey Metro* to see if the story was running. They told me you don't actually work there. I even asked if anyone with your name freelanced for them, and they said no. Given that you lied to me, and now you admit you've lied to others, it's difficult for me to accept what you say at face value."

Mimi lost whatever composure she had. The words flooded out with dizzying speed. "I can explain everything. I worked for *The West Jersey Metro* for almost ten years, until I left to work for a website. I did that for a couple of years and they laid me off and now I'm trying to get back into journalism and am writing pieces on spec—"

"I don't have time for a long story." He was patronizing her—again.

Mimi stamped her foot. "I'm not crazy!" Now she was saying it.

"Listen, ma'am. I appreciate you sharing your theories with me. As I don't have a lot of time, please tell me this. Do you have any evidence— and please note that word, evidence, as it's the only thing we can go by— that you believe shows the deceased was the victim of a homicide?"

Mimi could only eke out a quiet "not really."

"Thank you. If you'll excuse me, I have work to do." He lifted up a piece of yellow tape and disappeared behind it.

MIMI SPENT THE REST OF THE AFTERNOON with her mind running in a million directions, none of them pleasant.

In a strange way, she would miss Larry. Yes, it didn't make sense to miss a guy who pointed a gun at her and she mostly tried to avoid. In the end, they were, as she put it in their last phone conversation, friends. He was so dedicated to "the investigation" it may have killed him.

On the other hand, he could have killed himself. He clearly had a shaky relationship with the truth. He may have lied about not having bullets in his gun. Matthews could have been investigating *her* death.

That thought profoundly unsettled her. She decided the detective was right. She could only go by evidence. She was in danger of becoming paranoid, like Larry. From now on, she would stick to the facts.

Mimi longed to mull all this over in a warm bath with some cold wine. Except, tonight she was due to visit Channah. She had driven her car into work because of it.

As she walked to her parking spot in the Forty-Eighth Street garage, she saw Jimmy once again nodding off in his security booth. She got in her car and was about to drive off when he ran up to her.

"Hey, did you see your friend?"

Mimi rolled down her window. "What friend?"

Jimmy poked his head in. "The guy looking for you."

"Someone was looking for me? Are you sure?"

"Oh yeah. He described you perfectly. He even knew your car."

"Who was he?"

"I got no idea. He was Hasidic. And kind of intense."

CHAPTER EIGHTEEN

MIMI'S FATHER USED TO SAY his daughter had a "mouth that speaks before it thinks." Many times, Mimi wished she could take back what she said, flick her tongue and retrieve it, like a frog with a fly. Other times, Mimi worried about what she'd say, often to excess, like she worried about everything.

Mimi spent most of the ride to Channah's thinking about the man in the garage—so much so that, when she arrived at Channah's house, she realized she had no idea what she'd tell her friend about Yosef. Over the weekend she rehearsed different approaches; one started, "I found out some distressing news." They all sounded stilted and stupid. There's no easy way to inform someone their dead sainted fiancé was probably a crook. As she trudged up the driveway, she figured she'd wing it—though that rarely worked for her before.

One of Channah's four little brothers opened the door, holding a prayer book and stuffed animal, *payis* dangling from each side of his head. Mimi walked through a narrow hallway to find Channah's parents again stationed in the kitchen, her mother leaning over the sink, her father sitting at the table reading the newspaper, like they hadn't moved since her last visit. The oven was lit up with something cooking. It looked like beef.

Channah's mom greeted her with the standard hug and offer of food, without a smile this time.

"How's Channah doing?" Mimi asked.

"Not great." Her mother wiped her hands on her apron. "It's only been a few weeks since Yosef died. These things take a while."

"By the way," her father looked up from his newspaper, "she says you're helping her with this investigation of hers."

"I am."

He lay the newspaper down on the table. "Be smart. Don't get involved. The police are looking into this. Let them do their jobs."

"I'm just talking to people," Mimi sputtered. "Seeing what I can find out."

Channah's father peered at Mimi over his glasses. "I don't think you understand what is going on here. Channah is very fragile right now. I've never seen her like this. The things she says, some of them are a little out there. The last thing she needs is someone telling her a bunch of wild stories."

"I would never say anything to upset her," Mimi said quickly.

"Good. Be careful. She has been through enough. The slightest thing you say could send her over the edge."

Mimi said she understood, and headed to the basement.

Down there, things hadn't changed much. No progress had been made with the much-discussed redecorating. Channah had gained weight and didn't appear to be taking care of herself; she seemed a little too comfortable sitting around all day in her pajamas. Another half-finished bag of Butterfingers sat by her bed, and *The Jewish Guide to Grief and Mourning* looked even more well-thumbed.

When Channah saw Mimi, she offered a big smile and warm hug, which made Mimi feel the trip was worthwhile. Until Channah brought up the investigation.

"I've compiled a list of the people you've met with." She pulled out a pen and piece of paper. "Let's go over what each one told you." She seemed eager for any scrap of information, or just confirmation that she wasn't, as her father put it, a little out there. "You met with someone at the USGR. What did he say?"

Mimi opened her mouth and, for a moment, considered telling Channah everything—about the reports, the bribery, and Yosef. She couldn't do it. Channah couldn't handle that. Mimi couldn't either.

"He didn't say much." Mimi stared at the back wall. "I wanted to know if the pink was synthetic, and he said it wasn't."

"Huh. My father said some big shot over there just got fired for taking a bribe."

"That was the guy I met with. Paul Michelson."

"How do you know he's telling the truth? Think about it. You can't trust someone who'd do something like that."

"He claims he didn't take any money. I believe him."

Channah's eyes fluttered. "Why?"

"He seems trustworthy. On the level. Like a good guy."

Channah stared at her. "Mimi, do you—"

"What?

"The way you're talking about him, it's like you have a thing for him."

Mimi flushed. "Kind of."

"Wow." Channah chuckled, clearly pleased with herself. "I should be a reporter."

"It didn't go anywhere."

"Probably for the best." Channah surveyed her notes. "The rabbi didn't tell you anything?"

"Not really."

"How about Garstein?"

"He didn't say much, either. He asked me on a date."

"*Oy.*"

"*Oy* is right. Though I told him yes."

"Really?" Channah raised her eyebrows in surprise.

"I figured I'll get info out of him."

"Probably better than going out with the bribery guy."

Mimi forced a smile. "Don't know about that." She remained protective of Paul. She wasn't sure why.

"How about Bernard?"

"He did tell me something. The money from that pink diamond is going to a scholarship that will combine—"

"Children and sports," Channah interrupted. "He told me that too." She scanned her list. "What about that guy you met with the other night? The one you texted about? You thought he had information."

"Turned out to be nothing."

Channah's face tightened. "Why did you think he knew something?"

"I don't know. I was wrong." She avoided Channah's gaze.

"You're having all these meetings and not learning anything?" Channah crumpled the list, loud enough that Mimi heard every crinkle. Her eyes locked on Mimi, making her feel pinned to the chair. Channah *would* make a good reporter.

"You're acting weird, Mimi. Like you're hiding something. I thought we were doing this together. As a team."

"I know. I need to be sure of certain things. I'm not yet."

"You said you'd tell me everything tonight!" Channah's hand pounded the bed.

"I'm sorry," Mimi mumbled. "It's not the right time."

"Thanks a lot." Channah started tearing up. "You were the only one who took me seriously. Everyone else just rolled their eyes. Now you're using this investigation as your dating service."

Mimi's body tightened. "That's not fair!"

"I just wish you were—" Channah paused. "More honest."

All Mimi's life she'd been loose-lipped. She was finally exercising some self-control, and getting flak for it. "Give me more time. Please."

"I don't have a choice, do I?"

Mimi chose her words carefully. "Trust me. I need to do it this way. I have my reasons."

"I understand," Channah growled. Clearly, she didn't.

Mimi tried to change the subject, but the air was too charged, and the conversation soon petered out. Channah announced that she was tired with a loud yawn, and she uttered a quick good-bye, followed by an equally quick hug. As Mimi climbed the stairs, she turned around to see her friend burying her red face in her pillow. She considered going back down and comforting her before deciding it was best to go.

The investigation had started with them together. Now, Mimi was on her own.

CHAPTER NINETEEN

THE NEXT DAY, AS MIMI SAT at the receptionist desk, her phone rang. She was surprised to hear Paul on the other end.

"I need to apologize." He sounded rushed. "I shouldn't have accused you of talking about me to the USGR. I jumped to conclusions. I hope you can forgive me."

"It's no big deal." His apology made her feel worse. "Did they take away your severance?"

"No. They dropped the whole thing. They called the publication, and it turns out the reporter didn't even work there."

Mimi cringed. How many people had asked *The West Jersey Metro* about her?

"They told my lawyer that whoever this person was, they were either crazy or a good BS artist."

"Glad it worked out." She uttered this as clipped and tight as possible, hoping to brush him off.

Paul didn't take the hint. "If you're not mad at me for being a jerk, I wondered if you'd be interested in meeting for a drink." On the last few words, his voice jumped an octave.

It took Mimi a second to realize he was asking her out. She replied she'd have to check her schedule, which she did, even though she knew it was empty. They both agreed to meet at 7 PM on Friday in a bar in Paul's neighborhood.

"I'm looking forward to it," she said. And she was.

As FRIDAY APPROACHED, MIMI ANALYZED PAUL'S invitation with the rigor of a Talmudic scholar. They were having a drink. Did that mean they were going out or just hanging out? Maybe he wanted to cross-examine her again about her article.

Plus, a drink wasn't dinner, and didn't most dates involve dinner? Or maybe dates no longer existed. Maybe today people met on the internet and had sex and that was that.

If this was a date, or whatever they called it these days, that brought her to a new level of anxiety. Mimi was never a big dater, even when she was single—unless getting drunk and hooking up at a bar counted. She went on a dozen or so fix-ups with Jewish guys arranged by her parents and hated them. The journalist in her liked hearing people's stories, but people weren't that honest on dates, trotting out rehearsed and sanitized summaries of their lives.

During one listless encounter, the guy stood up after 20 minutes and declared, "This isn't going well." He slapped down money on the table and strode out of the diner.

At the time, she was mortified. Looking back, she appreciated his honesty. When something wasn't working, you might as well cut your losses, go home, and watch TV. Mimi never liked dating, and she couldn't imagine liking the whole tortured ritual any better now.

Plus, did she now have to text? To sext? To Tinder, whatever that was? Or chronicle the relationship on Facebook?

There was also the journalistic ethics issue, which Mimi had put out of her mind but was now staring her in the face. Paul was a source for her story and reporters shouldn't date sources, even though Mimi had done that before. Of course, going for drinks with a source was different than sleeping with one. Though Mimi had done that, too.

For all her reservations, Mimi was going on something that might—or might not—be a date. That made her happy. And excited. And anxious. Before she left, she scribbled a list of emergency conversation topics, in case things bogged down. As the clock ticked down to Friday at 7, Mimi tried on one outfit after another and generally felt like a teenager. She also remembered being a teenager kind of sucked.

THEY MET AT A DIMLY LIT WINE BAR in Brooklyn Heights and sat side by side on stools facing the front window. Paul looked well put-together and handsome, in a freshly pressed blue button-down shirt and brown slacks. Mimi, after a half hour of mulling over what to wear, and three wardrobe changes, opted for a casual look of tight-fitting jeans and a nice-but-not-that-nice orange sweater from eBay. He was dressed nicer than she was, which left her both embarrassed and flattered. It was a clue this was indeed a date.

They both ordered white wine. Paul seemed more confident than the tittering, throat-clearing bundle of nerves she met last week; he navigated the wine bar stool with far more dexterity than the one at the coffee shop. Mimi asked how his job search was progressing.

"Not well, regrettably. By the way, everything I say is off the record."

Mimi's mouth went dry.

"Just kidding," he laughed. "I know you're not writing about me." He apologized again for accusing her, and she quickly changed the subject. Paul tilted his wineglass, and a drop of wine leaped out, producing a noticeable blotch on his khakis. He quickly wiped it up with his napkin, hoping she wouldn't notice. She acted like she hadn't. He seemed nervous. Another clue.

"I'd love to set up my own laboratory. I just don't know if I could attract much business, given some of the negative perceptions out there. Everyone assumes I'm guilty. Nothing I do can convince them otherwise." He gripped the napkin and began tearing a straight line through its center. "I have been completely abandoned by my former colleagues. They won't even return my calls. Those people were my friends. I feel like a leper." He started shredding the napkin with greater intensity. This wasn't the nice evening Mimi hoped for.

Which gave her an idea. If she and Paul talked about the USGR all night, she'd spend it in reporter mode, cataloging and analyzing every morsel of information. She longed not to think about Yosef and his big pink, if only for an evening. Besides, she was on, she hoped, a date. Dates should be fun.

"Hey, Paul, before you go any further, let's agree that, for the rest of the night, we don't talk about labs, or diamonds, or anything related to our careers. Let's talk about other stuff."

She wasn't sure how he'd take that suggestion. He quickly smiled and agreed. It turned out, there was plenty of "other stuff" to talk about. Paul's face lit up talking about his children—a ten-year-old boy and an eight-year-old girl.

"Do you have photos?"

"You know how parents hate to show pictures of their kids." He reached for his phone. "I warn you, their cuteness may be overpowering."

Even with that buildup, Mimi produced an "awww" at their gap-toothed grins. "They *are* adorable."

"I don't disagree."

Mimi looked again. The girl was pretty—freckled with ponytails—though she appeared somewhat sickly. The boy was a splitting image of Paul.

"Your son looks like you did."

"Aside from the pizzaface thing."

Mimi winced into her wine. "You knew about that?"

"That I was called Pizzaface Paul? How could I not? My own brother called me that. My parents freaked out when they heard. Their reaction made everything worse."

"I have a confession. Sometimes, behind your back, I called you that too."

"I can't believe you were working against me." Paul shook his fist with mock outrage. "You'll be happy to know I am way over being called 'Pizzaface Paul.'"

"You sure?" Mimi laughed.

"My mother's family escaped from the Nazis when she was five. There are worse childhood traumas."

As long as they were clearing the air, Mimi apologized for not thanking Paul for defending her on the playground. He looked amused and assured her he had no memory of that incident, other than a dim recollection of dinner that night, when his mother asked about the bruise on his face. He told her he was hit by a volleyball in gym.

After the second glass of wine, Paul asked if she was interested in dinner. Mimi said yes, as offhandedly as she could. Paul brought up a nice Italian place down the street where he always wanted to take a date. He had used the d-word. Mystery solved.

THEY SAT AT A CORNER TABLE in the nice Italian place. It was an old-fashioned tile-laden bistro trying to modernize itself; the walls featured the standard frescos of the Tower of Pisa alongside abstract artwork done by locals.

After a little wine and lot of pasta—Mimi didn't order pizza because of the sensitivities around Pizzaface—Paul asked, "What's it like working for your father?"

"I thought we weren't talking about work!"

"That's more a family question. I guess it's all intertwined in this business."

"True," Mimi said, as she twirled buttery pasta on her fork. "I'd prefer a more meaningful job. For now, it's fine."

"He's okay, your dad?"

"For the most part. It's been two years since my mom died, and sometimes I think he misses her more than ever. He has eight grandchildren. They keep him busy."

"Eight? Impressive."

"And counting. My sisters are observant. They don't waste time."

"And you're not?"

"No. My mom wasn't really either. Though, as my father says, 'she was quiet about it. You let everyone know.'"

Paul laughed. "I call myself a hard-core agnostic. I'm certain I have no idea if there's a God."

Mimi smiled. "I like that. Though I do feel there is more to life than just this table and these chairs and this restaurant. And when you do good, you're rewarded, and when you don't, it catches up to you."

For a second, Paul grew quiet, then snapped out of it. "Sometimes I feel I can never really leave my background behind. My sister isn't religious either. She got married at twenty-four, and I did at twenty-seven, which was way younger than most of our friends. And while my marriage produced two beautiful kids, it was a pretty big mistake."

"Yeah, I made my mistake around thirty," Mimi replied, half listening, half mulling this over. She'd considered her wedding to a non-Jew a supreme act of rebellion. In truth, she had just done what was expected of her, with a twist.

"You don't have kids?"

"My ex-husband and I tried. We couldn't."

"Sorry. My wife and I had issues too. You see your nephews and nieces a lot?"

"Not as much as I'd like. Which is hard, because they mean a lot to me, not having kids myself. One of my sisters lives in Israel. The other lives in New Jersey, but we don't really get along. We had a fight because she didn't come to my wedding."

"Why not?"

"My ex-husband wasn't Jewish."

"That'll do it."

"Though, in retrospect, I shouldn't have gone to my wedding either."

Paul let go a soft chuckle. "How did your parents take the non-Jewish thing?"

"Okay. They came to the wedding. My father even gave a halfhearted toast. He never could hide his feelings though. He'd say things like, 'don't worry, we accept him.' I'd think, 'I wasn't worried until you brought it up.'"

"Did the religion thing capsize the marriage?"

"In the end, it didn't even make the top ten."

"If you don't mind me prying, what was number one?"

"He was having an affair."

"Ouch."

"With a friend of mine."

"Double ouch."

"It was rough. It left me pretty battle-scarred. That's why it's good to spend time with my father. Even when he drives me nuts, I know he's a decent man. He restores my faith in humanity."

Paul nodded, smart enough not to interrupt a date mid-spiel.

"I'll be honest with you, Paul." She looked him in his eyes. "I haven't gone out with anyone since my divorce. It's been difficult for me to trust people. Now I want to get back in touch with the better parts of life."

God, I sound like a Broadway musical. How much wine have I had?

She massaged her forehead. "I'm sorry. This was supposed to be a fun night. You don't want to hear about my messed-up life. Who wants to listen to a depressed rambling woman?"

That was even worse! Mimi looked down at her half-eaten plate of seafood pasta, and up at Paul, anxious how he'd react.

A sly smile formed on his lips. "Depressed rambling women are my type. I belong to a depressed rambling woman fetish site."

It took Mimi a moment to realize he'd made a joke. She let out a long, surprised laugh.

"We all have our low moments." Paul hoisted his wineglass. "Here's to better days."

They clinked, and Mimi was both relieved and impressed. She had been honest—too honest—and he hadn't bolted for the door. Instead, he smiled, listened, and cracked a cute joke. That wasn't meant as a test. He had passed anyway.

Time for her questions. "How are your parents?" She tapped her wineglass with her finger.

"Okay. Slower and greyer, of course. My mom's as feisty as ever. She calls me up and says"—Paul put on a convincing Eastern European accent—"'Tell me, Paul, vy did you get divorced?'"

"Tell me, Paul—" Mimi swilled her wine. "Why *did* you get divorced?" His face turned blank. "I'd rather not discuss it."

"Come on! I told you about my divorce!"

"Trust me. You don't want to hear this. You wanted a nice night."

"Too late," Mimi grinned. "I already ruined it."

"I don't want to talk about it." His face grew long as he dug into his remaining chicken.

Quiet descended on the table. They were now listening to other people talk and clink their knives and forks.

Mimi reminded herself she was off duty tonight. She summoned her list of emergency topics, going with number one, what TV shows they watched. That got the conversation back on track. Up to that point, she hadn't thought about the list, or how the night was going. The best sign it was going well.

Paul's mention of his mom triggered something in Mimi; she only faintly remembered his parents but recalled them as sweet people. It would be nice, she daydreamed for an instant, to see them again, as Paul's girlfriend. Of course, there was the not-so-slight issue of Mimi's father thinking Paul was a crook. She was now more convinced than ever he was innocent. There he was, sitting right in front of her, talking and laughing and acting smart and funny and kind. How could he be anything but?

AFTER DINNER, MIMI AND PAUL WALKED the cobblestone streets of Brooklyn Heights. It was a cool, pleasant, early March night. Stars dotted the sky and the air was filled with the tantalizing first hints of spring. Mimi and Paul both wore light leather jackets, and the streets were packed with people, mostly couples. As they walked, Mimi and Paul talked about favorite places they've travelled, where they dreamed of going, and what they'd do if they had a million dollars. Paul's soft, supple fingers made brief visits to Mimi's elbow, hands, and the small of her back.

At the Brooklyn Promenade, they sat on a park bench, facing the East River and the Manhattan skyline. Paul surprised Mimi by leaning over and kissing her. Mimi surprised herself by kissing back.

Mimi knew this was crazy. She shouldn't be on a park bench with Paul, never mind locking lips with him. She had kissed him once; it was too late to turn back now. She might as well do it again.

Maybe it was all the wine she drank, or that Pizzaface Paul was a surprisingly un-clumsy kisser, or just because, after weeks of thinking about murder, bribery, and corruption, Mimi really did want to get back in touch with the better parts of life. The second time they kissed, something inside of her changed, and she felt happy and at peace. It didn't take long for her remaining reservations to fade away.

CHAPTER TWENTY

O F ALL THE THINGS MIMI IMAGINED would happen when she started working for her father, she never dreamed she'd end up in the arms of her childhood friend. Yet, there she was this Friday night, snuggled up next to Paul, as the two sat on a park bench on the Brooklyn Heights Promenade, staring at the downtown skyline set against the cloudless sky.

Mimi had spent her life living around New York City and the city rarely fazed her. Nestled against Paul's firm chest, gazing at that majestic collection of downtown buildings, she felt like she was looking at the most full-of-possibility, amazing place on Earth. She wouldn't mind if the world faded away and she could spend the next few weeks with him on that bench.

They kissed again. Paul's breath tasted sweet, with just the hint of alcohol.

"Just think," he said as she rested her head on his shoulder. "This all started when you came to ask me about synthetics."

Mimi laughed softly. "Did you know I spent the interview checking out if you were married?"

"Is that what you were doing?" Paul chuckled and crossed his legs. "You didn't seem interested in gemology, that's for sure."

As he talked, he stroked Mimi's hair. She liked that.

"That was a fateful meeting. I met you, and I saw that report for that pink diamond." He released a breath. "One good thing, one bad thing."

Mimi sat up. As much as she wanted to relax and enjoy the moment, she had something to say. "Paul, I've been thinking about your situation.

I know your lawyer said you shouldn't file suit against the USGR. I think you might have a case. You could say you signed that separation agreement under duress. The USGR called you a 'bad apple' in a trade publication. That's a clear case of defamation."

His mouth curved down. "I've thought about that. They will just come back at me with their phony computer records showing I took a payoff."

"So what? You can say you discovered that second report. If you find a copy of that other certificate, that will back up everything you've said."

Paul took off his glasses and rubbed his eyes. "It's probably been erased from their system."

"You don't know that. Someone in the industry might have it."

"I guess." He put his glasses back on. "I just need to move forward. I don't have the money for a big court case." He turned toward the river.

"I hate to see bad things happen to good people. You're obviously not the type of person who would ever take a bribe."

Paul fell silent. His Adam's apple bobbed, and he turned to Mimi. "I have a story to tell you."

Two years ago, Paul's daughter developed a possibly life-threatening heart ailment that required emergency surgery. "We wanted her to see this doctor in Ohio, who was supposed to be the best at this type of procedure. The insurance company wouldn't pay because he was out of network. The entire thing would cost about eighty thousand dollars, with airfare, hotels, and everything. Which I didn't have at the time. I had two young kids, and my wife was staying home taking care of them. We had just bought this beautiful four-bedroom home in Westchester. I was basically living paycheck to paycheck. I didn't have eighty grand at the ready, certainly not without drowning in debt. This was my daughter we were talking about. She was six at the time, and I'd do anything for that little girl. I love her so much, it's painful sometimes."

As he spoke, his face twitched and temple throbbed. "Around this time, I was friends with a major USGR lab client. We didn't socialize or anything. We just knew other professionally, and our parents had done business together. We would occasionally talk on the phone. One day, I started unloading to him about this. I wasn't looking for charity, just venting, really. The guy told me, 'I can give you the eighty grand.' I said he didn't have to. He insisted on it, it was a *mitzvah*, he said. A few days later I went to his office, and he handed me two fat envelopes stuffed with hundreds.

"Of course, this was against lab rules. You're not supposed to take gifts from clients, never mind large stacks of cash. I wasn't going to say anything because this guy had completely solved my problem. While eighty grand wasn't that much to him, I swore a million times I'd pay him back. I didn't know how I'd do that, because even after my daughter had the surgery, she needed follow-up care, and that wasn't cheap either. But that was one hundred percent my intention.

"About a month later, this guy called me up. Again, I thanked him and promised to pay him back. He said, 'you don't have to do that. I did a *mitzvah* for you, now you do a *mitzvah* for me.' That was how he put it, a *mitzvah*. He had this fifteen-carat stone coming through the lab, and he wanted me to bump it up a few grades. I was pretty uneasy about that request, but I had no choice. This guy had given me all that money, and if he wanted to, he could have turned me in and gotten me in trouble. I went into the computer system and increased his stone two color grades and one clarity grade. It took about two seconds. Afterward, I did a back of the envelope calculation. I'd just made the guy around one hundred and fifty thousand dollars on an eighty-thousand-dollar investment. That's close to a one hundred and fifty percent return, certainly a better margin than you can make selling most diamonds. For weeks afterward, I was petrified I'd get caught.

"At one point, the guy reached out to me and said he wanted to keep giving me money for upgrades. He said I could have a nice side business and pay for my kids' college. I'll be honest, I was tempted, because I was definitely having trouble making ends meet. There was no way I could agree to that. In the meantime, this guy wouldn't stop asking me. I tried to avoid him, and he kept leaving messages. I wrote him this big long email thanking him and trying to extricate myself from the situation. I was stupid enough to write it from my work email. That's how they caught me."

His eyes stayed focused on the river, as if it held the answer to this craziness.

"The board held this disciplinary hearing. I had to hire a lawyer and I had no idea if I would lose my job or even go to jail. In the end, I got suspended for two months without pay. They added restrictions on me meeting people on my own, which is why it was such a big deal we had that interview. And the dealer got banned from submitting to the lab again. Considering what could have happened, we both got off easy. I still had a job afterward, and he could always send in stones through someone else. Everything was kept hush-hush. Clearly, Tanner and the board didn't want the news getting out.

"The whole situation caused some rocky times in my marriage. At one point, my wife said, 'I can't believe I married a crook.' That's when I realized the marriage was over. She knew why I did what I did. I couldn't be with someone who thought of me that way."

Mimi's brain was swimming. The timing didn't make sense. "Didn't this happen two years ago? You got fired last week."

"Correct. That's why I think they set me up. They said they had evidence I took another bribe. That was a lie. I took only one payoff my whole career. That's it. When you've admitted it once, it's hard to claim you're innocent. I was just happy they gave me severance. I took the money and left." His face flushed with panic. "Don't tell anyone about this. Please."

"Of course not. You have my word." She raised her hand.

"Even my parents and closest friends don't know this story. I probably shouldn't have told you. You brought it up and it just came out.

"This whole episode really screwed up my life in a myriad of ways. I'm now divorced and unemployed. I can only see my kids every other weekend. The important thing is, my daughter got help when she needed it. That's what really matters."

He stuck out his lower lip and exhaled. "It was good to get that off my chest. I really do feel lighter." He turned to her with a gleam in his eyes. "Anyway, now that we've both spilled our guts, would you like to come up to my place?"

Mimi's stomach lurched. A few minutes ago, she would have jumped at the chance. Hell, she would have jumped him. Now, she needed to mull things over. "I should get back to New Jersey. It's kind of late."

Paul's face sank. "It's fine if you don't come home with me." His voice grew small. "Are you upset about what I told you?"

"A little." Mimi avoided his eyes.

He frowned. "Come on, Mimi. I'm not proud of what I did. I had no choice. My daughter was sick. You understand that, right?"

"Of course I understand. Your daughter was sick. I just need to go home."

They rose from the bench and walked to the subway in silence. While Mimi had just had a great night with Paul, she needed to get away from him. She was no longer sure who he was.

CHAPTER TWENTY-ONE

Bᴇғᴏʀᴇ Mɪᴍɪ ʟᴇғᴛ Pᴀᴜʟ, ꜱʜᴇ ɢᴀᴠᴇ ʜɪᴍ ᴀ ᴋɪꜱꜱ, said she would call him soon, and acted like everything was fine. It wasn't.

When she returned to her apartment, she saw the outfits she'd tried on pre-date piled high on her bed. Thinking of how excited she was then, and how conflicted she felt now, she lay down amid the rejected outfits, nuzzled her face in her grey wool sweater, and cried.

She'd promised to call Paul when she got home. She didn't; she needed time to think. The next day, she was still thinking. On Sunday, he called, reached voice mail, and hung up. The day after, he sent a short sad text. "Hi there. All good?" Mimi didn't write back. She was now one of those people that promised to call and disappeared. A jerk.

Every rational voice in her head told her, not always politely, she should not see Paul, at least not in "that way." After dealing with her ex-husband's moodiness and infidelity, she vowed to never again get involved with a man with issues. It was hard to find a man with more issues than this guy. Hearing someone confess to a crime wasn't her idea of dream romantic banter.

Dating him also violated every tenet of journalistic ethics. She'd considered Paul an innocent bystander. Now, he might play a bigger role in the story than she thought. To properly investigate Yosef's murder, she'd need professional distance, and emotional distance too.

Yet every time she vowed not to see him, another, equally insistent voice piped up. *Sure about that?* She never was. Several times throughout the day, she thought about him and smiled, despite everything. He was the kind of guy she had hoped to meet if she resumed dating—which, in a way, she just had.

If she could only be sure of Paul's tales of second certs and bribery mitzvahs. He'd struck her as a decent person. Yosef had, too. Now, she wasn't sure about either of them.

Mimi's old newspaper editor's mantra was "Trust, but verify."

"Don't put anything in print," he'd wave his arms, "unless you're one hundred percent sure it's true. No matter the source, verify, verify, verify."

Mimi couldn't verify anything Paul said. The only thing left was trust.

After a sleepless night, she did something she hated. She asked her father for advice. "Dad," she walked back from the reception area for a quick break, "you know how you say being a dealer is as much about sorting the people as sorting the diamonds?"

"Those are wise words." He grinned. "Sometimes I'm quite intelligent."

"How do you sort people? How do you determine who to trust?"

"Why do you ask?"

"Just curious."

"That's the hardest part of this business." Max cupped his hands behind his head. "If you're not careful, you can lose a lot of money. There aren't many people in the world I would lend one hundred dollars to. Yet, last week, I gave Sol a decent-sized stone worth far more than that, and all I got back was a receipt scribbled on paper." He patted a pile of papers, couldn't find it, moaned, and went on.

"You used to trust people in this business one hundred percent. When you said *Mazal* and shook on a deal, it meant something. Your word really was your bond. You'd go to the club and see notices, 'found: two-carat diamond.' In those days, if someone found a stone on the floor, it would be an insult to his honor to even think about not returning it."

"You still see those signs at the club."

"The board is still there. Except now there's many more lost notices than found ones. The business has changed. It used to be all about relationships. My customers were like family. Now, they go to the big guys down the street to save one percent."

The conversation had wandered off into the problems of the industry. Why shouldn't Max be wistful for the old days? Back then, his wife was alive, his business was thriving, and his daughter wasn't a secular divorced woman warning him his company was going bust. He roused himself and returned to the subject at hand.

"Anyway, who do you trust? Sometimes it's obvious. If someone appears out of the blue and wants to buy a ton of goods and doesn't *hondle* you on price, he'll probably take everything you have, dump it at a pawnshop, and disappear without paying. Most *ganefs* know not to act that way.

"You go by gut, by feel. You ask yourself: Does the person seem decent? Do they smell right?"

That didn't help. Mimi had been on wary terms with her gut ever since it advised her to marry her ex-husband. "That's it? You do huge deals just by your gut?"

"Yeah." Max shrugged. "What else am I gonna do? There's no magic formula. I'm just a person. I've made a lot of mistakes over the years. Eventually you learn. You can just tell.

"I know Sol's a good guy. I don't know why, I just do. We get along. He shoots straight. In forty years of doing business together, he's never proven me wrong. It's a leap of faith. Your judgment is all you have in this world. It's about trusting yourself. That's just as important as trusting other people." He peered at Mimi. "You're having some kind of problem, aren't you? Is it with a man?"

Mimi felt a blush creep up her neck. "I'd rather not go into it."

"OK. If you ever want to talk, I'm here for you."

"Thanks." Mimi kept her head down. "That was a good guess."

A smile spread across Max's face. "That's what happens when you have three girls. See? Sometimes my gut's not too bad."

Mimi returned to reception. If she was going by her gut, there was only one thing to do. She took a deep breath and dialed Paul's number.

He picked up right away. "Hi, Mimi. Good to hear from you."

They hadn't talked in three days.

"Sorry I haven't called. I had to think about things."

"I understand."

She sensed an undercurrent of hurt, like he expected a good-bye.

"Sometimes it takes me a while to sort things out. Sorry I haven't called. I would like to go out again."

He sounded puzzled. "Okay. On Friday, you seemed uneasy about, you know, the bribery thing." He stumbled over the word, like he hated to even say it.

"No, that's fine." Mimi immediately thought she should amend that statement, as she wasn't okay with bribery. Better to change the subject before she changed her mind. "I had a great time with you. We did kiss."

"That's true. Kissing on a date is generally considered a good sign."

Mimi laughed. "You sound like an expert."

"We're hot commodities, us middle-aged divorced unemployed men."

Mimi laughed again. "It was very nice. And if we get together, perhaps we can kiss again."

"Whoa. You must think I'm easy."

Mimi chuckled once more. Three laughs in one conversation. Not bad.

They talked and joked a little while longer, and Mimi felt the old chemistry re-ignite. They made a date to get together on Wednesday. Mimi knew she'd made the right choice.

Leap of faith, taken.

LATER THAT DAY, AS MIMI WAITED on the building security line after she returned from lunch—she still hadn't gotten her building ID—she heard the woman in front of her ask for Larry Greenbaum's office. The woman said she was Larry's daughter and was cleaning out his things. She had a different last name than her father, and there was a little confusion while they sorted everything out. The guard discovered she'd been coming for the past few days and let her up. Mimi followed.

Mimi watched the woman fumble with her keys and enter Larry's office. She spent a minute pacing the hall debating whether to buzz his door. When she did, she was let right in.

The furniture was mostly gone, and the office looked smaller than before. It was no longer Larry's personal fiefdom of craziness and disorder; just a hollowed-out room with overflowing garbage cans and boxes on every desk.

Larry's daughter was tall and brunette. Mimi saw a bit of her father in her earnest, intense eyes. She was young, probably in her early 20s. Her face was lined like she'd seen hard times. She greeted Mimi with a Starbucks cup in her hand and a quizzical look. Her coat was tossed on a desk.

"I heard you say you're Larry's daughter. I was a friend of your father. We were working on a project together."

"Nice to meet you." She extended her hand and introduced herself as Ellen.

"What kind of project?"

"It was kind of an investigation, about the USGR."

"Interesting. I saw some files on that."

Files? This piqued Mimi's curiosity. She'd only seen the one. "Could I see them?"

"Sure." Ellen walked back to the boxes. "I was planning to throw them out."

She rummaged through a box, pulled out two folders, and handed them to Mimi.

"Thanks." Mimi eagerly grabbed hold of them. "We did a lot of work on this. I'd hate to see it go to waste." Without realizing it, Ellen had just acted as her father's dead man's switch.

Mimi gave the folders a quick glance. On the top one was written in magic marker, "USGR Important," underlined with exclamation points. She smiled, remembering how Larry loved his exclamation points. "I'm sorry for your loss. I really liked your father."

"Were you close friends?"

"Not really. Aside from this project, I didn't know him that well."

"Me neither. We had lost touch."

"He mentioned that."

Ellen looked up. "Did he talk about me?"

"Sometimes. He said you weren't speaking."

"Yeah." Ellen dragged out the word so it sounded like a sigh. "I feel bad about that. When my mother remarried, he didn't handle it too well. After that, we didn't talk. Maybe it was his fault, maybe mine, maybe my mom's. Too late now." She shrugged and sipped her coffee, like she'd long ago come to terms with it.

"Sorry. I know he cared about you."

"It's so strange. Sometimes you don't know someone 'till they're gone. I've been going through his things. I had substance abuse problems in high school, and I discovered he paid for my rehab. All of it. Which is crazy, because that wasn't cheap, and he didn't have a lot of money. No one ever told me." She averted her eyes. "Sorry, I shouldn't be going on about this."

"It's okay. His death has been hard for me too."

"My father was a good guy. A little overdramatic sometimes, but a good guy."

"Yes, he was."

"Overdramatic or a good guy?"

"Both."

She and Mimi laughed.

"My father was, what do you call it, a *mensch*."

Larry would be so happy if he heard his daughter call him that. Maybe he did. They were in his office. Mimi felt his presence all around them.

"Why did he kill himself?" Ellen asked. "Was he depressed?"

Mimi wasn't sure how to answer that. "It's complicated. How about we get together sometime, and I'll tell you what I know?"

Ellen half-smiled. "I'd like that." She handed Mimi her card. She was, as her father once said, a police cadet. A crime fighter, like her dad.

When Mimi returned to her office, she dove into the folders. At first, she was disappointed. They were filled with the same old USGR reports he showed her last week. Oh well. She could keep them as a souvenir of her time with Larry.

Underneath them, she saw a folder labeled "undeniable evidence," with the requisite underlines and exclamation points. It contained one piece of paper: A printout of an email from Paresh@mehtacoloreddiamonds.com from the morning after Larry and Mimi met.

"Hi, Paresh," Larry wrote. "I remember you originally owned a 3.2-carat pink radiant. I've heard it's now being sold with a different report. Do you have a copy of that original cert? It's REALLY IMPORTANT that I get it!!!"

The reply was brief. "Larry, I cannot and will not give you that report. Do not contact me about this again. Too risky."

That was indeed evidence of a second cert. The dealer had basically admitted he had the report but wouldn't give it to Larry because it was "too risky." That was interesting in itself.

Granted, this wasn't undeniable proof; Larry *did* like to exaggerate.

Regardless, it was a huge break. Mimi now knew who had the second cert. Wherever Larry was, he deserved a gold star. Underlined, with exclamation points.

Later, Mimi realized something else. If the second cert existed, that backed up a crucial part of Paul's story. She could trust him after all.

Her gut wasn't too bad either.

CHAPTER TWENTY-TWO

Mimi's next move was contacting Paresh@ Mehtacoloreddiamonds.com and getting that report. Which could be challenging. His email to Larry made it clear he wanted no part of this.

She spent all night strategizing. She would appeal to Mr. Mehta's conscience and explain why it was so important she get that second cert. She would be direct and honest.

But first, she'd lie.

Online research said his company specialized in colored diamonds. She called and said she was doing a story on that topic for *The West Jersey Metro*. She secured an interview for the next day.

Before heading over, Mimi asked her father if he knew the Mehtas. He didn't, and sounded surprised an Indian dealer specialized in colored diamonds.

"I keep thinking that Indian companies only sell small diamonds. The world has really changed."

"India only got into the business recently, right?"

"They started in the eighties, cutting low-grade material everyone considered *chazerai*. Before that, no one cut those stones because the labor costs alone would be worth more than the diamond. Labor is so cheap in India; they made a business out of it. Luckily, the Indian dealers were a good fit for the industry."

"Why's that?"

"Most Indian diamond dealers are Jains. Their culture stresses family and hard work. Like religious Jews, they have a very particular diet."

"They're hard-core vegetarians, right?"

"That's putting it mildly. The really devout Jains don't eat honey, because collecting it hurts the bees. Their diet is so strict it makes ours looks normal."

He gave a slight shrug. "The Indian community is taking over this industry. What am I saying? They *have* taken over. Nearly every diamond is cut and polished in India. They just keep a few old Jews like me around for decoration."

AT 4 PM THAT AFTERNOON, Mimi ventured to the other side of the street and Mehta Colored Diamonds. She was greeted at the front window by Paresh Mehta.

He was medium-height and wore a button-down shirt and slacks, with a well-maintained mustache and thinning jet-black hair separated by a prominent part on the side. He was also in his socks.

"Before you enter, please remove your shoes."

Mimi did. Slipping them off felt liberating.

The website described Paresh as company president and CEO. It was clear that, like her father's company, this was mostly a one-man show. He introduced Mimi to his wife, Swapna, a plump woman with lines under her eyes. She was draped in a red and yellow sari and her hair was in a bun. Her card read, "vice president." Mimi figured she helped out around the office, like her mom.

The Mehtas' office was more modern than Mimi's father's, and way neater. A statue of Ganesha, the green-skinned multi-armed elephant god, stood on one desk, next to a framed picture of the Mehtas with their family.

A trade ad for the Mehtas' company hung on the wall. It was slick and professional, showing gleaming colored gems floating atop a rainbow, with the tagline, "If you're looking for it, we have it." This couple did not run the biggest operation, yet they knew how to market themselves. It seemed to be paying off. Paresh had an impressive stack of purchase orders on his desk.

"May we get you some tea?" Swapna offered.

This sounded good to Mimi. When Swapna delivered the steaming cup, she warned Mimi not to touch the sides, lest she get burned. The tea was potent, flavored with cinnamon and served with two sugar cookies on the side. All nice and cozy. She liked this couple.

Mimi liked them so much, she reminded herself she had a thorny job ahead. She set her recorder on her lap and dove into her pre-prepared list of colored diamond questions. Most of the Mehtas' answers were a glorified commercial for their products, done with a wink, as if to say, "we don't take this stuff seriously, and neither should you."

At one point, Paresh pulled out a parcel to show off a particularly impressive specimen—a two-carat yellow. He held it to the light. "The color is like bathing in the rays of the sun. It is a joy to be surrounded all day by such beautiful objects."

"Do you have a favorite diamond?" Mimi asked.

"That is like asking who is your favorite child." Paresh smiled. "They are all special. I always say colored diamonds are like people. Each one is unique, and their flaws make them interesting."

"Talk about how the celebrities wear them," Swapna prompted. "That is good for the newspapers."

He turned to his wife. "I was getting to that. Jennifer Lopez recently wore a lovely pink—"

"Don't bring her up." Swapna waved her hand in her husband's face. "She's old news."

"Do not interrupt, Swapna. I am talking to the woman." This seemed the latest round in an argument that stretched back decades. "You have no notion who the hot celebrities are."

She turned to Mimi. "We don't pay attention to such rubbish."

"Do not say things like that, please, Swapna. She could print it."

On it went, the Mehtas chatting and bickering, interspersed with musings about how they would sound in the newspaper.

They give great quotes, Mimi thought. *Shame this isn't a real interview.*

Meanwhile, Mimi kept wondering when to drop her big pink bomb. She let the interview drag on, sipping her tea and stress-eating the cookies. Once she'd asked three variations of the same question, and received three variations of the same answer, she knew the time had come.

"Obviously grading reports are important for colored diamonds." She eased into the subject with care, as if she were lowering herself into a hot bath. "I recently heard about a three-point-two-carat pink radiant cut that was graded fancy vivid, though not everyone thought it deserved that grade."

Mimi felt the energy in the room shift. Or maybe she imagined it.

"Yes, having your diamond certified by the right lab is of paramount importance," Paresh declared.

"This was graded by the U.S. Academy for Gemological Research. The USGR is the best lab there is. Speaking of which," Mimi walked even farther out on the ledge, "I have heard that your company once owned that three-point-two-carat pink radiant."

"Really?" Paresh gave a mock shrug. "You cannot put much stock in trade gossip. We have countless diamonds come through here."

"We can't remember every stone," said Swapna. "Who can keep track of such things?" She discharged a forced titter that sounded like a high-pitched machine gun.

"A moment ago, you said your diamonds were like your children," Mimi said. "You don't forget your children, do you?"

Swapna's jaw flapped as she groped for a response.

Her husband was studying Mimi with a new intensity. "May I ask," an edge crept into his voice, "who told you we owned this particular diamond?"

"A dealer. Larry Greenbaum."

"Larry was a friend of mine." Paresh's head jerked back.

"He was my friend, too."

"We will have to take your word for that, as he cannot inform us otherwise." Paresh's eyes narrowed to slits. "What else did your friend tell you?"

"That you have a report for that diamond that shows a different, much lower grade."

Paresh turned to his wife, and they talked feverishly in Hindi for a minute. He pivoted back to Mimi. "We have no idea what you're talking about."

"I think you do." Time to step all the way off the cliff. "In fact, I know you do."

The air grew heavier. Tea and cookie time was over.

"Who are you?" Paresh pointed his finger at her. "Who sent you?"

"I'm a reporter for *The West Jersey Metro.*"

"Swapna," he barked. "Call *The West Jersey Metro* and inquire if she works there."

His wife shot up from her seat and scurried to the phone until Mimi called out, "Don't." She couldn't bear for her old newspaper to field yet another question about her.

Swapna stopped in her tracks. She twirled around and stared at Mimi.

"I don't work for *The West Jersey Metro*. I mean, I did. I don't anymore. The point is, we need to discuss that grading report."

"We do not want any trouble." Paresh looked nervous. "We are decent humble people."

Mimi sensed she held the upper hand. She summoned the sternest expression she could. "I didn't come for trouble. I came for that cert."

"Is that all you want?" Paresh's eyes dashed around the room.

Mimi nodded and didn't change her expression.

The Mehtas exchanged more words in Hindi, more agitated this time, until Swapna rushed across the floor.

"We will get it for you," Paresh declared.

Mimi exhaled. Her bluff had worked.

Everyone watched Swapna open a desk drawer and rifle through papers until she found the report. She handed it to her husband with trembling hands. He glanced at it and nodded. He placed it on his lap and looked at Mimi.

"If we give this to you, you must promise to leave us alone."

"Hand it over," Mimi declared, "and I won't bother you again."

Paresh delivered the report to Mimi with the utmost delicacy, like it was an explosive. Mimi glanced at it. It backed up Paul's story. The color grade was fancy light—several notches below fancy vivid—and its clarity was SI. The stone had been artificially treated to improve its color. Yosef's diamond was indeed a dog.

"Thank you for this." Mimi kept up her serious front. Inside, she was doing cartwheels. She had prepared a long speech beseeching the Mehtas to hand over the report. She wouldn't have to utter a word.

"We gave you what you want," Paresh declared. "You must keep your word and go."

"I'm begging you please, leave us alone." Swapna's eyes grew red. "Do not hurt us. We have children."

Mimi's victory had a bitter aftertaste. She hated seeing this woman upset. "Why do you think I'd hurt you?"

"You know why," Paresh said. "We have seen what happened to other people who have become involved in this matter, including another former acquaintance of mine. Yosef Levine."

This stunned Mimi. She'd always believed Yosef's death was connected to the different grading reports but hadn't found anyone else who did. Now, she had, and this person seemed to know a great deal. Time to drop the act.

"I'll be honest with you. No one sent me here. I *am* a journalist, though I am not writing about colored diamonds. I'm investigating Yosef Levine's death. He was my cousin. I'd like to hear everything you know about him and this report."

The Mehtas looked mystified.

Go slow. Build trust.

"I'm one of the good guys. I want to find out who did these awful things." She reached in her pocketbook. "Here's my driver's license so you can see exactly who I am." She handed it to Paresh. "You can photocopy it, scan it, whatever. If I was engaged in something sinister, would I show you my ID?"

Paresh turned it over and stared at it.

"We can work together on this. By giving me this report, you're shining a light on corruption in the industry. You should be proud."

Paresh handed back the license. He looked deep in thought until he shot his wife a glance. "Take it from her."

Mrs. Mehta pulled the report from Mimi's hands, sparking a fierce tug of war. Swapna was a determined woman with a fierce grip, and she wrested the report from Mimi, leaving her with nothing more than a small torn corner.

Mimi sat flabbergasted, like a toddler whose toy has been snatched away. "Give that back!" She watched in horror as Mrs. Mehta placed the report on her chair and sat on it. "You don't understand—"

"No, ma'am, *you* don't understand," Paresh intoned. "We will not talk any further. You must vacate our premises."

"Please. Give me that report. I'll make you the heroes of my story. I'll write a big article about colored diamonds—"

"Perhaps I have not been clear," Paresh interrupted. "When I said remove yourself from our office, that was not a request."

Short of throwing Mrs. Mehta from her chair, Mimi had no choice but to leave. She stuffed the torn corner of the report in her purse, scooped up her tape recorder, and trudged out of the office. Paresh trailed her through the double security doors, like an insistent if unimposing bouncer.

As she exited, Mimi issued a final plea. "Let's talk about this."

"I will only say one thing to you, miss. Be careful what you're getting involved in, or you will end up dead."

The door slammed on her face.

Mimi meandered down to the hall in a daze. She was nearing the elevator when she heard a noise. She turned around and saw something hurled toward her. She jumped out of the way and threw her back against the wall. The object landed with a thud on the green carpet before her. She stood there a minute, her heart beating so hard it was almost painful. Finally, she summoned the courage to look down.

It was her shoes.

CHAPTER TWENTY-THREE

A N HOUR AFTER SHE WAS KICKED OUT of Mehta Colored Diamonds, Mimi went to meet Paul at Connolly's, a classic gold brass Irish bar near Forty-Seventh Street. It was just filling up with office workers coming in for Happy Hour.

Mimi was discombobulated after meeting the Mehtas and thought about cancelling. She decided that she wanted to see Paul. She had even spent the prior night tidying her apartment . . . just in case. The thought of him spending the night at her place made her even enjoy scrubbing the bathroom.

As she waited at the bar, nursing a white wine, she realized she was exhausted and needed a break. A weekend getaway with Paul might do the trick. She worked out how she'd ask. She'd look him in the eyes and say, "Would you be interested in going for a romantic weekend together?" She had never done anything like that in the past, but she was a modern, mature woman who shouldn't feel bashful about such things. Mimi swore to herself that, no matter what, she'd raise the topic that night—or better yet, the next morning.

Through the window she spotted Paul walking with a tall 30-ish guy who looked familiar, but she couldn't quite place. They laughed, shook hands, and parted ways. Paul entered the bar, looking as cute as Mimi remembered. He wore a winter coat, baseball cap, brown sweater vest with a tie peeking out, and knapsack propped on his shoulder. He spotted her and gave a quick wave. Just seeing him navigate his way through the crowd, politely asking people to step aside and squirming through the tight spots, lifted Mimi's spirits. He gave her a peck hello, ordered a beer from the bar, and scooped up both their drinks and led Mimi to a table in the corner, away from the growing hum of the after-work crowd.

Paul seemed in a good mood, and Mimi said so.

"I just came from a meeting, where I made huge progress with my lab." He crossed his legs with confidence. "This dealer, who I hadn't spoken to in years, called me out of the blue and said he'd give me all the funding I need."

"That's great," Mimi beamed. "Here's to your new lab." She raised her glass and they clinked.

"I still have a ton of work getting this thing set up. This is just a huge load off my shoulders." He gulped some beer. "How are things with you?"

Mimi let out a breath. "Eh, okay." Her attempt at an upbeat front crumbled. "I just had this messed-up experience." She took a sip of wine.

Paul's brow wrinkled. "What happened?"

Mimi wasn't sure she should go into it, but she needed to unburden herself and had decided she trusted Paul. This would be a good first step.

"Remember I told you I was doing an article on synthetics. I'm actually looking into a lot of things. One is the death of my cousin, a diamond dealer."

Paul took a tentative sip of his drink. "Okay."

"I've discovered it might be related to the bribery at USGR. I've started looking into that too."

Paul put his beer down. "You're writing about what's going on at USGR?"

"In a way."

"Will you cover my case?"

"Possibly. It won't be my main focus."

"Whoa, whoa, whoa." He held his hand up like a stop sign, fingers together, rigid and straight up. "You told me you weren't writing about the USGR. Otherwise, I wouldn't have told you my story."

"I would never write about your story without permission. You told me that in confidence." She punctuated this with a reassuring smile.

He didn't smile back. "Will you mention me losing my job?"

"If I do, it will be a small part of it."

"I don't want you writing about me at all."

"Come on, Paul. I would never trash you. I know you're one of the good guys." She took his hand. "I trust you."

"I understand that." He pulled his hand from hers. "I am not sure I trust *you*."

Mimi shuddered. "Whoa!"

"You repeatedly told me you weren't looking into the USGR."

"The USGR is only partially related to my main story. But, yes, I am."

"Hold it. That was you who asked Tanner about me, right? You know, the question they nearly pulled my severance over?" His mouth became a tight line. "Be honest."

"Yes. That was me." Mimi looked at the table. A series of concentric circles in the wood momentarily caught her eye.

His fist pounded the table. "I knew it! That was the only explanation that made sense. You told me it wasn't you. I believed you. I even apologized! How could I be so stupid?" He gazed at her with scientific detachment, like he was looking at a particularly flawed rock. "You also told the USGR that you worked for a publication that you didn't. Right?"

"Kind of."

"Kind of?"

She didn't look up. "I used to work for that newspaper. But yes." What more could she say?

After a few agonizing seconds of silence, she spoke, soft and low. "Paul, I'm sorry for lying to you. When you called, I panicked. That was the first thing that came out of my mouth. I apologize. I've been honest about everything else."

"Like what?"

"I admitted I called you 'Pizzaface.'"

"That was thirty years ago!" he said, a little too loud. "How about being honest about things that are happening now?"

Mimi felt backed into a corner. "Paul, I admit I made mistakes. You haven't been completely truthful with me either. When we met at the coffee shop, you didn't tell me everything about why you were fired."

"What do you think?" He stretched his arms so far he nearly hit the guy next to him. "I'd tell you the whole story right then?"

"Please, let's not make a big deal out of this." Mimi gave his elbow a slight tap. She didn't know if she had permission to grab his hand. "We can work together on this story. You can be a source. We'll let everyone know what's going on at USGR. We'll expose the dealer who bribed you."

"I would never expose that person!"

"Why not?"

Paul pursed his lips. "He's funding my lab."

"You're taking money from him?" She squinted. "Again?"

Paul folded his arms. "I don't have many other options. There aren't that many funding sources out there for a lab executive who resigned under a cloud. And he made me a generous offer."

"Paul, think about this. This guy doesn't do charity. Aren't you worried he's trying to pay you off so you don't say anything about the past?"

"He could be. That's fine with me. I don't want anyone to know about that anyway. The only other person I told about that was you. What a brilliant move that was." He smacked his hand against his forehead. "Of all people to tell, a reporter."

"If it's that important, I promise I won't write about you." She raised her hand. "I give you my word. Diamond business. My word is my bond."

Paul snickered. "We know how well that's going these days."

"It'll be okay, trust me."

Paul sipped his drink.

"Are you sure you want to take money from that guy? What if he wants you to change a grade again?"

"We'll cross that bridge when we come to it."

"You have to consider that."

"I have thought about it. I need funding, he offered it, and I'm taking it. Sorry if you don't like it. I wasn't asking for permission." He was breathing heavy.

"The whole thing just seems kind of . . ." She searched for the right word. Paul wasn't holding his tongue. She wouldn't either. "Gross."

"Wow!" He slammed his palm on the table. "Pardon me if I don't take ethics advice from an admitted liar."

"Okay, Paul. Now you're being a dick."

"Whatever. I'm getting out of here."

She watched with horror as he slung his knapsack over his shoulder. Her first promising relationship in ages was falling apart.

He put on his coat, giving firm tugs to each sleeve. He placed his hands on the table and leaned over it, staring at Mimi through knitted eyes. "Since I've met you, I've been fired, disgraced, and now my biggest secret might get out. I hope you know you've been a blight on my life."

Mimi felt unsteady, like someone had picked up the bar and tilted it 90 degrees. "That's a terrible thing to say." Tears gathered in her eyes.

"Can I just ask you one thing?"

Paul didn't try to hide his annoyance. "What?"

Mimi drew a breath. "Would you be interested in going on a romantic weekend together?"

He looked at Mimi like she was insane. He turned around and faded into the crowd, leaving Mimi with an empty glass on the other side of the table.

CHAPTER TWENTY-FOUR

THE ARGUMENT WITH PAUL RATTLED MIMI; it wasn't every day someone called her a blight on his life. The next day, after yet another sleepless night, she got some good news. She needed it.

Channah called and announced she would return to work on Monday. Mimi was comforted by her familiar friendly voice; they hadn't spoken since last week's meeting in the basement.

"I'm not doing great," Channah said. "I don't think sitting around here all day is helping. My rabbi thinks it will be good for me to get out of the house."

For a second, Mimi hoped they could pick up where they left off, eating lunch and swapping stories. Until Channah brought up the investigation. "I'm sorry I gave you a hard time last week. That wasn't right of me."

It was a weird thing about apologies. Sometimes they made people feel better. This one did.

"The fact that you're investigating Yosef's murder means so much to me. If you don't want to tell me what you're finding, that's up to you. Of course, if you do want to tell me, I wouldn't object." Channah laughed afterward, to signal she was joking, though she clearly did want to know.

And Mimi did want to tell her. For the last month, the investigation had dominated her thoughts and invaded her dreams. She needed to talk about it, with *somebody*. She no longer had much reason to hold back. She always thought she'd wait until she had firm proof Yosef bribed somebody. Now, she'd seen the second cert with her own eyes.

"How about I tell you when you come back to work?"

"That would be great." Channah paused. "Though, remember, you said you'd tell me last time and didn't. Not that I'm pressuring you or anything." She laughed again.

"This time, I promise. I'll tell you everything."

"Great. And you'll be at work on Monday?"

"Sure. Why wouldn't I be?"

"I don't know," Channah hedged. "Before my time off, you only came in part-time. I didn't know if you were going back to that."

Come to think of it, Mimi wasn't sure of that either.

The question nagged at her all afternoon: Once Channah returned, her job entailed . . . what exactly? She'd already done her father's books.

Mimi walked to her dad's desk, where he was sorting invoices, licking his finger before he turned each page.

"Channah's coming back Monday," she announced.

Max glanced up and smiled. "Terrific. So she's doing better?"

"Good enough to return to work, I guess."

"That means you're finally off the phones. *Mazal tov.*" He went back to his invoices.

Mimi stood looking down at him, until her father noticed she was still there.

"Will I go back to working three days a week?"

"I hadn't really thought about it. If you want that, sure." Back to the invoices.

Time to confront this. "What's my job now that Channah's back?"

Max stopped paging through the bills. "I don't know. You help out. I like having you around."

"Dad, I appreciate you letting me work here. I definitely need the money. I'd like to earn my salary. I'm not a just-being-around kind of person. I want to help out. I have opinions."

"I'm well aware that you have opinions. What else would you do? You don't want to go into the business."

True enough, though he'd never asked.

"I couldn't deal diamonds like you do. I don't have the fire for it. There are other things I could work on." She thought about the Mehtas' ads. "Have you ever thought of advertising?"

"I ran an ad years ago. It didn't work."

"You mean that 'to the Max' thing?"

That ad ran in the eighties, and a framed copy of it lay amid the piles of papers on one of the desks. It featured a group of diamonds under the words "Rosen Diamonds. Service to the Max."

"Of course that didn't work," she said. "It didn't say anything."

"I came up with that," Max shot back. "It was clever. Sure it said something. My name is Max. It said 'to the Max.' At the time, that was a very big expression. They said it in all the videos."

"Did the ad work?"

"No. That doesn't mean it wasn't clever." His arms crossed.

"It didn't say why your company is unique. How many times did it run?"

"I don't know, two or three."

"Dad, for advertising to really make an impression, it has to a) have a message and b) run more than two or three times."

"That takes money." Max rubbed his hand over his scalp. "I'm not sure we have all that much to spend." He squeezed his forehead and looked sheepish; it was the first time he'd even come close to admitting his company's financial problems weren't just a figment of her imagination.

"I realize that. This is kind of a Hail Mary pass."

"What's that?"

Mimi knew she shouldn't have used a term referencing both football and Catholicism.

"It's a gamble when you have nothing to lose. We could do this for cheap. I'll write the copy and design it. The biggest expense would be buying the ad space, and we're aiming for trade publications, which aren't all that costly, especially if it's only online. You know the business needs new customers to continue."

"*Meh*," he replied, as if that answered her argument.

"Come on, Dad. I've been thinking about getting into copywriting. This will give me something for my portfolio."

"All right. Put an ad together, and I'll look at it."

"I'll have a mockup by tomorrow."

Mimi strutted back to the front desk to answer the phones. Of all the arguments she trotted out, the one that prevailed was running the ad would help her career.

That was her father. He had his flaws. Deep down, he was a caring man who put others first.

No wonder he was going out of business.

MIMI NEEDED A CONCEPT, a way to sell her father. That made him unique.

She couldn't think of one. Her father was a diamond dealer. He dealt diamonds. As did countless businesses on Forty-Seventh Street. She could tout his years in the industry, his expertise. When she scoured trade publications, she realized that every ad said that.

The investigation had consumed so much of her mental energy that at first the ad provided a welcome diversion. Next came three hours sitting at her computer getting frustrated. At about 10 PM, inspiration stuck. She stayed up until 3 AM fine-tuning her design and wrestling with the words until every one clicked.

When she awoke four hours later, she poured some much-needed coffee and sat at the kitchen table with her creation. It was good.

The idea came as her mind wandered back to Yosef's murder. She spent so much time wondering who to trust. She never doubted her father. He was a man of complete integrity.

That would be his selling point. From there, the ad wrote itself, as he had written it for her. For the headline, she used that Max Rosen classic, "This business isn't about sorting the diamonds. It's about sorting the people."

"My name is Max Rosen," said the body copy. "I believe integrity and relationships matter in this industry. My customers are like family to me.

"Diamonds are valuable. But a dealer who truly cares about you, who treats you like a person rather than a dollar sign, is the rarest and most precious thing of all.

"Let's do business the old-fashioned way. The way with heart."

She designed a mockup around a rare photo of Max smiling. When Mimi arrived at work that morning, she was so convinced she had a winner, she marched to her father's desk and thrust it before him.

Max appeared puzzled, like he barely remembered their conversation the day before. He looked at the ad. Mimi lingered over him, scanning his face for a reaction. Finally, he put it down. "I don't like it." He pushed it away.

"Why not?"

"It's too much about me. Can't you just say I have nice diamonds?"

"Are your diamonds nicer than anyone else's?"

He shrugged. "Not really."

"Yeah, Dad, great sales pitch. 'Buy my diamonds. They're the same as everyone else's.'"

He picked it up again. His lips moved and as he whispered the copy to himself. He held it out in front of him. "I don't like the picture. I look like an old Jewish man."

"Dad, you *are* an old Jewish man. Besides, I like the photo. You have a nice smile."

"My teeth look crooked."

Mimi didn't know what that meant. "We can have a new picture taken. I can hire a photographer."

Max frowned. "I don't want a big production. What is this, Hollywood?"

"These are minor things."

He handed the ad back to her. "I'll take it under advisement." That was Dad code for "I'll never mention this again and hope you forget about it."

He turned back to his computer. "Can you go up front? The phones don't pick up themselves."

"I'd like to talk about this."

"Later. Right now, you have to answer the phones."

Mimi didn't move. She hadn't gotten any sleep the night before, or for that matter, in the past month. Her father had dismissed her accounting. Now he'd brushed aside her writing. What was she doing there?

"I stayed up until three in the morning doing this, to save your company. Could I at least get a thank you?"

"Thank you." Max barely opened his mouth to say the words. His eyes returned to his computer.

"I want real gratitude, not some halfhearted mumble."

His face registered annoyance, as well as surprise and a little fear. "I said thank you. What are you getting upset for?"

"You never take anything I do seriously."

"Of course I do. I seriously need you to answer the phones."

"Did you listen to what I said yesterday? I don't want to just be your bookkeeper and office manager, like Mom was. I want a real role here."

"You don't know what you're talking about." A vein on his forehead bulged. "Certain things have been asked of you, and you need to do them. You're working for me, remember? This is my company."

"If you don't get with the times, it won't be your company much longer. It'll be the bank's."

Max rose from his seat, his face red. He was warming to this fight. "If you don't like how this company operates, you can always leave."

"Fine! I don't need to stay in a place where I'm not appreciated. I can quit."

"Go ahead. I don't really need you here. I just hired you to be nice."

That was the worst possible thing Max could have said, whether or not he realized it.

"I'm giving two weeks' notice, starting today." Her voice trembled as she said this, and afterward, she felt a headache come on.

"Go ahead." Max sank into his seat, his breath heavy.

Mimi stomped up front for another boring day answering the phones. They barely rang on Fridays anyway, giving her plenty of time to sit and stew. The office closed early for *Shabbat* in the winter, so when 2:45 came, she bolted out the door without saying a word.

Thankfully, it was the weekend, and Mimi wouldn't see her father for another two days. Right now, she couldn't stand the sight of him.

CHAPTER TWENTY-FIVE

AFTER MIMI STORMED OUT OF THE OFFICE on Friday, she considered never coming back. That was followed by a weekend clicking through job boards. The market for writing positions hadn't improved much since her last search. She would need those last two weeks of salary.

Monday morning, Mimi swallowed her pride and returned to the office, where she was happy to see Channah at her familiar perch in the receptionist area, dressed in a black blouse and long grey skirt. As she entered, Channah flashed a wide smile, like she'd never left. They shared a long tight welcome back hug and made plans to go to lunch.

It was so good to have Channah back, Mimi was even happy to eat at Kosher Gourmet again—though it still wasn't gourmet. It was there, over trays topped with oily Chinese, that Mimi told Channah that she'd given notice.

"That's so crazy!" Channah's plastic chopsticks kept a precarious grip on a clump of rice. "What are you going to do?"

"Go back to publishing. I'll find something. I hope."

"Real nice." Channah mock pouted. "I finally come back, and now you're leaving."

"I know. I feel awful. I had to do it. I can't work in an office where I'm not appreciated."

"Your father appreciates you. You know how he is. He can be a little set in his ways. Sometimes it's just a matter of handling him right."

Mimi wasn't in the mood to consider this. "I need to move on." She popped a rust-colored noodle in her mouth.

"I can talk to him. I'll tell him how important it is to run the ad."

"You haven't seen it."

"I'm sure it's good. I've told you many times, Mimi, you're very smart."

That was a reference to the investigation, a subject they had delicately danced around all morning. Mimi would have to address it sooner or later. She might as well do it now. She put her fork down on the pile of lukewarm lo mien, and declared it was time for an update.

Channah tried to act nonchalant. "Yeah, what's happening with that? Have you interviewed anyone lately?"

"I am having dinner with David Garstein tomorrow. There's some things I need to ask him."

"Like what?"

"That's what we need to discuss. Let me warn you. Some of it may be upsetting."

Channah laid her chopsticks on her tray, rapt.

"That pink diamond Yosef was selling, it had two reports. Yosef's report had much higher grades than the first one. It appears there was . . ." Mimi struggled for an easy way to relay this. There was none. "A payoff to raise the grade."

Mimi had more to say to soften the blow. She didn't get a chance.

"Mimi, you're not saying that Yosef—"

Mimi sighed. "Unfortunately, I am." She touched Channah's hand. "I'm sorry. I'm sure it's difficult to hear. That is what I found. My theory is he had an attack of conscience and was going to come clean."

"I don't know, Mimi." Channah's neck turned a faint shade of pink. "You're very smart. But you're wrong about this."

"I was surprised too. Yosef was my cousin. I liked him a lot. Everyone did. You yourself said that he was under a lot of pressure to make something of himself."

"Sure he was. He still wouldn't do something like that."

"I believe he would have done the right thing in the end."

"He did the right thing, always." Channah shook her curls with fervor. "You made a mistake somewhere."

Mimi had done so much work on this, been through so much, her first reaction was to feel offended. She tried to put herself in Channah's shoes. "I hate having to tell you this. That stone had two certs. Yosef submitted the stone when it got the upgraded report. What other explanation could there be?"

"Sometimes grades differ."

"Not this much."

Channah grimaced. "How do you know all this?"

"When I met Paul Michelson, he found a second report for the pink in the USGR computer system. He said the grade must have been changed deliberately."

"Isn't he the guy who took a bribe?"

"That's what they say. I think he's innocent."

"Why? 'Cause you have a crush on him?"

"No, because I think he's a good person."

"What?" Channah moved her face forward. "Are you dating him now?"

"We went out once. That's it." She wasn't happy where this conversation was headed.

"If he's such a good guy, why did you only go out once?"

"Because—" Mimi tensed up. "That doesn't matter."

"I don't know about *your* boyfriend. Yosef would never do anything like that. He was very religious. Every morning he would be in *shul*, *davening*, and learning Torah."

"I don't know about that–"

"Well, I do! Yosef wouldn't even know how to bribe somebody!"

"What do you mean?"

"Think about it. You have to know what you're doing to pull off something like that. Yosef wasn't a good enough dealer to be a crook."

This stopped Mimi short. She didn't know how to respond to that. "I guess he figured it out."

"Do you have any proof of what you're saying? You think this Paul guy is telling the truth because you went out with him?"

"I saw the other report with my own eyes."

Channah crossed her arms. "I'd like to see it, too."

"I have part of it." Mimi reached in her pocketbook and placed the torn corner of the report on the table. "Here you go."

Channah looked puzzled. "That's just a scrap of paper."

"It's part of a report."

"It doesn't say that. It could be anything."

Mimi became annoyed. "What do you think? I carry random scraps of paper in my pocketbook?"

"I have no idea!" Channah threw it on the table.

"Be careful! I went through a lot of trouble to get that."

"You went through a lot of trouble to get a scrap of paper?"

Mimi scooped up the corner and stuffed it in her pocketbook as Channah's eyes popped.

"You always had something against Yosef. Right before he died, you told me I should find someone else. Like I could do better. What a thing to say about your cousin. You were just worried that you and I wouldn't be friends anymore." Her lips started to quaver. "I knew Yosef. I loved him. I could never do better than him."

This hit Mimi like a blow to the gut.

"We're just different people, that's all." Channah's voice was tipped with ice. "Very different."

While she didn't elaborate, Mimi sensed what she was getting at. The gap between her and her religious friend suddenly loomed large.

Mimi tried to keep cool. "Channah, I really cared about Yosef. I miss him terribly. Think about it. You could never understand how Yosef could afford a four-million-dollar stone. And you told me the pink was ugly, that it didn't deserve a good grade. This is the only logical explanation."

Channah sat without speaking, her head hanging over her body.

"I know it's a lot to take in," Mimi said in a soft voice. "You wanted to hear what I found. This is it."

Channah started to cry, quietly but insistently. People were staring.

"You're right. I did say that." Channah looked stricken. "I gotta go."

In quick succession, Channah picked up her tray, dumped her food in the garbage, and darted out of the restaurant. This wasn't the happy reunion Mimi had in mind.

For the rest of the workday, Channah and Mimi didn't talk. At closing time, Channah walked back and said good night. They hugged, but it was perfunctory and awkward, not at all like their tight embrace that morning. Mimi searched for something to say that would make everything better. She considered telling Channah she was sorry, only she wasn't sure she was and didn't know if that would help anyway. Instead, she took Channah's hands and looked her in the eyes. "It's really great to see you again."

Channah gamely smiled in return. It looked like she regretted ever coming back to work.

LATER THAT NIGHT, AS MIMI AGONIZED over the day's events in her recliner, accompanied by "La Vie en Rose" and cheap chardonnay, she got a call from an unknown number. She picked up. It was Bernard.

"I just talked to Channah. She's devastated."

"I know." What else could she say?

"Did you tell her that Yosef bribed someone at USGR?"

"Yes." Mimi sighed. "Unfortunately, that's true."

"Again with this nonsense." He let out an annoyed grunt. "You're really going to write a story that says my dead brother was a briber?"

Mimi hadn't been thinking about her article. It wasn't her most pressing concern. "If that's the truth, I'll have to."

"Even if that means dragging a dead man's name through the mud?"

Mimi had no response.

"I hope you seriously consider how such an article will impact our family. We've all been shattered by Yosef's death, and if you print terrible stories about my brother, that will make things a million times worse. It would also hurt your friend Channah. More than you already have."

His last words made her wince.

"I don't understand how you could spread such terrible lies about a member of your family." His standard rat-a-tat delivery gained speed and force. "Is it because Yosef and I didn't attend your wedding? Have you not gotten over that?"

This stunned Mimi. "That's ridiculous, Bernard! That has nothing to do with this." She sat up on her chair. "I'm investigating who killed Yosef. Don't you want to know that?"

"Of course I do. They just got the guy."

"What?"

"The police arrested someone yesterday. They called me a couple of hours ago. It'll hit the newspapers tomorrow. I called Channah to tell her, and she hit me with this *narishkeit* about my brother the crook."

Mimi clutched the phone. "Who'd they arrest?"

"I don't know. Some gang member, some animal, his name isn't worth repeating."

"Look, Bernard. You have my word; I would never do anything to cause pain to our family. I will think about what you've said."

A few hours later, Mimi saw the article on the internet.

Gang Member Arrested in Diamond Dealer's Murder

Manuel Carmen, a Colombian national who police say was part of a gang that terrorized traveling jewelry salesmen, has been charged with first degree murder for a cold-blooded killing that shocked the Diamond District.

Yosef Levine, 25, was shot point-blank in a parking garage on 48th St. on Feb. 10, in what local detectives described as a robbery attempt gone wrong.

Carmen, 33, was already sought by police for a string of violent robberies of travelling gem couriers. Sources say he was linked to the crime with the help of DNA evidence found at the scene.

"The diamond industry is grateful for the quick work of the New York City Police Department in this case," said David Garstein, president of the Consolidated Diamond Bourse of New York. "This was an appalling tragedy, but people in the industry will sleep better knowing this reprehensible criminal has been captured."

Except for Mimi. She didn't sleep a wink.

CHAPTER TWENTY-SIX

"**Y**OU MAY REMEMBER, WHEN WE MET a few weeks ago," Mimi told Rabbi Hirshhorn the next morning, "I was writing an article about the murder of Yosef Levine." She was dressed in her most modest outfit—a turtleneck and skirt that extended to her ankles.

"I remember." The rabbi was no less forbidding this time. He was at least looking at her. "I hope you remember I am duty-bound not to disclose what Yosef told me."

"I know. You told me you counsel people about issues of ethics or conscience. I'm here for—" She paused because she couldn't believe what she was about to say. "—advice."

It had come to this. Mimi needed someone to talk to. She couldn't discuss the investigation with her father, or Channah, and certainly not Paul. She had no money for a shrink. The only person left was this guy, the representative of a faith she never had much interest in.

"Go on."

"I always thought that Yosef's murder was more than just a regular robbery. Yesterday they arrested someone for it. A gang member."

"Yes." The rabbi nodded. "I saw that in the newspaper. Very good news."

"The problem is, during my investigation, I discovered some things that reflect badly on someone I used to respect. You know who I'm talking about, don't you?" Mimi squirmed in her chair.

The rabbi didn't move.

"It's Yosef. I've discovered he bribed graders at a diamond lab. I'm not

sure what to do with this information. Since they've arrested someone
for Yosef's murder, I wonder: Should I keep looking into it? Or will it just
be hurtful to people close to him?"

The rabbi listened with his standard mix of nods and methodical
beard-stroking. When Mimi finished speaking, he bowed his head and
sat silent for a second. "I thought I'd see you again," he said finally. "You
seemed like a sharp cookie. You have what I call a Jewish head.

"I also appreciate that you're wrestling with this dilemma. It shows
you have a good heart. That is far more important than a good head."
He drummed his fingers on his chest. "The question you are asking is,
should I keep searching for the truth, even if it hurts people?"

"Yes."

"I think you know the answer, or you would not be here. The truth
is not always pretty. It's quite possible that, the more you investigate, you
will uncover things that are even uglier than you are seeing now."

Is that a hint?

"Looking for the truth can mean looking at unpleasant things. That is
not what human beings like to do. We don't like to look at ugliness. Sadly,
sometimes we must. To do otherwise is to abdicate responsibility. We all
know of terrible events that occurred in the last century because people
closed their eyes.

"The crime you are discussing, bribery, is something that needs to be
exposed. I advise you to keep looking for the truth. Because appearances
can be deceiving. It's easy to jump to conclusions."

That seemed like another hint. Mimi couldn't let it go. "Are you
suggesting I'm wrong about something?"

He stared ahead. "Do you remember what I said about Yosef the first
time we met?"

"You didn't say anything. You said I should read your eulogy."

"Did you?"

"No. I heard you deliver it."

"What did I say?" He looked at her, unblinking.

"You talked about what a decent and upstanding person Yosef was."
It clicked. "What are you telling me? That Yosef wasn't involved in the
bribery?"

"Draw your own conclusions. Speaking generally, one does not
hail someone as a model of virtue if he has confessed to a crime a few
days before."

Mimi felt her brain was being reshuffled. "So, what you're saying is—" She paused and re-grouped. "Actually, you're not saying it, because you haven't violated your confidence with Yosef, and I'm figuring this out on my own."

The rabbi nodded.

"Yosef would never bribe anybody," she continued. "In fact, he may have been the one who discovered the bribery and wanted to expose it. Am I on the right track?"

"I can't say more. Just that Yosef was an honorable man, and you are using that good head of yours."

She mulled this over. "Did Yosef tell you anything else? Like who actually did the bribing?"

"Even if he did, I could not tell you."

"Right." Mimi folded her notebook. "Thank you, Rabbi. In your own way, you've been helpful."

"I try. Anything else?"

"I notice that you call Yosef a man. Everyone else called him a boy."

"When a person does the right thing, at great personal sacrifice, that makes him a man."

"I hope you told him that."

"I did."

Mimi smiled. "I guess I better be going." She picked up her pocketbook and rose from her chair.

"Miss, as long as you've found me so helpful, can I interest you in attending services at this *shul*?"

"I'll think about it. I'm not religious, though."

"That strikes me as a polite no."

Mimi laughed. "I guess." She lifted her coat from the chair.

"I take it you will pursue your investigation?"

Mimi gave a slight nod. "I don't have a choice. I have to find the truth."

"May I ask you to sit down?"

Mimi did as she was told. The rabbi closed his eyes and mumbled in Hebrew. Afterward, he lifted his head. He ripped a piece of paper from a pad and started writing on it.

"That was something I should have done for Yosef." He handed her the paper. "I said a prayer for your safety."

CHAPTER TWENTY-SEVEN

IT MADE SENSE. YOSEF WASN'T INVOLVED in the bribery. He discovered it. Her cousin was exactly who she thought he was. She couldn't wait to tell Channah. She couldn't wait to tell Bernard. If she could, she'd tell the world.

When she returned to the office, Channah was on the phone with FedEx. Mimi waited in her jacket and gloves until she finished the call. The minute Channah hung up, Mimi launched into her litany. "I just learned some great news."

Channah cut her off. Politely. But she cut her off. "Is this an investigation thing? If it is, I don't want to hear it."

This confounded Mimi. "Channah, you got me into this. It was our thing."

"I know. That was wrong of me." She spoke calmly and deliberately, with an unmistakable undercurrent of anger. "They've captured Yosef's killer. There's nothing left to investigate."

"Come on, Channah. You don't really believe that, do you? You told me how Yosef wouldn't have fought back, all the weird things you noticed—"

Channah again cut her off. "I was wrong about that. Just like you're wrong about Yosef bribing people."

"Yes! That's what I've been trying to tell you. I *was* wrong about that. I found out new information. Yosef wasn't a briber. He—"

"Enough already!" Channah snapped. "You know how you made me feel yesterday with your *meshuga* theory? Today, you change your mind, and I'm supposed to be happy about it. We're talking about someone I loved. You're bouncing me around like I'm a ping-pong ball."

Mimi watched in horror as Channah's face grew redder and harder. She struggled to connect with her. "I'm sorry about yesterday. I know the truth now."

"You said you knew the truth yesterday!" Channah slammed the desk with such ferocity it startled Mimi. "Last night was terrible for me. First, you tell me Yosef's a briber. Then I get home, and I hear they've caught Yosef's killer. Everyone tells me I should be thrilled. And I'm thinking, what's to be happy about? Yosef's still dead, I'm still alone, and I can't even turn on the TV because that's all they're talking about and it makes me sick all over again. I come here to escape, and you tell me your new revelation, which is the exact opposite of what you told me yesterday. I feel like I'm on this horrible roller-coaster I can't ever get off!" Her welled-up eyes gave way to full-blown sobs. Mimi watched as Channah sat, beet red, crying over her desk.

"Bernard thinks you're crazy, you know," she said after a torrent of sobs. "Your own cousin."

Mimi moved to give Channah a hug. Channah lurched away and buried her face in her arms. Mimi crouched down and placed her hand on Channah's hot back and felt it move up and down with her sobs, grateful she didn't swat it off. "I feel terrible."

"Leave me alone," Channah grumbled from her arm-cave.

"I will." Mimi stood up and backed away. "Let me know if there's anything I can do."

Channah lifted her head slowly and turned to Mimi. "You can stop investigating. You're just making everything worse."

Mimi took a breath. "Okay."

Channah just sneered. "Oh, please. I know you, Mimi. You won't stop investigating. You don't stop when you think you're right. That's how you are."

Mimi focused on the floor. "Yes." She repeated what she had told the rabbi. "I don't have a choice. I have to find the truth."

Channah became so angry Mimi was afraid she'd lunge at her. "Do what you want, Mimi! Spread a million lies, go on dates with everybody. I don't care. Just don't talk to me about it. I can't bear to hear you mention it one more time." She struggled to catch her breath. "I'm glad you're quitting."

They both froze, stomachs bouncing with their breaths, as Channah's statement hung in the air. Channah put her head down and continued crying, leaving Mimi to stare at her mass of vibrating curly hair. When she realized Channah wasn't going to apologize or even look at her, and this was the end of the conversation and most likely their friendship, Mimi threw her shoulders back and headed to her desk, trying to look proud but feeling like her guts had been ripped out.

Mimi told herself Channah was still grieving and not to take anything she said personally. But that was all Mimi thought about all day.

Mimi never wanted to work at her father's company. Yet, she always felt at home there. Now, she wasn't speaking to her father and Channah wasn't talking to her. Mimi was glad she was quitting too.

Mimi longed to go home and try to make sense of everything. However, this was the night of her dinner—he'd say "date"—with David Garstein. It was first scheduled for three weeks ago. Mimi cancelled because she wasn't in the mood. Last week, she postponed again because she was meeting Paul. Garstein insisted they make plans a third time.

She wanted to back out again, especially after his secretary called and said she had made reservations at the S&R Bistro, a swanky steakhouse near Forty-Seventh Street. She was in no mood for a night of Garstein plying his supposed charms on her. Even so, she had to go. Garstein seemed to know things.

She would have to change her outfit. She had dressed modestly for the rabbi but couldn't go out with Garstein looking like a *rebbetzin*. She ceased work for the day—she had little to do anyway—and headed for the PATH train back to Jersey. She didn't tell anyone at the office she was leaving. No one there cared about her anyway.

AFTER AGONIZING OVER WHAT TO WEAR for her maybe-date with Paul, Mimi felt no such anxiety about her strictly-dinner with Garstein. While things didn't work out with Paul, at least it got her over the dating hump.

Entering the restaurant in a form-fitting, though not *too* tight, brown dress and her best pair of heels—at least the best pair that she'd bought on eBay—Mimi thought this might be fun. She hadn't eaten at a nice place in a long time, and the S&R Bistro had candlelit tables, a tuxedoed pianist, and a four-star rating out front. The tablecloths and waiters were both well-pressed. She spotted Garstein at a front table, spread out on his chair, barking into his phone, hair pulled into a ponytail, his black silk shirt undone two more buttons than Mimi wanted. And she lost her appetite.

Garstein motioned to her and finished his conversation. He tapped the face of his Rolex, making sure Mimi could see it was a Rolex. "You're a little late."

Mimi mumbled something about the trains. Three seconds into this dinner that wasn't a date, she already wanted to tell him to screw himself.

"It's okay. Let us enjoy. This place is excellent. I eat here all the time."

On cue, a waiter appeared, sporting white hair and a white jacket, greeting him as "Mr. Garstein," even as Garstein called him "Herbert." They bantered about how it was March and when's it finally going to be spring already, as Garstein snuck glances at Mimi, making sure she was watching this testament to his popularity. At the end of the conversation, Herbert delivered a napkin-covered breadbasket, which Garstein greeted with a grin. "Here you go, Mr. Garstein. Nice and hot."

"This is perfect, Herbert, thank you." He pivoted to Mimi. "These are the special olive rolls they have. They were going to get rid of them, and I said no, this is the best bread you have, you must keep it." He raised his finger to illustrate his firmness on this point. "They make them, just for me, and they give them to me every time I come." His hands hovered over the basket and parted, as if he were a magician who'd conjured these rolls on the table. He grabbed one and pushed the wire basket, and its tower of identical brown speckled rolls, across the tablecloth toward Mimi. "Have one."

Mimi put her hand up to stop the encroaching basket. "I'm okay."

"I'm telling you, they're very good." He took an eager bite of a roll and chewed it so vigorously Mimi could see it twirling in his mouth. "The olives give them a very interesting texture."

"It's okay."

"We need wine. Herbert!" He waved his hand and the waiter scooted to the table. "Two glasses of the usual."

Herbert nodded and walked off.

Garstein turned to Mimi. "I always have the Cabernet sauvignon. It is very good."

Mimi usually drank white wine. It was looking like a long night.

The wine arrived, and Garstein raised his glass. "Let's toast to the good news. You were writing about Yosef's murder. There's no more reason for it. They caught the killer. Here's to the case being closed."

They clinked glasses. Mimi did so without enthusiasm, but she clinked.

"You deserve credit too," he grinned. "I know some of the top people at the police department. I said a reporter was going to write on this, and if they didn't solve this case soon, it wouldn't look so good. That lit a fire under them. We should toast to you, too."

He held out his glass again, and both his smile and arm stayed frozen until Mimi realized she had no choice but to clink.

"Of course, terrible things like that murder aren't good dinnertime conversation." He stretched out on his chair, giving Mimi an unasked-for view of his chest. "Let's get to know each other. I'll bet you don't know where I grew up."

"No." She didn't care either.

"I grew up in South Bend, Indiana." He pronounced it like it rhymed with "mama." "My father worked for a jewelry chain over there. I am what they call a Hoosier. I was the only Israeli immigrant in my school. Probably in the whole state."

This piqued Mimi's curiosity. "What was that like?"

"What do you think it was like? I barely spoke English, and when I did, I had a thick accent. Even the Jewish kids thought I was from outer space. I never felt so alone in my life. Whenever we visited Israel, I begged my father to move back. He told me that every time I complained about living in America, he'd make sure we stayed another year. He said it would toughen me up so I wouldn't be such a soft kid. Now I realize he was right. When you're at a disadvantage, you learn how to fight. You look for angles. How to read people. I have no hard feelings."

Yet, all these years later, he was still talking about it. Mimi was sensing a person behind the bluster.

"One thing I've learned," he continued, "is if you want to know someone, meet their parents. It puts them in, what's the word, context. I remember your mother very well. She was a smart lady. She may not have been the entire brains behind your father's operation, though she played a major role in his success."

"No, she—" Mimi squinted in disbelief. "My mother just did the books."

"Please!" he laughed. "Your mother was involved with everything at that company. Your father is an extremely intelligent man. He just didn't always keep with the times. Your mother, she had a pleasant way about her. She nudged him in the right direction. If it weren't for her, he'd probably still use a slide rule. I'm sure he misses her personally. Professionally, it's a huge loss."

"Wow, that's—" Mimi took a sip of wine. "I didn't know that."

"They never talked about it openly, of course, because that was the old school. Everyone in the industry knew. You didn't?"

"No." Mimi stared into the flame, trying to digest this.

"To me, it's obvious which parent you take after. Your father."

"No, no, no," Mimi declared. "My sisters are more like my father. They're the religious ones. I'm more like my mother. She was into the arts—"

"I'm not talking about who's religious and all that. I mean what you're like as people. You're both very stubborn. You get on the high horse a lot. You are, what do they say, the peas in the pod. I'll bet the two of you argue a lot."

Mimi released a rueful laugh. "Sometimes." She was growing intrigued with Garstein. Maybe it was the wine.

"Like him, you are very serious. You need to smile more."

"I've had a hard day."

"You want to tell me about it? That is part of my job, hearing people's stories."

"It's no big deal. I had a fight with a friend."

"A fight with a friend is no small thing. What was it about?"

"Nothing, really." Mimi gulped some wine. "An article I'm writing."

He cocked his head. "What article? The one about Yosef?"

"Well, no—" Mimi's breath got caught in her throat. "I mean—"

Garstein smiled. "This is a friendly dinner. Why be cagey?"

It hit her. She was here for information. So was he.

Mimi went back on alert. "I probably won't write about Yosef. It's so sad, the whole thing."

"Definitely." Garstein buttered his bread. "Though, if you have any questions about Yosef, I'll be happy to answer them."

"As long as you mention it"—Mimi tried to sound nonchalant, even as her pulse quickened—"there are a few items I've wondered about. I was never clear what Yosef talked to you about before he died."

"I told you all I remember." His tone was flat. "If anything more occurs to me, I'll let you know."

"Now *you're* being cagey." Mimi forced a smile to her lips. She was about to press more, until she realized something. "You know I'm still writing about this, don't you?"

Garstein leaned back, seeming pleased with himself. "Forty-Seventh Street is a small community. I keep tabs."

Mimi fiddled with her fork. *Time to recalibrate.* "You're right. This is supposed to be a friendly dinner. We don't have to talk business. We can talk about other stuff. It would be nice to get to know each other better." She underlined this with a smile.

She worried Garstein wouldn't fall for it, that it was too soon after she tried to quiz him about Yosef. He perked up and produced a wide grin. Never underestimate the male ego.

"I would like that quite a lot." He popped a piece of roll in his mouth. "I have told you all about me. I don't know much about you. Obviously, you're single. Ever been married?"

"I got a divorced a year ago."

"I'm sad to hear that."

Mimi twitched in her seat. "It's okay."

"I don't think it is. An attractive girl like you shouldn't be alone." He moved the breadbasket toward her. "You sure you don't want a roll?"

"No thanks." She pushed the basket back.

"It's always better when you have someone in your life. For support, for companionship, and for you-know-what." His eyebrows fluttered and he clutched his knife, like he wanted to make her his next meal. "Lucky for you, David Garstein knows how to make a woman smile."

He reached over the table and covered her hand with his. Mimi's fingers felt trapped under his thick paw. She tried to remain calm. When his sweaty fingers stroked hers, she couldn't play along anymore. She snatched her hand away so quickly it startled them both.

"I'd prefer you not touch me like that." Mimi moved both her hands under the table. "I don't get involved with people I write about."

Garstein lifted an eyebrow. "Not what I heard."

"What do you mean by that?" Mimi sputtered. "You heard about me and Paul and now you think—" Her throat burned. "Yeech!"

What happened next surprised her. He looked hurt. "It's okay if you are not interested." His eyes turned down. "You don't have to make a yuck noise."

For a moment, Mimi felt bad. She was about to apologize when Garstein looked up, a fierce glint in his eyes.

"As you've insulted me, I guess it's time I put the cards on my table. You cannot write about USGR. You could greatly hurt the industry."

Mimi almost laughed at this. "I will speak frankly too. I am doing an article. It will talk about Yosef. It will talk about the USGR. We all have a responsibility to look at the world's ugliness."

Garstein seemed puzzled. "Yosef said the same thing."

Mimi smiled to herself. Yosef had met with the rabbi before Garstein too.

"All this high and mighty talk, it gives me a headache. If I want to, I can stop you. I'd rather not get into that."

"Is that what you told Yosef? That you'd stop him from talking publicly about the USGR?"

He clucked his tongue and shook his head with disapproval, like she was a child. "You think you know the whole story. You don't. Yosef came to me, crying. He couldn't eat or sleep. He didn't want to say anything."

"Why not?"

"He had his reasons. He was a good boy. I believe he would have done the right thing."

"Someone killed him before he could make that choice!"

Garstein's eyebrows rammed against each other so fast they almost collided. "Yosef was killed by the South Americans!"

"That's what they say. That's not what I believe."

Garstein raised his chin 20 degrees. The candle threw a dark shadow on his face. "I don't want to do this. It's regrettable that I must." His face moved across the table, slowly, like a shark. "I know about your father. How he's not paying his rent. From what I hear, he's really hanging by a thread."

A chill ran down Mimi's spine. "That is none of your business!"

"On the contrary." He reclined in his seat. "Everything on Forty-Seventh Street is my business. His landlord is a good friend of mine. He's always happy to do me favors."

"What are you saying? If I write something, he'll be evicted?"

"When someone doesn't pay their rent, that is always a risk."

"You're threatening me, and I will print that."

"Where? In *The West Jersey Metro*? The place you said you worked for, and didn't?" He smiled. "I know about that too."

Mimi's breath turned rapid and shallow. "I'll find a place."

"Go ahead. No one will have sympathy for your father. Businesses

have to pay rent. And by the time you print it, he'll be out already."
He took a sip of wine. "This isn't pleasant for me. David Garstein does
not like to play bad guy. You forced me into this. If I have to decide
between the well-being of my entire organization and one man who
can't afford his rent, it's not such a hard choice. Your father isn't even
a member."

Mimi wanted to cry. She wanted to scream. She wanted to kick his
stupid teeth in.

"I will get this printed, and I will expose you for the vile piece of
vomit you are. My father calls you 'that *shmuck* Garstein.' I realize now,
that's being kind."

She kept up the stream of insults. He appeared unfazed by her
hostility, even seemed to draw strength from it. Her voice grew louder
until Herbert approached the table.

"Miss, please, no shouting."

"I'm sorry," Mimi said. Her throat felt sore.

"We apologize, Herbert. Sometimes people get emotional. I'll make
sure she keeps it down."

"I appreciate your consideration." Herbert bowed and walked away.

"That was embarrassing!" Garstein fumed. "Everyone is looking at
us. I'm a regular at this restaurant. If this continues, I'll be ashamed to
show my face here. Let's discuss this calmly. Nothing bad has to happen.
We can make a deal, diamond business style."

"I'm not making a deal with you," Mimi sneered.

"You have to. You have no choice."

Mimi tried to stay calm, until she realized: Why should she?

"The reason I won't make a deal with you," she declared, as loud as
possible, "is you aren't a real politician. You're not that important."

Garstein exploded out of his chair. "How could you say that? I'm
president of a major diamond organization."

She waved her hand. "Big deal."

"It *is* a big deal." His voice grew louder. "I oversee hundreds of people.
Ask anyone about David Garstein. I'm a prominent industry figure."

This brought on a return visit from Herbert, who came to the table
and intoned, "I'm afraid I'll have to ask you to leave."

Garstein settled back in his chair. He snatched his napkin from the
table and spread it on his lap. "Don't worry, Herbert. She'll be gone soon."

Mimi began stuffing her arms in her coat sleeves.

"Apologies for being unclear." The waiter looked past him. "That was aimed at both of you."

Mimi was putting on her coat as she heard this. She stopped to see Garstein's reaction. His nostrils swelled and he bared his teeth. He sprung from his chair and started screaming at Herbert. He protested what a terrible injustice this was, how it was all her fault, how he always spent lots of money and left big tips. She knew the bigger commotion he made, the more he hurt himself. It would be a long time before he'd be welcomed back with warm greetings and olive rolls.

She could hear him yelling as she sprinted out the door. He *had* made her smile.

A few minutes later, Mimi was hurrying down Forty-Seventh Street to the subway. It was a cold night, the sky black and free of stars. The stores had shut, and the block was deserted, except for a bundled-up hawker that roamed the street in a futile hunt for passersby to trade in their gold.

Mimi was about to descend the steps to the subway when she felt a tap on her shoulder. *What the—*

"Would you like to sell your gold, miss?" asked the hawker, thrusting out a handbill.

She spun around to deliver an epic tell-off. "No, and I'd appreciate—"

Her body froze. A scarf covered the hawker's face, and he was no longer dressed in Hasidic garb. There was no mistaking those eyes, like poison darts aimed straight at her. Seeing them up close made Mimi gasp—even before she saw the knife.

CHAPTER TWENTY-EIGHT

THE HAWKER'S EYES LOCKED IN ON MIMI. He grabbed her throat. His hands felt like claws that pierced through his gloves to her skin.

Mimi tried to scream but couldn't; her throat was filled with blood. Her eyes bulged as she gasped for air. She tried to wrest herself from him. His grip was cast-iron.

He lifted the knife and aimed it at her chest. She could see it coming at her, almost in slow motion. She clutched her pocketbook against her stomach as a barrier and leaned back.

The only part of her body she could freely move was her legs. She lifted the right one and smashed the heel of her shoe against his kneecap. It didn't have much impact; his knee felt like it was made out of wood. She did notice the faintest glimmer of surprise in his eyes.

She lifted her leg and rammed her heel into his groin, harder this time, with a force that came from deep within her.

His eyes grew wider, his body jerked, and he emitted a faint groan. He loosened his hold on her neck, and she broke free of his grip. His hold was the only thing that was keeping her upright. She lost her balance and tumbled backward, as the world slipped away.

She flew through the air until she landed with a series of sharp, jarring knocks to her head. When the bumps stopped, she opened her eyes to see the world spinning. She had tumbled halfway down the flight of subway steps.

Her pocketbook had opened, and she saw her lipstick, phone, and other random objects of her everyday life scattered on the stairs. The hawker stood atop the staircase, framed against the night. He ran down the stairs, led by his knife.

Mimi could barely move; her body felt stuck to the steps. She mustered all her strength and rolled herself down the few remaining cold hard stairs—bump after bump after horrible bump, each one feeling like she had been punched with a fist made of sandpaper. She reached the subway station with a final knock to her nose.

She lay on the dirty subway floor, inhaling the too-sweet smell of a nearby piece of gum. The station was spinning wildly. Her body ached on and off; her blood was pumping so fast that the pain only came in small awful bursts. Her right eye was covered with a film of blood. Through the splotches she could see the hawker was coming down the steps. Her mind attained a kind of hyper-focus, and she prayed, *Please, God, don't let me die tonight.* She wasn't expecting to, but many things had happened lately she didn't expect.

She saw her assailant was getting closer. With her remaining energy, she lifted her head and screamed for help as loud as she could. She dropped her head to the ground and tried to grab hold of the concrete floor as the station spun out of control. Everything went black.

The rest passed in a haze. Someone knelt beside her, and she was petrified it was the hawker. It was a burly transit worker who shook her and called for help then barked into his phone that an ambulance was needed immediately, because someone had fallen down the steps and was seriously hurt. *Wow*, Mimi thought. *I am seriously hurt.*

She heard a siren and saw an EMT in a bright white parka peering down the subway stairs. Two men lifted her onto a stretcher and stuck a plastic breathing tube in her nose. As they carried her up the stairs, she spotted the spilled contents of her pocketbook and called to them, "Don't forget my phone. I don't have the money for a new one."

The EMTs lifted the stretcher into the ambulance. Mimi asked if she would be okay. One told her yes, and that made her feel better, though he probably said that to everyone. It was just sinking in that she was headed to the hospital because someone had tried to kill her.

She was mostly passed out during the ride to the emergency room, with the occasional bump jolting her awake. At the hospital, a fleet of doctors descended on her, bombarded her with questions, and scissored off her dinner dress. When they determined she was conscious and not seriously injured, they disappeared as quickly as they came.

She felt relieved later that night when the friendly forty-something internist with the Australian accent and warm hands looked her over and declared she was going to be all right, just a little worse for wear.

"Try not to make a habit of falling down subway stairs," he said with a grin. He asked how it happened.

"Someone tried to stab me."

His smile faded.

After that, a young nurse, probably no older than Channah, wordlessly sewed stitches into her eyebrow, side, and leg. With all the pain in her body, the pinch of the needle didn't register.

An hour later, a businesslike orderly sat her in a wheelchair and brought her to a small cold area, separated from the rest of the emergency room by a thin white curtain. He lifted her on an examining table that doubled as a bed, next to a cart that held a brown water pitcher, a Styrofoam cup, and a box of tissues. Before leaving, the orderly asked if she needed to call anybody. She decided against phoning her dad; he'd probably panic and make her feel worse.

She spent most of the night in the ER, with only a few white sheets that smelled like bleach for company. She clutched them and tried to sleep amid the noise and cold. An IV fed pain medicine through her arm, but the aches flashed all over regardless, as if her various body parts had agreed to take turns hurting.

She heard doctors tending to the night's other emergencies. A shell-shocked teenager described his friend getting shot; another woman cried in Spanish over what seemed to be her husband's heart attack. An unattended elderly woman lying on a gurney bleated "help me" for a few agonizing minutes, while the rest of the ER tried their best to ignore it. One thing about a hospital, Mimi's father always said, however bad you have it, you'll find others there who have it worse.

Early on, Mimi gave a policeman a quick description of her assailant. An hour later, another visitor came through the curtain.

"Ms. Rosen?"

It was Detective Matthews. He was dressed in a heavy black overcoat, opened to a loosened tie. Mimi felt groggy but sat up.

"They tell me you fell down some subway steps."

"Yes. Someone tried to stab me." That made it real again, and she shivered and reached for the cup of water on the nearby table.

"You got pretty banged up."

My God. I must look terrible. The EMTs had delivered her pocketbook. She couldn't bear to look in the mirror.

Matthews took out his notepad. There wasn't much space between her table and the curtain; his bulky chest towered over her. "Do you have any idea why this man attacked you?"

"I believe it's related to my investigation of the murder of Yosef Levine."

He registered no reaction. "Do you know who this man was?"

"He was a hawker on Forty-Seventh Street."

He jotted something in his notepad. "Have you ever seen him before?"

"Yes, twice. But then he wasn't hawking. He was Hasidic."

Matthews stopped writing. "He was a Hasidic hawker?"

"No. When he was Hasidic, he wasn't a hawker."

"Just Hasidic?"

"Yes, although I'm not completely sure of that. He looked at me once when I was immodestly dressed."

Matthews' face fell. He always unnerved her, even now.

"Actually, I saw him one other time. I can't remember where it was."

She tried to summon that memory. With all that had happened, she couldn't think straight. The answer was stashed away somewhere in the junk drawer of her mind.

Matthews cleared his throat. "When he looked at you when you were immodestly dressed, was he Hasidic or a hawker?"

"It was when I—" She stopped. "I don't want to play this game anymore, Detective."

"I don't consider this a game, ma'am."

"I don't either. That's the point." She took a sip of water. "I know we got off on the wrong foot, and sometimes I get nervous around you. I told you I work for *The West Jersey Metro* so you would take me seriously. Obviously, that didn't work too well, and I'm sorry I didn't tell you I'm just an unemployed former reporter who can't get a job and barely writes for anybody anymore.

"Everything else I've told you is the God's-honest truth. I'm investigating Yosef's death. I have uncovered genuine corruption and last night someone tried to kill me." The last line made her queasy, and she broke down, unable to continue.

Detective Matthews plucked a tissue from the box and handed it to her. He watched Mimi dab her eyes and blow her nose. She heard him click his pen. He had big puffy bags under his eyes. It was past midnight, and he looked as tired as her.

Mimi regained her voice. "How about this? Can we talk tomorrow in my hospital room? We'll both get some sleep and I'll tell you everything I've discovered. If you're still skeptical of me, fine. I think there's a lot you should know." She put her cup of water on the table. "Please, Detective."

His features softened. "All right. I'll stop by tomorrow."

Just then, an orderly entered with a wheelchair. It was time for the move to a hospital room. The orderly took Mimi's hand and held her torso as she sat up. She felt jolted by a sharp pain, which quickly subsided. It was nothing she couldn't handle. She'd almost gotten used to it.

"Can you walk?" the orderly asked.

Mimi lowered herself off the table and her legs seized up, like her nerves had been slammed in a desk drawer. She clutched the table and gritted her teeth. "Give me a sec. I can do this."

With one arm holding the orderly, the other resting on the detective's shoulder, Mimi walked, slow and wobbly. She felt like a baby taking her first steps.

"Let's put you in the wheelchair," the orderly said, and before Mimi could respond she was lowered into it.

"Want me to call anyone, to let 'em know what happened?" Matthews asked out of the blue.

Mimi thought again of calling her father but said no.

"Feel better," Matthews mumbled as she was wheeled away. That was the nicest thing he'd ever said to her. He still appeared puzzled by Mimi, but there seemed to be a decent guy underneath it all.

CHAPTER TWENTY-NINE

WHEN MIMI AWOKE THE NEXT DAY, it took her a second to realize where she was—in a small hospital room that contained a bed, a cart with a breakfast tray, a TV, and not much else. The clock on the wall read noon.

She had vague memories of nurses and interns tending to her throughout the night and morning. Her body ached and felt stiff, but she could move, which was more than she could do last night. She felt well-rested, possibly because a nurse had given her a pain pill in the middle of the night.

Her arms were studded with multi-colored bruises. A half-dollar-sized lump rose from the middle of her left leg like an anthill. She opened her pocketbook and saw her possessions had survived the trip. She snuck a glance in her makeup mirror and winced. Her face was also covered with scratches and bruises. She put the mirror away, resolving not to look at her reflection for a while. It made everything hurt again.

She felt hungry and spotted some food on the table by her bed, probably left there from breakfast. She wolfed down two cold slices of toast.

A doctor visited and diagnosed her with a slight concussion and bruised rib. He advised her to take it easy and let everything heal and contact the hospital if she experienced any dizzy spells or felt faint. He said she looked ready to be released and she should wait for her discharge paperwork. After he left, Mimi fell back asleep.

She was awakened a little while later by Detective Matthews. After quick pleasantries, which were, as usual, not that pleasant, he pulled up a chair and whipped out his notepad, not taking off his coat. In a weird way she was glad to see him. Even when you had a tortured history with someone, it was still a history.

"You said you had information for me."

Mimi propped herself on some pillows and unfurled the whole twisted tale. Despite a mind hazy from pain pills, she remembered everything, the pink diamond, the second cert, Tanner, Larry, Garstein, and the rabbi. She edited out only one part: Paul's riverside confession. She had promised Paul she wouldn't talk about that, and her word was her bond.

As she talked, she hoped the detective would acknowledge her work. He registered little reaction, only offering occasional questions and sporadic "uh-huhs." A few times he bit his lip; once, he might have raised an eyebrow.

When they got to present day, she told him about the attack and again described her assailant. The detective closed his notebook and said they knew of no witnesses to last night's attack, and, while they would keep a lookout, in all likelihood her attacker was a hired gun who had already fled town. He said they'd send a squad car to periodically check on her and instructed her to call immediately if she noticed anything suspicious or threatening. Then he left.

Lunch came, and Mimi devoured the bland turkey sandwich and chocolate pudding. She felt full and ready for a nap. She checked her phone. Max had left five messages and a text. She played the first message. "Hey, where are you? It's your father. Are you coming in today? I have something I want to talk to you about." On the second message, his voice was louder and quicker. "It's a little strange I'm not hearing from you. You left early yesterday without saying good-bye, and now I'm getting worried. There was a story about a woman getting attacked last night on Forty-Seventh Street. I'm sure it's not you. I'm just being a worrier. Call me, please. Goodbye." She didn't bother to listen to the next three but saw the text, which said simply "Call ASAP. Dad." She was impressed he texted; Channah must have shown him how.

Mimi took a deep breath and called.

"Where are you?" Max just about screamed. "I know you said you're quitting in two weeks. Are you ignoring me now? I was worried sick about you."

"Dad, don't freak out. I'm in the hospital."

He freaked out.

"It's fine. I was attacked and fell down some subway steps. It's no big deal."

"You were attacked and fell down subway steps? How is that no big deal?"

"I'm fine."

"What hospital are you at? I'm coming over."

"New York Hospital. Please, don't—."

"I'm coming over."

"You don't—."

"I'm getting in a cab."

"You don't need to come over!"

About 15 minutes later, he was standing by her bed, along with Channah, after they both barely concealed their shock at the state of her face. Yesterday, Mimi was feuding with both of them; today, things felt back to normal, or as normal as they could be, given she was in the hospital after nearly being stabbed.

"Mimi, do you think you were attacked because of the investigation?" Channah asked, her eyes round.

Mimi nodded. "I think so."

"By the way, let's talk about this investigation." Max raised his voice. "Channah told me you're trying to solve Yosef's murder. Are you insane? You want to get killed?"

"Dad, you don't have to worry. I won't get hurt."

"What are you talking about? You're in the hospital!" He threw up his hands. "Tell her, Channah."

"I'm so sorry I got you into this, Mimi. I couldn't handle it if, God forbid, something else happened to you."

Mimi grabbed her hand. "Channah, yesterday you told me to drop this and I didn't listen. Whatever happened from that point is on me." She gave Channah's hand a squeeze. "You know what this means, don't you? We were right. There *is* something more to Yosef's murder. It wasn't just a gang robbery. This shows I found something. I just don't know how it all fits together."

"I'm glad you feel so validated," Max exclaimed. "Of all things. What made you think you could investigate a murder?"

"I was a newspaper reporter."

"You covered town council meetings!"

"I did a lot of good journalism back then."

Max grew flustered. "Let's not argue, Mimi." He wrapped his hands around the metal bar by her bed. "I did have something I wanted to talk to you about. I'm running your ad."

Mimi wasn't having it. "Dad, don't run my ad because I'm in the hospital. I don't want charity."

Max scowled. "This has nothing to do with charity. I decided this morning, before all this. It's not bad. I like the part where you quote me. Sometimes I'm very wise." His voice dropped. "At this point, I might as well run it. It's my only chance to save my business."

This stunned Mimi, though Channah didn't appear surprised. She and Max seemed to have discussed it.

"You know, Mimi," he gripped the metal bar, "when you came to me a few weeks ago, you made it seem like a big revelation that I was going out of business. I already knew that. I've known it for years. I'm not stupid. I figured I could go out of business right away or spend a couple of years doing it gradually. That's what I've been doing. What else am I going to do? Sit home all day? It's just not something I like to talk about." The words came slowly, as if every syllable hurt. "My time has finally run out. The landlord called this morning and told me if I didn't pay my back rent, he would bring eviction proceedings."

That shumuck Garstein!

"It's not worth draining my savings to save a dying business. I made a deal with him. I'll pay part of my back rent, and I'll stay the next two months, and after that, the business is finished. This way I'll have time to pack up my things and tell everyone good-bye. The market's not too bad. I should be able to liquidate my inventory. Who knows, maybe I can turn things around. I'll run your ad. It's—what do you call it? A Hail Mary pass."

"Dad, listen." Mimi sat up. "This is my fault. I caused the problems with your landlord."

Max scowled. "No, you didn't."

"Yes, I did. Last night I went to see David Garstein, and he got mad that I was looking into the USGR situation. He said he would call your landlord—"

Her father interrupted. "Mimi, stop it."

"I can fix this! I'll go on a date with Garstein and maybe he'll call off the landlord—"

Max recoiled. "Please! I'd rather see you back with your ex-husband."
Mimi laughed.

He took her hand. "*Bubelah*, this was inevitable, as you well know.
I enjoyed forty-five good years in this industry. My business was living
on borrowed time. Nothing lasts forever. Maybe diamonds. Just not
diamond companies."

His mouth broke into an unconvincing smile. He looked pale. He
looked thin. It was hard to reconcile the frail figure standing before her
with the often-formidable father of her youth.

Mimi gripped his hand. "How do you feel about this?"

"I was upset most of the morning, until I heard about my daughter in
the hospital. Puts things in perspective."

He let go of the metal bar and turned to the window. "It'll be a change.
I'll have to find ways to occupy myself all day. There's some things I'll
miss. There's a man who stands outside my building asking for money.
Every morning he says to me, 'hope you have a wonderful day, Mr.
Rosen.' Not just a nice day, a wonderful day. And I give him a dollar, and
he gives me a wide smile. That's the kind of thing I feel bad about leaving.

"I won't miss the stress, the constant worrying that the industry has
passed me by. Sometimes you have to move on to the next chapter in life
whether you're ready to or not. I always hoped when I retired, your mother
and I would travel the world. I guess some things aren't meant to be."

His eyes misted and he turned back to Mimi. "From what my lawyer
tells me, it's not so easy to shut a business down. I have inventory to
sell off, and there is a lot of paperwork. I'll need help with that. And
occasional moral support.

"I know you gave your two weeks' notice. I hope you change your mind
and come back. You'll only have to put up with me another two months."

"I want you to come back, too, Mimi," Channah chimed in. "We can
both look for jobs together!"

"O.K.!" Mimi smiled. "We'll all go down with the ship!"

"Good. And don't worry," Max said, "you'll have plenty to do."

Her father had finally given her a real job. She only had to destroy his
company.

"Please don't think I don't respect you or any of that nonsense. Part
of me will always consider you my little girl. I was raised with a different
concept of women than you were.

"You have always been a person who made up her own mind about things. And even when you look at the world a little differently than me, I've always been proud of you. More than you'll ever know."

It sounded stilted, and it was clearly not an easy thing for him to say. Mimi got a lump in her throat just the same.

"You should rest up. When are you getting out of here?"

"Soon. I have to fill out some forms. You want to grab some lunch and come back?"

"Sure. Just please, Mimi, end this investigation." Max shot her a look that brought back memories of childhood scoldings.

Mimi knew he meant well, even if he was coming off as another man in the diamond industry telling her what to do. "I'll be okay," she said. She really didn't know how okay she'd be. She no longer had a choice. She had to find the truth.

"Mimi, if you keep this up, I'll spend every minute worrying that something will happen to you. I won't get a minute of sleep."

Mimi's father was an artist, and guilt was his medium.

"Can't the police look into this?" he asked.

"They are. I had a long talk with the detective this morning. I don't think they really understand what's going on. There's a terrible person out there. He killed Yosef, he killed Larry, and he just tried to kill me."

"All the more reason you should stay out of this!" Max bellowed. "Let the police take care of it. They're the experts. You aren't."

Mimi had a sudden inspiration. She fell silent. "You're right. The police should handle this."

This idea so pleased her, she couldn't help smiling, even though it made her face hurt.

LATER THAT DAY, MIMI WAS DISCHARGED from the hospital with some prescriptions and strict instructions from the doctor to take it easy. Her father insisted she spend the night at his house in Queens. He gave her a long speech about how, being in the diamond business, he always had good security and he would set it to the highest level so that if anyone even came near the place, the cops would arrive just like that. Mimi told him that wasn't necessary; the police pledged to keep tabs on her. She didn't give him a big argument over it. Before they went to bed, her father stacked chairs against the front door for protection. Mimi told him that was silly, given his talk about his great alarm system. She didn't argue much about that either.

Mimi had visited her old family home several times after her mom died. This was the first time she'd stayed for more than a few hours. The floorboards were creakier, the furniture more weathered. The mantle over the fireplace always held lots of pictures, but now it was cluttered with them; it had become a mom shrine. There were also subtle but clear signs of deterioration—the way the medicine cabinet was stocked with pill bottles past their expiration dates or how her father hadn't changed several burned-out lightbulbs.

After her father's nightly before-bed ritual of sitting in the kitchen, and enjoying a kosher Belgian chocolate while listening to classical music on the radio, Mimi retired to the cramped room she grew up in. Her old twin bed was way too small and not very comfortable, yet it felt familiar, like her body fit in it.

Even so, she couldn't sleep. Her body thrummed with nervous energy. Someone wanted to kill her. She was a target. Was she safe here? Was she safe anywhere?

The room's windows had their old child safety bars. They might not deter a killer. She needed a weapon. She retrieved a knife from the kitchen to keep beside her while she slept. She worried she'd fall asleep and roll onto it, so she tucked it under her pillow and replaced it with a nail file. She didn't know what she'd do with the nail file; really, she had no idea what she'd do with the knife either. She felt better with it beside her, like it was a teddy bear.

She continued to toss and turn. She couldn't banish all that had happened from her mind. She could see the hawker's eyes boring into her, feel his hands pressing on her throat.

Something else bothered her. She knew she'd seen him another time, not as a hawker, not as a Hasid. She just couldn't recall where.

After an hour, she took a pain pill and, at last, relaxed. Just as she was drifting off, Mimi bolted upright. She remembered where she saw him.

Outside Connolly's, the Irish bar. He was the guy talking to Paul.

CHAPTER THIRTY

THE NEXT DAY, MIMI, CLAD IN SUNGLASSES that only partially hid her bruises, rang the bell at Paresh Mehta's. Through the door, she heard Paresh and his wife shout to each other in Hindi. Finally, Paresh came up front.

"Miss," he hissed through the door, "I have told you I want no more to do with you."

"Mr. Mehta, there is someone I want you to meet. Larry Greenbaum's daughter."

Ellen peered up at the camera.

Paresh cracked the door open and stuck his face out. "Ellen?"

"You know my name?"

"Of course. Everyone who knew Larry heard about his daughter."

Ellen beamed.

"I do not wish to speak with you. However, I am sorry for your loss." He slammed the door.

"Mr. Mehta," Ellen shouted through the door, "this isn't a social call. I'm a cadet at the New York Police Academy. I'm here because you might be in big trouble. You either speak with me now, or to one of my friends on the force later today."

Mehta opened the door. "What are you talking about?"

"This is about you possibly being involved in an assault on Miss Rosen," Ellen responded. "Can we come in?"

Without waiting for an answer, the two women barreled their way to the main office. There would be no taking shoes off today. Swapna watched from her seat, not getting up or saying hello.

"We are interested in what you told Miss Rosen on this tape." She held up Mimi's recorder. "I imagine the police will be interested as well."

"This is an absurdity." Paresh folded his arms.

Ellen pressed play. Paresh's words filled the room. "I will only say one thing to you, miss. 'Be careful what you are getting involved in, or you will end up dead.'"

"A few days after you said that," Ellen said, "Ms. Rosen here was attacked and nearly killed."

Mimi removed her sunglasses to show her black eye and scars.

"We can show you the police report if you like."

"You don't need to." Paresh stared at Mimi's face. "I can see it."

"How did you know to make that threat, Mr. Mehta?"

"That wasn't a threat." His squeaky protests sounded very different from the stern man on the recording. "It was a warning."

"A quite accurate warning. A little too accurate, if you ask me."

"This is insane." He put his hands up, as if in surrender. "I assumed something might occur, because of all the events that had transpired."

"What events?"

"I saw what happened with—" His face contorted, like it was being squeezed. "Why are you bothering me? Why is *she* pestering me?" He shook his finger furiously at Mimi, as if it was a magic wand that could make her disappear. "We are total bystanders here. Tell them, Swapna. Tell them we know nothing of this."

All eyes turned to his wife. Who broke down in tears.

The Mehtas then retreated to a corner and engaged in an animated huddle in both Hindi and English. At one point, Swapna suggested getting a lawyer.

"The only lawyer we know is your brother," responded Paresh. "He does real estate."

A few minutes later, they were all sitting at a white table in the Mehtas' office. There was a vase of flowers on the side, and the same colorful Indian patterns and gem pictures dotted the office as before, but no one was smiling. It was grim faces discussing a grim situation.

Mimi talked the most, sitting forward in her seat, while Ellen sat back, eyeing both Mimi and the Mehtas. Indian music played on the radio, and its hypnotic jagged rhythms floated in and out of Mimi's consciousness.

"After Yosef posted the three-carat pink radiant on the online network, we recognized it immediately as a diamond we had owned," said Paresh. "One that originally received a different report. The proper one."

"The proper one?" asked Mimi.

"There is no doubt the initial report bears the correct assessment. That was an extremely flawed stone. We asked Yosef to our office, and showed him the original report, with the lower grade and notice of a treatment."

"Treatment?" asked Ellen.

Mimi turned to Ellen. "That means the diamond was chemically altered to improve its characteristics." She turned back to the Mehtas. "Then what happened?"

"He instantly knew that something unseemly had occurred. We have heard those rumors about USGR for years, but you don't expect evidence of this caliber. He was very upset. Yosef was—what is the colloquialism? A boy scout."

"A Jewish boy scout," said his wife.

Paresh shot her a dirty look.

"Did Yosef say anything more?"

"He said he would discuss it with his partner on the diamond."

Whoa. Mimi had never heard that Yosef had a partner before. "Did he say who the partner was?"

Paresh turned to his wife. "Did he say, Swapna?"

"No. He just left with a copy of the report. He said he planned to inform the U.S. Attorney. A few days later, we heard that he died."

"Why didn't you tell the police about this?" Mimi asked.

"They said it was one of the South American theft crews. We thought it was appropriate to let them do their jobs. Where I come from, we do not question officers of the law."

"Come on," Mimi insisted. "The police need info from people like you."

Silence followed until Swapna piped up. "We were very scared." Which said it all.

"Ever since I have heard of Yosef's passing," Paresh said, "I have been beyond tears, beyond grief, beyond any consolation. I do not like to think we played any role in it, however inadvertent."

After all this time as his adversary, Mimi wanted to hug him.

"Can you give us the certificate?" she asked.

Paresh sighed and nodded to Swapna, who trotted off and pulled the report from a desk drawer. She handed it to Mimi—torn corner and all. Mimi immediately stuffed it in her pocketbook.

"What you say makes sense, Mr. Mehta," Ellen said. "We have no more questions."

The Mehtas audibly exhaled.

"Who would like tea?" piped up Swapna.

For the first time since they arrived at the Mehtas, Ellen and Mimi smiled. They made some small talk, and Swapna offered cookies, but it was clear the Mehtas preferred they leave.

Before Mimi left, Paresh shook her hand, wished her luck, and looked her in the eyes. "Miss, I would never hurt you. Those words I said, they were not a threat. Please understand that."

"I know." Mimi smiled. "Honestly, I knew the whole time."

ON THE ELEVATOR ON THE WAY DOWN, Ellen asked Mimi, "This report, is it a big deal?"

"In this world it is."

"What are you going to do with it?"

Mimi hadn't really considered her next move; she was amazed they'd pulled this off. "I don't know. Want to go for coffee?" She'd feel safer in the company of a police cadet.

"I have to go back to class. You'll be safe, right?"

"I hope so."

"You asked great questions, by the way. You're a good reporter."

Mimi smiled. "I appreciate that."

The elevator reached the bottom floor. She and Ellen said good-bye with a hug. They hadn't known each other for that long, but working together on this made Mimi feel close to her.

Mimi walked down Forty-Seventh Street, happy and astonished. At last she had her hands on the second cert. She clutched her little prize close to her chest like a baby and grinned to herself. She was learning to play this game.

CHAPTER THIRTY-ONE

Mimi felt too jumpy to head home. She couldn't get her mind around the idea that someone out there wanted her dead and would probably try to kill her again.

After Ellen left, Mimi went into a local bodega and asked the clerk for the biggest, most powerful can of pepper spray he had. Seeing the bruises on her face, he quickly complied.

She figured she'd be safer in public. She set up camp at a coffee shop near Forty-Seventh Street.

Her long-sought-after prize—the second report—lay in her pocketbook, right next to her extra-large bottle of pepper spray. She held the purse close to her breast, frequently lifting her sunglasses to observe her surroundings.

She hadn't eaten all day, but wasn't hungry. She ordered an apple Danish. It just sat there on her plate, which annoyed Mimi so much she covered it with a napkin.

Ever since she left the hospital, she had felt an ever-present anxiety, a slimy, pulsing ball of fear that had taken up seemingly permanent residence in the stomach. She mostly tuned it out, the way one ignored a low-grade headache.

Every so often, she could feel the ball of fear pulsate and grow, crawling up her chest, spreading its cold tentacles throughout her body. She tried to not give in to it or acknowledge its existence. For if she really thought about what was going on, she would fall apart, and might never get herself back together again. The darkness would swallow her whole.

She turned her mind back to the investigation. She took out a piece of paper and made up a list of suspects.

First, Yosef's partner on the stone. She didn't know who that was.

Second, that *shmuck* Garstein. She considered him a suspect; she just couldn't think of a motive. Yes, he wanted to protect the industry. He was probably too selfish to kill over that. Regardless, he was a jerk and deserved to make her list of suspects for that reason alone.

Third, the person at the USGR who issued that upgraded cert. She now had the report. That was clear proof someone had been paid off.

Paul said that only someone in the executive office could have done that. Which meant Tanner and, well, Paul.

There were plenty of reasons to suspect Paul. She had seen him with her assailant. That morning, she had called Matthews to tell him that. "Interesting," he replied. "Paul Michelson is definitely someone we're looking at."

When Mimi hung up, she realized: Despite all that had happened between her and Paul, she couldn't believe he was a bad guy. It didn't make sense. It didn't smell right. He was Pizzaface Paul.

Paul might know how to run a diamond lab. He might have taken a payoff. He still didn't seem like a killer. Like Yosef, he wasn't competent enough. When he received a bribe, he inadvertently turned himself in. The guy had trouble handling a wineglass, never mind a gun.

Her father told her to trust her judgment about people. Every bone in her body believed Paul was innocent.

The problem was, the police were now looking at him, because of her. It felt like they were back on the playground, and she'd gotten him in trouble again. This time, she wouldn't leave him to the wolves.

If Paul didn't change that grade, Tanner must have. She hadn't thought about Tanner in a while. He was an intriguing suspect. He had told her the second report didn't exist. It did. He had accused Paul of taking a bribe, and never reported him to the police. She should talk to the USGR's chief excellence officer.

Of course, in their last interview, Tanner had kicked her out of his office. She needed a way to get his attention.

She thought a bit and realized it was sitting in her pocketbook.

"Dear Mr. Tanner," read her email. "During our interview a few weeks ago, I asked you if Paul Michelson was fired for finding a second report for a 3.2 carat pink. You told me no. I now have that second report in my possession. Why did you lie to me?"

How he responds to this will be telling.

Within five minutes, she received a message from Brenda Russell, executive assistant to USGR lab director Arthur Tanner.

"Mr. Tanner has seen your message. Can you come to his office ASAP to discuss?"

That told her something.

Ten minutes later, Mimi arrived at Tanner's office. Entering the reception area, she removed her sunglasses; she wanted to observe Tanner's reaction to her still-battered face. Brenda nodded at Mimi and ushered her in immediately.

Tanner greeted Mimi with a half-hearted attempt at a smile. He slammed the door, and every hair on Mimi's body shot up. She was alone in a room with a maybe murderer.

She tried to calm herself. The secretary had seen her come in. Besides, people didn't get killed in fancy office suites in the middle of the day. At least, she hoped they didn't. She didn't want to be the first.

She kept her pocketbook open and on her lap, with the pepper spray lying up top for easy access. She had the rabbi's safety prayer in her front pocket. She didn't know if that would help. It couldn't hurt.

Tanner sat down and placed his fist flat on the desk. He was as well put-together as the first time Mimi met him, but his faced looked creased in a way it hadn't before. He started to talk, until he stopped, and gazed at Mimi. "Have you been injured?"

"The other night someone tried to stab me." She uttered this as matter-of-factly as she could and scanned his face for a reaction.

His expression registered shock, or at least a decent facsimile. "My word. I'm sorry to hear that." He re-arranged some papers on his desk. "In any case, Miss Rosen, I wasn't sure I should speak to you, given that you're not a real journalist."

"Maybe I'm not," she fired back. "I'm enough of a journalist to get that certificate. Which proves you're a liar."

"Miss Rosen—"

"It also shows, pretty clearly, shady stuff going on at your lab. A lot of newspapers might be interested in that story. Either you talk to me now or wait until the article comes out."

Tanner seemed to spear her with his eyes. "How do I know you're not working with Paul Michelson?"

"I'm not. You have my word." She put up her hand.

"I'll have to trust you on that," he sniffed. "Regardless, I did not lie to you, Miss Rosen."

"How could you say that? That second report backs up everything Paul said."

"That certificate does not back up Paul's story. It could be considered evidence against him." His eyes turned down. "I'll admit I didn't tell you all the facts when we first met. Perhaps that was wrong of me. Suffice it to say, you are correct, that stone had two reports. And the second received an illicit upgrade."

"Which was discovered by Paul Michelson."

"That's what he claims. That's not what we believe." He played with a paper clip. "What appears to have happened is, when you interviewed him, he saw that the first report was still in the system and attempted to erase it. Fortunately, our executive assistant, Brenda, discovered what he was trying to do. We investigated and found that Paul had upgraded that stone."

"Why would Paul change a grade?" Mimi asked, conceding something she did not want to. "For money?"

"He didn't admit to that. He didn't admit to anything. We do know that he *had* taken money before."

"If Paul did all those things, why didn't you report him to the police? Isn't that standard in situations like this?"

Tanner dropped his chin to his chest. "In retrospect, we should have. Please understand, we were acting with the best intentions. We care about this institution. It has a very important mission."

"Again with the mission!" Mimi broke in. "You realize you're not curing cancer."

Tanner seemed startled by this, even wounded. "We're helping our industry." He straightened to his full height. "This trade has helped us earn a living. We are giving something back. That may not mean much to you. It does to me."

He rubbed his temples. "In any case, the police called us today about Paul. They think he may have something to do with a recent murder. He might not escape justice after all."

Mimi gulped. Paul really *was* a suspect.

"I am pained this happened on my watch." He sank into his chair. "Paul fooled a lot of people. He certainly fooled me. I shouldn't have trusted him. You shouldn't either."

Mimi couldn't ignore the implication of that. "You keep referring to me and Paul, like we're together or something. I told you I have nothing to do with him."

"Well, I had heard that the two of you were once—" He hunted for the right word. "Involved. I assume that's why you're defending him."

"We were not 'involved.' And even if we were, that's none of your business."

Tanner cringed. "I apologize. This is not an easy time." Clearly, Mimi's anger was one more headache he was in no mood to deal with. "If you do write about this, I just ask you get across that we did try to do the right thing. Maybe we made mistakes. We made them for good reasons." He slumped further. "Anything else?"

Mimi had one more question, but it had slipped her mind. "Wait a minute," she called out.

She frantically paged through her notebook. Finally, she found it: The old note she wrote to herself. She aimed her eyes on Tanner. "According to you, the first time you heard the pink was upgraded was from Brenda, correct?"

"Yes."

"According to David Garstein, Yosef Levine called and left you a message about the pink one week before that. Is that true?"

Tanner crinkled his forehead. "I don't recall such a message." He dialed his secretary on speakerphone. "Brenda, did a Yosef Levine contact us a few weeks ago?"

Mimi heard Brenda click some keys. "Yes," she came back. "He called about a meeting. He didn't say regarding what."

"What was the result?" Tanner demanded.

More clicking. "Paul Michelson saw the message in the system and decided that he would meet with Mr. Levine."

"Paul had a meeting with Yosef?" Mimi asked. "Just the two of them?"

"Yes," said Brenda.

"On what day?"

"February tenth."

"February tenth." Mimi repeated, a little stunned. "That was the day he died."

As SHE RODE DOWN IN THE ELEVATOR, Mimi tried to wrap her mind around everything. It sure seemed like Paul was guilty of *something*.

Perhaps her gut was wrong. It wouldn't be the first time.

Maybe she was only sticking up for Paul because, long ago, he had stuck up for her. Or maybe, like Tanner said, because they had gone out on a date.

Hold it. That was strange. How did Tanner know she went out with Paul? Garstein knew too. Paul may have told them. Why would he?

Come to think of it, quite a few people had known what she was up to. The hawker knew when she was meeting with the rabbi and Garstein. Someone knew she was talking to Larry. She hadn't told anyone about those things.

Leaving the building, it hit her. She had told one person all that. Channah.

CHAPTER THIRTY-TWO

WHEN MIMI LEFT TANNER'S OFFICE, IT was 5:30 PM and getting dark. She wanted to pop up to her father's office and ask Channah a few questions.

Her phone rang. It was cousin Bernard.

"I just spoke with Channah. She told me you no longer believe Yosef was a briber."

"Yes." Mimi said. "It turns out there was a partner on the stone."

"I'm glad to hear you won't besmirch my late brother's memory."

"Bernard, I've told you a million times, I would never do anything to hurt our family."

"You say that. I know how ruthless journalists are. You act nice, then screw everybody."

Bernard's insinuations particularly annoyed Mimi today. Considering all she had been through; he should be thanking her.

"By the way," Bernard cleared his throat, "I'm at the probate lawyer going through Yosef's effects. You might be right about certain things. We found an agreement that lists Yosef's partner in the pink. A Phil DeMasse. Ever heard of him?"

"No." Mimi made a mental note of the name. "Is there anything in Yosef's papers about a meeting with Paul Michelson?"

"You mean the guy that got canned from the USGR? I might have seen something on that." He rustled papers. "Yeah, here it is, in Yosef's appointment book. He had a meeting with Paul Michelson at 3:30 on February tenth. I guess that was right before Yosef died."

"Interesting. Can I see that appointment book?"

"Sure. If you come to the lawyer's office."

"I'll drive over right now." Mimi clicked off and hurried to her car; she was avoiding the subway for a while. Suddenly, something occurred to her. She pulled out her phone and Googled "Phil DeMasse."

Up popped his picture, on one of those public mugshot sites. Even without his hawker or Hasid guise, those eyes were unmistakable.

Mimi nearly dropped the phone. She now knew who killed Yosef.

It made her sick. It was someone who she had known since she was a child. Someone who she cared about. Someone who, despite his flaws, she never thought capable of such a thing.

She couldn't live in denial any longer. She had to face the truth.

She needed to check one more fact. She called Paul. He quickly picked up.

"Paul, it's Mimi. You're in a lot of trouble."

He chuckled. "It's good to hear from you too, Mimi."

"Do you know guy named Phil DeMasse?"

"I met him once."

"Did he work for that dealer? The one who bribed you?"

Paul paused for a second. "Yes."

"I need you to tell me the name of that dealer."

"I can't do that, Mimi. I've explained why."

"Paul, my life may be at stake. So might yours. There's a good chance you're being set up for murder."

"What?" he sputtered. "That's crazy."

"Paul, I know that, deep down, you trust me. And I trust you." She stopped walking, forcing annoyed pedestrians to circumvent her. "How about I tell you who it is, and you just confirm?" She uttered the name.

Paul mumbled a quick "yes," and hung up.

Mimi had one more call. He picked up with a curt "Matthews."

"Detective, think about it." Mimi's speech and pace quickened as she neared the garage. "Who else would Yosef have been reluctant to turn in? Who has been talking to Channah this whole time? How could Bernard check a date in Yosef's appointment book, when I have Yosef's appointment book? Finally, if Yosef was careful about who he dealt with, why would he take as a partner someone whose mugshot was on Google?"

There was a brief silence on the other end. "I'm sorry. Who am I speaking with?"

"Mimi Rosen." She didn't take a breath. "I've put it together. Bernard Levine killed his brother Yosef." Her voice broke on the last part. "I'm going to confront him right now."

Matthews gave one of his vast repertoire of world-weary sighs. "Ma'am, that isn't a smart thing to do with someone you suspect of murder. And why do you have Yosef Levine's appointment book?"

"Detective, I want my life back. That can only happen if I stop Bernard. He is a dangerous man. He is setting someone up for this crime. He must be stopped before he does more harm."

His voice quickened to match hers. "Are you meeting Bernard now?"

"Yes. At the probate attorney's office. Ninety-Five Riverdale Parkway in the Bronx."

"I'll go there and talk with him. You need to head home. I don't want you involved with this anymore. Do you understand? Go home!"

"I understand. We can talk later."

Matthews grunted and hung up.

Mimi smiled. *That worked.*

She rushed into the familiar garage on Forty-Eighth Street. While visiting the murder site had lately not bothered her, today it made her feel raw and emotional. She felt the ball of fear in her stomach pulsate and grow.

As she exited the elevator, Mimi saw Jimmy the security guard slumped in his booth, asleep as usual. She gripped her phone as she sped through the garage. She needed to get to her car and get home.

She heard a loud sudden bang. Her heart jumped into her throat. She had no particular reason to be frightened of it or consider it different from any other loud noise one hears in New York City. Yet, she sensed that the noise and her were connected somehow. She froze between the rows of parked cars, listening to the echo grow softer and fade away.

She heard rustling, another sound she wouldn't normally think twice about. Only her life was not normal now. The garage felt dark and menacing. She felt alone and exposed. She wanted to run. She didn't know where. She stood a few feet from the elevator, a few feet from her car.

"Jimmy, did you hear that?" she called out.

He didn't answer.

How could he sleep through that noise?

"Jimmy, are you there?"

No response. She clenched her phone so tight it was almost painful and rushed to her car. She was just about there when she saw a big black lump behind her rear fender. She made out the stomach, the head. He was clad in a body stocking, crouched and poised to strike.

Mimi swallowed a scream. She spun around and sped to Jimmy's security booth, the first oasis she could see. She pounded on the glass, hoping to wake him up. He didn't move.

"Jimmy!" she screamed, banging as loud as she could. Finally, she stopped and peered inside. She saw the hole in Jimmy's stomach, the soupy mess of blood on the floor.

Her hands trembled as she called Matthews. His line was ringing when she felt the gun at her back.

CHAPTER THIRTY-THREE

BERNARD'S HAND SHOOK AS HE PRESSED the gun against her spine. He may not have been used to killing someone in cold blood. But he was about to.

"Drop the phone," he barked.

Mimi did as she was told.

"Hand it over."

Mimi knew, as with Yosef, Bernard wasn't after a million-dollar diamond. Yosef wouldn't have given his life over something so trivial.

Mimi tried to think about the situation logically—as logically as she could think with a pistol pressed against her. She remembered Sol's rules for robberies. Keep calm, give the crooks what they're after, and the bad guys will go away.

She reached into her purse and handed over the report. He stuffed it in his pocket. The gun didn't leave her back. She couldn't give this bad guy what he wanted. He wasn't going away.

Mimi figured Bernard would kill her and plant the report on Paul, who would then "commit suicide" out of guilt. Mimi could almost admire the plan if it wasn't so evil.

She had to get the pepper spray. She moved her hand to her purse.

"I see what you're doing," Bernard growled. "Drop it."

Mimi watched her pocketbook fall to the floor. She no longer had access to her best weapon. She had only one weapon left, though it was a dangerous and unpredictable one. Her mouth.

"Bernard, you can't kill me." Her voice trembled. "I'm family."

"That's why I'm doing this. For *my* family."

He's talking and hasn't killed me yet. That's a good sign.

"That's right," Mimi said. "And it's because of your family that you have to make a deal with me. You have no choice."

He scoffed. "You have nothing to offer me."

"Actually, I do." Mimi suddenly felt focused. "Just before Yosef died, he wrote down every date, every meeting, everything you two discussed. You know how meticulous he was about taking notes. If the police ever get that document, you'll be in big trouble. And just in case you get any ideas about killing me, I've set up a dead man's switch."

"A what?"

"That means that if I die, the police will get a copy of Yosef's note. You need to make a deal with me. Diamond-business style." She let this sink in. "I'm willing to destroy it for one hundred thousand dollars."

"What a ridiculous story," he snarled. "You would never come up with a plan like that. You're a softie. Like Yosef."

"I'm a journalist. Didn't you say all journalists are ruthless?" She breathed out. "If you don't believe me, I can show you the note. It's right here in my front pocket."

He was silent for an agonizing moment. "Hand it over," he growled.

She removed the paper filled with Hebrew scrawl from her front pocket. He snatched it from her. She heard him read it to himself, until he angrily tossed it to the floor. "This is a prayer!"

He probably would have killed her then and there. Except, while he was reading, Mimi reached down, picked up her purse, twirled around, and hit Bernard in the face with it. With the giant pepper spray bottle on top, it packed quite a wallop. That thing finally came in handy.

Bernard toppled over and fell to the floor. He lay on his back, his arms and legs wriggling like an insect that's been swatted by a newspaper. Mimi dropped her purse on his face, and he screamed—an angry roar that sounded like it came from an animal.

Then she ran, as fast as she'd ever run from anything. Her only hope was getting to the elevator. She heard Bernard scramble to his feet and run after her. She didn't look back, though she heard him getting closer. She reached the elevator and gave the button a few frantic pushes. She ducked behind a nearby car as the elevator light descended with excruciating slowness. A loud bang rippled through the garage. He was shooting at her. *Come, elevator. Come.*

Finally, the ding rang out that would bring her to safety. The metallic doors parted, and Mimi ran into the elevator in a crouch. More gunshots rang out, and she felt a bullet whiz over her head. She dove in the elevator, which gave her a quick sour taste of the floor. She scurried into the rear corner of the elevator and watched the doors slowly close.

Until they stopped. Bernard had forced his hand between them.

She watched, horrified, as he wedged his arm, his shoulder, and his torso in the gap between the doors. They buzzed and dinged and repeatedly closed on him. He didn't stop. He was fueled by pure manic rage.

He worked his way into the elevator, red-faced and grunting. He raised his arm and pointed his gun at Mimi. He no longer seemed to care if he got caught. He just wanted her dead.

Mimi scrunched into a ball in a corner of the elevator. "Bernard, please don't," she begged. She held up her hand, as if that would stop a bullet. Her worst fear was coming true. She would die in an elevator.

When the shot rang out, she didn't feel it. Maybe her body had gone into shock or she was in a place where you no longer feel pain. Mimi lifted her head to see an intense, overpowering light.

She stared at it until she heard the cavalcade of noise. Screaming. Screeching tires. Barked orders. She blinked and looked again at the light. It was the fluorescent bulb on the elevator ceiling.

Bernard rolled on the ground in front of her, crying and grabbing his arm, as it gushed blood onto the floor. Normally, that sight would make her jump. She was too numb to do anything except sit at the rear of the elevator, her breath and pulse cascading wildly.

The elevator motor stopped, and the doors parted. Detective Matthews poked his head in.

"I'm calling an ambulance. Don't go anywhere."

She wasn't planning to.

The police dragged Bernard out of the elevator. A sandy-haired middle-aged EMT walked in afterward. He shone a flashlight on Mimi and asked if she could move. Mimi said she could. In reality, she wasn't sure of anything anymore.

The EMT helped her to her feet. She wobbled but could stand, which was better than two nights ago, the last time she was nearly killed. The EMT escorted her out of the elevator until she came face to face with Detective Matthews.

"Are you okay?" he asked.

"*Baruch Hashem*," she replied. What else could she say? "How did you know where I was?"

"We tracked your phone's GPS."

"How is Bernard doing?"

"He'll be well enough to stand trial."

Mimi surveyed the commotion around her—the cars, the ambulance. She could only say one thing. "Thanks for saving my life, Detective."

"It's my job." He walked away. As warm as ever.

The EMT sat her on a folding chair and asked if she wanted water. She nodded robotically; she had no idea if she was thirsty or not. She took a quick sip. The cold water felt good in her throat.

She was too stunned to register much emotion, although at one point she broke into tears, because she had to. She was drawn to a moth circling the police car headlight, impervious to the insanity surrounding it.

Nearby, Bernard lay on a stretcher in handcuffs. The black mask was off his face, and she could see his mussed hair and askew yarmulke. A blood-soaked tourniquet was wrapped around his arm. His teeth were gritted, and his beard was soaked with sweat, and he emitted an occasional anguished cry. As much as she thought he was despicable, as much as she hated what he had done to her life and to Yosef's and Channah's and Larry's and Jimmy's, at that moment, she almost felt sorry for him. Almost.

Many times, she had imagined what she would say to Yosef's killer. She dreamed of delivering an impassioned lecture letting him know what kind of man he murdered. Bernard knew how good Yosef was. He killed him anyway.

As the police lifted the stretcher into the ambulance, Bernard looked at Mimi. In her cousin's eyes she saw fear and bewilderment, like he couldn't wrap his mind around how he had landed in this insane position. He looked like a little boy, confused and scared. Like his brother used to.

CHAPTER THIRTY-FOUR

IT TOOK MIMI A LONG TIME TO RECOVER from the events in the garage. She started seeing a counselor who put her on medication. At one point, the therapist remarked that Max and Channah were probably just as devastated as she was. From that moment, Mimi put all her energies into supporting them. And that helped her, too.

About two months after Bernard's arrest, Mimi started to think about writing her story. She pitched her piece to a variety of places. It received little interest. An editor emailed back "You're telling me you solved a murder? Gimme a break!"

One publication bit: *The West Jersey Metro*. Her old editor Lewis laughed that he had gotten so many calls inquiring if she worked there, he knew she was on to something big. Mimi phoned Detective Matthews and asked if he would grant her an off-the-record interview to fill in some gaps. To her surprise, he said yes.

The next night they met for drinks in a Midtown hotel. Bernard had just pled guilty to killing Yosef and Jimmy and arranging Larry's murder. His associate, the one who dressed like a Hasidic man and a hawker, had also been nabbed and was working out a plea.

She and Matthews moved to a corner of the bar. They sat on red velvet chairs, hunched over a small black table. Low-level techno music thumped in the background. Mimi ordered a cranberry vodka; Matthews, straight scotch.

"Before we start," Matthews swirled his drink, "I need to apologize. I should have paid more attention to what you were saying. I deal with the worst in people. It makes me overly suspicious sometimes." He looked up, and he appeared vulnerable, his eyes soft, his mouth eager and open. Quickly, this passed, and his face returned to granite.

"My fellow detectives and I really dropped the ball on some aspects of this case." His double chin bounced as he talked. "One thing about Bernard Levine, as stupid as he was about some things, he was occasionally very smart. He had some dealings buying stolen goods from South American crews, and he placed certain objects at the scene, which is why we thought we had DNA evidence. When he found out we had talked to you, he developed a scheme to frame Paul Michelson. He did a good job sending us on wild goose chases."

"It's okay. I made mistakes too," Mimi said. "For a long time, I believed Yosef was the briber."

"It's a little more serious when it happens to us."

Mimi didn't want to consider the implications of this. "In the end, it's good I got involved, right?"

"Actually, no," Matthews leaned back and hugged himself, his bulky frame tilting to one side. "I understand reporters want to look into crimes. The way you did it, you nearly got yourself killed. I would advise you to be more careful in the future." He glanced at his watch. "What can I help you with?"

Mimi started with the main question. "Why did Bernard kill his brother?"

"You first have to know the background." He picked up a coaster and tapped it on the table. "After Bernard Levine was banned from submitting to the USGR, he recruited a front man to send in stones while he paid off graders. Eventually, that individual decided it was too risky.

"When Bernard bought a three-carat pink diamond that was unsellable without an upgrade, he figured he'd use Yosef. From what we could ascertain, Yosef never wanted to do business with his brother. Thought he was sleazy."

"For good reason."

"Indeed. By that point Yosef was desperate and figured one deal wouldn't hurt. He didn't know about the payoff, of course. Which is where the problems started."

"Even so," Mimi interjected, "did he have to kill him?"

"From what Bernard told us, his plan was to dress up like a gang member, get the lab report, and maybe scare his brother into leaving the business. Yosef figured out who it was and fought back and—well, you know the rest. It appears the initial murder wasn't intentional, though everything that followed from that point certainly was."

"Didn't Bernard go crazy with guilt?"

"Having seen hundreds of cases, I've learned people have all sorts of rationalizations for what they do. In this instance, Bernard Levine was worried he would go to jail if his brother exposed his bribery. He also felt betrayed because he thought he was doing him a favor. Obviously, there were issues there."

They both stayed quiet for a second as Mimi arranged the pieces in her mind. "If Bernard was the briber, who at the USGR took the payoffs?"

"We have referred that aspect of the case to the U.S. Attorney."

"It's obvious who it was. At least it is to me. It wasn't Arthur Tanner, and it wasn't Paul Michelson. It was their assistant. Brenda."

Matthews looked surprised.

"She had access to everyone's system. On my last visit to see Tanner, she didn't say one word about my bruises. She didn't even look surprised.

"She also said that Paul met with Yosef on the day he died. That meeting wasn't listed in Yosef's appointment book, and Yosef was meticulous about that stuff. Plus, Paul wasn't allowed to meet with anyone on his own. Brenda knew that. She probably just took Yosef's message and never told Tanner."

Matthews' mouth curved into something resembling a smile. "Not bad. Confidentially, it's one hundred percent correct. It's quite likely that individual might be charged as an accessory to murder."

"Good. How about everyone else?"

"What do you mean?"

"Brenda may have been the ringleader at USGR. I can't believe she acted alone. Lots of people there took bribes. Lots of companies made payoffs."

Matthews groaned. "My guess is the U.S. Attorney won't pursue that aspect. All the USGR records have been doctored. Prosecutors today want slam-dunks, easy cases where they are sure to get a guilty plea. In this district, they have bigger fish to fry—Wall Street, terrorism, the mob."

"It's very sad," Mimi pouted. "Bernard killed his brother because he didn't want him going to the U.S. Attorney. Probably nothing would have happened anyway."

She took a drink. "I guess this means that all the graders that took bribes, all the companies that profited at the expense of innocent businesses, are just going to get away with it?"

Matthews shrugged a half-apology. "Unfortunately, yes. And in my line of work, you see that all the time." He finished his drink with a loud slurp. "Is that it?"

"Yes."

Matthews put his hand to his mouth and was quiet for a bit. "I'll say this. You have yourself one hell of a story. And if I had another drink, I might admit your involvement was somewhat helpful. Just don't do anything like this again."

Mimi laughed. Somewhat helpful. That was the best pat on the head she was going to get. "Don't worry, Detective. I'm not planning to."

"Good. As long as we're on the same page with that, let's talk about the reward."

Mimi froze. "There's a reward?"

CHAPTER THIRTY-FIVE

A FEW WEEKS LATER, MIMI RECEIVED THE $25,000 REWARD, which had been put up, ironically, by Bernard, following his brother's death. After paying off her bills and credit card debt, Mimi gave a portion to her father to pay his back rent. With the $10,000 or so left over, Mimi and Channah launched the memorial fund for Yosef, to teach sports to unprivileged children. Paresh and Swapna Mehta gave the first donation.

Mimi had less luck with her other reward, the chance to write the story of a lifetime. Whenever she sat down to write, the memories came flooding back and she was left staring at a blurry computer screen.

In the end, what did she have? The murder of a lovely person by a disgusting one. In the words of that disgusting person, that wasn't big entertainment.

She also worried how an article would affect Bernard's family—which was also *her* family. He had five kids. They had experienced more than their share of pain. An article might make things worse.

Mimi had also promised Bernard she wouldn't do anything to hurt them. And her word was her bond. Even to a killer.

After several tortured drafts that barely reached the second page, Mimi gave up. She had finally landed the blockbuster story she'd always dreamed of. It would never see print.

The West Jersey Metro said it understood. She did sell the newspaper articles on lab-grown and colored diamonds. She didn't want to waste those interviews.

After the grading scandal broke, the USGR enlisted an outside firm to investigate. Four graders and Brenda were eventually let go for "improper behavior," which everyone knew meant bribery. Shortly after, Tanner stepped down as head of the lab. A statement thanked him for his dedication to the organization's mission and stressed that he did nothing unethical. Mimi believed that. It didn't matter. He was in charge. The good soldier had to fall on his sword.

Amid all this, the USGR saw a huge drop in business. While this might not have been the downfall the Avenger longed for, Mimi hoped Larry and his father were toasting it up in Heaven.

Shortly after Bernard's arrest, Mimi and Paul went out to dinner. It was a long meal, as they compared notes on all that occurred, shaking their heads at all the craziness. Paul still seemed scarred from all that happened. Mimi was too. At the end of the night, he kissed her on the cheek, and they promised to get together soon.

Except, they didn't. With dealers no longer trusting the USGR, Paul's lab received a sudden burst of interest. He and Mimi made a few dates. He always cancelled, saying he was too busy. "Being an entrepreneur is crazy and stressful and I love it," he emailed. They soon fell out of touch.

Mimi occasionally thought about Paul, and her gut told her things weren't completely over between them. As her father would say, sometimes her gut's not too bad.

Meanwhile, Mimi was back working three days a week at her father's office. Things there had grown unexpectedly busy. Mimi's ad had struck a nerve with Mom and Pop jewelers throughout the country, who really were clamoring for that old-fashioned way of doing business. Max heard from customers he hadn't talked to in years. They didn't all buy from him. Many did.

"We've had constant phone calls all day," Max griped one afternoon. "I can't get any work done, and I don't have half the goods these people are looking for."

Mimi bit back a laugh. The father who had spent his life complaining about business was now moaning he was getting too much.

One night, Max invited Mimi to dinner at a nearby kosher restaurant, the Wolf and Dragon. Mimi could tell he had something on his mind, though he didn't bring it up until halfway through the meal.

"Your ad worked pretty well," he said, dipping a fry in his ketchup. "I was wondering if you had some suggestions for my business."

Mimi wasn't sure she heard right. Her father was asking her opinion, instead of cringing when she offered it.

Mimi played it cool. "I'll let you know if I think of any."

"Please do."

For a second, neither spoke.

"Who am I kidding?" Mimi slapped her hands on the table. "I have a million opinions."

"I'm shocked." Max broke into a smile.

"First, your computers need to be upgraded. You can't keep running your company like a Mickey Mouse operation."

"That's a bit insulting. I guess there's something helpful in there somewhere." He put his hand to his chin. "Okay. We have extra money now. Go buy me new computers."

"Me?"

"Who else? I'm Mickey Mouse, remember? That's how a small business works. You want something done, you do it yourself."

That seemed like a big job. Mimi couldn't worry about that now. She had more to say.

"Here's something else. No woman goes into a store looking for loose diamonds. You need to sell diamond jewelry. Why don't you hook up with a good young hungry designer?"

Max stopped chewing for a moment. "Great idea. You can handle that too."

"I don't know how to find a jewelry designer!"

"I don't either." Max stuck a fry in his mouth. "You're smart. You'll figure it out."

Mimi didn't want that also dumped in her lap. She didn't stop. She was on a roll.

"One more thing. The modern trend is ethical consumerism. Your company needs to go beyond saying it doesn't carry blood diamonds and only sell products where the proceeds help their local communities."

"Very noble." Max nodded. "You're welcome to work on that too."

"I'm beginning to get what's going on here. You're giving me an awful lot to do. I can't do all that working three days a week."

"That's the other thing I wanted to talk about." Max put his burger down. "I was thinking, maybe you could work for me full-time again. It would mean you'd get more involved in the business. We could use someone with a lot of ideas and energy. I could even give you an ownership stake. That won't make you rich or anything. It's not nothing either."

Mimi took this in. Her father was asking her to join his business. That was a tremendous compliment, even if uttered in his typical low-key Dad-like way.

"I'm flattered. Really, I am. I appreciate everything you've done for me. I would love to do those projects. And it's great working with you and Channah."

"I feel a 'but' coming on."

"I want to return to journalism. It's hard to freelance when you're working fulltime."

Max hid his reaction by bringing a burger to his face. "I understand. You need to listen to your heart. Be a reporter. Just don't try to solve another murder. I never want you doing that again."

"Yes, Dad, you've told me that a million times."

"Go ahead, then. Follow your passion." He put down his food. "I shouldn't have asked in the first place. It was a dumb idea. Why would you want to work at a washed-up old diamond company?"

"I'd love to help you, Dad." Mimi's fork bounced around her salad. "Journalism is my calling."

"I understand." He took a bite of his burger.

"Don't make me feel bad about this."

"I'm not making you feel bad!" Max protested, his mouth half-full.

"Yes, you are, you—" Mimi stopped. He was right. He *wasn't* making her feel bad. The only person doing that was . . . her.

She released a great sigh. "All right, Dad. I'm on board. Really on board. Full time."

Max looked surprised. "Are you sure? I don't want to stand in the way of your dream." His lips quivered slightly. Mimi noticed his lips quivered a lot lately. She wasn't sure what to do about that.

"It's fine." Mimi took a sip of wine. "It's probably time I accept that I will never be a famous reporter. And if I don't, that will be okay. *I'll* be okay.

"I like working at a place where I can make a difference. Besides, as a wise man once said, 'what am I gonna do? Sit home all day?'"

Mimi and Max talked about her suggestions, and she was surprised how her father enthusiastically embraced them. After dinner, she gave him a lift back to Queens. She dropped him off and said she'd see him tomorrow.

It was a warm, pleasant June night. Mimi drove home with the windows open, the only sound the purring of her car on the highway. The whole way back, her head was filled with new ideas for her father's company.

GLOSSARY
of Yiddish/Hebrew/Diamond Industry Terms
(But Mostly Yiddish)

Baruch Hashem–Hebrew. This expression translates to "Blessed be the name." Generally used as "thank God." (See *Hashem.*)

Beshert–Yiddish. Fate, fated. Generally refers to someone's soul mate.

Bubelah–Yiddish. Sweetheart, term of endearment.

Carat–Diamond industry. The units used to measure the weight of a diamond. The term is believed to have been derived from the Egyptian carob bean.

Chazerai–Yiddish. Junk, garbage.

Daven–Yiddish. Recite the traditional prayers.

Frum–Yiddish. Devout, pious.

Ganef–Yiddish. Thief, crook.

Gletz–Diamond industry. A flaw in a diamond, generally a crack or fracture.

Hashem–Hebrew. Translates to "the name." It is used by Orthodox Jews who don't wish to utter the word *God* out of respect.

Hondle–Yiddish. Bargain. (Verb form.)

I1–Diamond industry. I1, I2, and I3 are the lowest clarity grades for diamonds. "I" stands for "included." This means that the diamond contains flaws or blemishes that can be easily seen at 10x magnification or the unaided eye by either a grader or a layperson. These flaws can hinder the diamond's brilliance or fire.

Inclusions–Diamond industry. Flaws or blemishes that affect a diamond's clarity grade.

Kaddish—Hebrew. The mourner's Kaddish is recited at Jewish funeral services. It is meant to praise God and sanctify his name even at a time of grief.

Loupe–Diamond industry. A small handheld magnifying glass that lets dealers examine diamonds at 10x magnification.

Macher–Yiddish. Translates to "one who makes." It refers to an important person.

Maven–Yiddish. An expert.

Mazal Tov–Hebrew/Yiddish. Translates to "good luck." It is uttered as form of congratulations at happy occasions.

Mazal U'Bruche–Hebrew/Diamond industry. Translates to "luck and blessings." It is used, along with a handshake, to seal deals in the diamond industry. Sometimes shortened to just *Mazal.*

Mensch–Yiddish. A person who is mature and has integrity and honor. Someone to emulate.

Meshuga–Yiddish. Crazy, nonsensical.

Metziah–Yiddish. A good deal or bargain (noun form).

Minyan–Hebrew. A quorum of ten or more Jewish men who get together to pray.

Mitzvah–Hebrew. Translates to "command." It generally means a good deed.

Narishkeit–Yiddish. Foolishness.

Nebbishy–Yiddish. A weak, unfortunate person. Kind of nerdy.

Negiah–Hebrew. The concept in Jewish law that restricts contact with the opposite sex.

Nu–Yiddish. So?

Oy–Yiddish. An expression of dismay. Also: *oy vey.*

Payis–Hebrew. Sidecurls. Worn by some religious men and boys due to the Biblical injunction against shaving the "corners" of one's head.

Pepper spots–Diamond industry. Black spots in a diamond, caused by uncrystallized carbon, that sometimes look like specks of pepper. Considered flaws.

Pisher–Yiddish. An insignificant person, a nothing.

Princess-cut/princess–Diamond industry. A generally square-shaped diamond cut, though it is sometimes slightly rectangular. Considered the second most popular diamond shape, next to rounds.

Putz–Yiddish. A jerk. Kind of like a *shmuck.*

Radiant *cut–Diamond industry.* Another square-shaped diamond. Radiants are often used in colored diamonds, as they display color better than round shapes.

Rebbetzin–*Yiddish.* The wife of a rabbi.

Shabbat—*Hebrew.* The traditional day of rest and prayer in Judaism. It starts Friday night at sundown and ends on sundown Saturday night.

Schelp–*Yiddish.* To move very slowly, to drag.

Schmuck–*Yiddish.* A jerk. Kind of like a *putz.*

Schnorrer–*Yiddish.* Beggar, moocher.

Shul–*Yiddish.* Synagogue.

SI–*Diamond industry.* SI1 and SI2 are lower clarity grades. SI stands for slightly included. It means that the stone contains flaws a trained grader using 10x magnification can easily spot.

Sheitel–*Hebrew.* A wig worn by some married Orthodox Jewish women, to conform to the Jewish law that requires that married women cover their hair.

Shiva–*Hebrew.* The proscribed seven-day mourning period in Judaism.

Strop–*Diamond industry.* A bad buy.

Synthetic diamonds–*Diamond industry.* A gem that is grown by an artificial process, rather than by nature. Also known as *lab-grown* or *man-made* diamonds.

Talmud—*Hebrew.* The writings that form the basis for Jewish law and theology.

Treatment–*Diamond industry.* An artificial process, which can be either temporary or permanent, that enhances a gem's color or clarity. As a rule, treated stones are worth less than others.

Tuchus–*Yiddish.* Rear end.

Verkakte–*Yiddish.* Ridiculous.

Verklempt—*Yiddish.* Choked up, overcome with emotion.

VS–*Diamond industry.* VS1 and VS2 are mid-range clarity grades. VS stands for "very slightly included." It means the stone has minor flaws that are somewhat easy for a trained grader to see using 10x magnification.

VVS1–*Diamond industry.* VVS1 and VVS2 are the highest clarity grades next to flawless. VVS stands for "very very slightly included." It means the stone has flaws that are difficult for a skilled grader to see using 10x magnification.

R OB BATES HAS WRITTEN ABOUT THE diamond industry for over
25 years. He is currently the news director of *JCK*, the leading
publication in the jewelry industry, which just celebrated its 150th
anniversary. He has won 12 editorial awards, and been quoted as an
industry authority in *The New York Times*, *The Wall Street Journal*, and
on National Public Radio. He is also a comedy writer and performer,
whose work has appeared on *Saturday Night Live's* Weekend Update
segment, comedycentral.com, and Mcsweeneys He has also written for
Time Out New York, New York Newsday, and Fastcompany.com. He lives
in Manhattan with his wife and son.

CARROLL COUNTY

DEC   2020

PUBLIC LIBRARY

CPSIA information can be obtained
at www.ICGtesting.com
Printed in the USA
LVHW110029131120
671537LV00004B/302

9 781603 812214